A Loss Too Great

By

Lonz Cook

Published by: Elevation Book Publishing
Atlanta, Georgia 30308
www.elevationbookpublishing.com

Cook, Lonz, 1960-
A Loss Too Great by Lonz Cook
p.cm.
ISBN 978-1-943904-12-9 (hc)

BISAC FAM014000
BISAC FAM029000
BISAC FIC027020
BISAC FIC025000

Table of Contents

Chapter 1

Tom approached his townhouse door, pulled out his key, and managed to enter while holding a bouquet of flowers and his briefcase. He walked into the living room, dropped his briefcase near the coat tree, and noticed an empty glass on the living room coffee table.

He passed the open kitchen on his way to the master bedroom. "My sweet Mary," he called, and waited for a response. Silence replayed the reflection of his voice.

He went into the bathroom where the separate toilet door was closed and tapped on the door. "Mary, are you okay?" Again, no answer. Tom walked to the sewing room, what was supposed to be their son's room. He yelled, "Mary!" No answer.

Tom went into his bedroom, dropped the flowers on the bed, and changed from his work clothes to casual comfort. He returned to the living room with the bouquet in hand and walked towards the couch. "Mary!" There lay his wife of twenty-five years, on the floor in front of the couch. He dropped to her side and touched her cheek. "Baby, baby, are you okay?" She didn't move. "Mary, baby, wake up." She didn't respond. He touched her neck, feeling for a pulse. He touched her cheek in search for some indication of life. He raised her arm enough to grab her wrist and search for a pulse again. Tom picked Mary up from the floor and placed her on the couch, again feeling her neck for a pulse. "Baby, are you okay?"

He touched her heart and her shoulder, and then other parts of her, still searching for a pulse. Tom moved his fingers over her veins and placed his ear over her nose, hoping to feel her breathe. "Oh, baby, what did you do? Come on, come on."

He tapped her. Again, she didn't respond. "Oh, my God!" He ran to the house phone and dialed 911. "Send an ambulance, please. I'm at 5322 Hembrick - yes, 5322 Hembrick. It's my wife. I don't feel a pulse, and she's not responding. Send an ambulance, quick." He hung up the phone and went back to Mary.

"Baby, what did you do?" He put his head on her chest, hoping to find a heartbeat or feel her chest rise with a breath. Then his Army training kicked in. He performed CPR, pressing her chest and breathing into her mouth. He repeated the process: push, push, push, push, push, push, push... blow.

Minutes later, he heard a knock on the door. He hurried to let the EMTs enter. Tom watched the two men work on Mary. "What happened?" the tech questioned.

"I came home and found her on the floor next to the couch!"

"Okay." The technician looked at his buddy who was doing vitals check. "Was she taking any kind of medicine?"

"Something for depression and blood thinners."

The technician took notes and glanced at his partner. He put the clipboard down, and like clockwork, one EMT moved and the other adjusted. The younger technician pumped Mary's chest to massage her heart, and the other pressed a red balloon type of apparatus, pushing her lungs full of oxygen.

One technician grabbed the defibrillator kit and set it for an electric charge, to start Mary's heart. "Stand clear." The technician pressed his portable paddles together, creating an electronic spark. He placed the paddles onto her body and pulled the trigger. Mary's body jumped in response, but nothing happened. The technician repeated the process.

"Standby; all clear." Zap - her body arched and the other technician checked her for vital signs.

Minutes of doing everything within their power, they grabbed her body, placed it on the gurney, and rolled it to their truck. They drove quickly, transporting her to the nearest trauma center.

Tom was in shock, sitting in the back of the ambulance and holding Mary's hand. His mind was numb, and nothing seemed to register in his thought except the woman he'd loved for over thirty years. Tom's world crashed.

***

Three years earlier, Tom and Mary had finished their workout at their favorite gym. Of course, Mary actually danced her weight off, keeping as fit as the day Tom had met her. She was the hyper-energetic type and always watched what she ate, mindful of what contributed to her shape and muscles.

As on the day Mary had taken Tom's heart, it made him remember how he gave his all to her at first sight. He'd walked over to her after observing her bend over to tie her shoelace. She didn't squat; she bent, her extraordinary features inviting his response. Tom did just what she expected. He went over to her and struck up a conversation.

"I couldn't help myself." Tom smiled. "Did you call me?"

"How would I do that when I haven't met you?" Mary gazed at Tom's eyes. She saw the joy in his heart and the comfort of a strong soul simply by looking into his eyes.

"Actually, you're right." Tom offered his hand. "I'm Tom. I'm lucky to meet you." He spread his lips as far and wide as a canyon, baring his teeth.

"I'm Mary." She grabbed his hand. "Nice meeting you." She let go and turned back to the field, where she had planned on running.

"I thought you were inviting me?"

"I don't think so." She crossed one leg over the other and stretched her hamstrings. She switched legs and bent forward, stretching her other leg.

Tom saw the most beautiful bottom a man could ever imagine. She had the right curves, the slender legs, and the little gap between her thighs when she stood with her feet together. Tom stepped closer to her and tapped her shoulder. "You could at least give me your phone number so I can call you for..." he paused, gazing into her eyes, "...let's say, dinner?"

Mary laughed and then shouted "477-9522" as she took off, leaving him behind.

***

Tom grabbed Mary's hand, like he has done for many years, before they walked outside the gym to their car. She was happy at how Tom continually measured up, just like her father had whispered on the morning of her wedding: "He'll treat you like a queen for life." Mary looked at Tom after he closed the car door and she opened his, pushed it to break the tight seal as he grabbed the door handle. "Thank you," Tom said. He buckled his seat belt and looked at Mary while turning the key to start the car, putting the car into 'drive'. He took off, eased into traffic, and drove as though the importance of their destination had changed. Tom stopped at a traffic light and grabbed his lovely wife. He pulled her towards him and she stopped at the armrest, right where he kissed her. "Babe, I love you."

Tom parked in the driveway to their perfect house, where

Mary had created the perfect nest, built with affection. She was proud of her accomplishment, where she managed to work with Tom on multiple decorating or fixer-up projects. She felt their home was the best on the block. Their yard was a creation filled with color, and the greenery from tree foliage influenced their take on a renovated, 19th century four-bedroom, beach-style structure with a widow walk. The house sat in one of Baltimore's prestigious neighborhood areas. Tom had found the house after driving through the neighborhood at the end of his work shift. He saw it as the perfect investment for a fixer-upper.

***

"Where are you taking me?" Mary asked.

"Hold on, I have something to show you." Tom drove north on I-895 and crossed the bridge. "You always said you like this part of Baltimore."

"I do, but why are we coming here?"

"Hold your horses, you'll see."

Mary observed the exit Tom took off of the interstate. She knew the neighborhood was not luxurious like the mansions located nearby, but the houses were keepsakes of a unique era, the kind of structures she'd dreamed of living in. It was close to the harbor, but not mixed with row houses, and the streets were wider, so cars were able to park on either side and still allow two lanes of roadway.

Tom drove down one street and turned west at the intersection. His slow drive gave Mary a view of each house and each style, allowing her to enjoy what she dreamed of having. "I love these houses." Mary smiled and touched Tom's arm. "Slow down, there's one for sale."

Tom stopped the car on the curb. "You like this one?"

"I love it." Mary got out of the car.

"Where are you going?"

"I'm going to look closer." Mary looked over her shoulder. "Maybe the owner will let me walk through it."

"Mary, baby, wait." Tom drove forward to a street parking spot, parallel parked, and ran to Mary's side. "Look." He raised the keys in his hand. "You don't have to ask."

"What?"

"You don't have to ask the owner. Come on." Tom walked to the house and went to the front door. "Are you ready?"

"Oh, my God...you didn't."

"I did."

Mary grabbed Tom, pulled him tight, and kissed him. "I've never loved someone so much."

"I love you too, baby, with every ounce of my heart."

***

Mary fell in love with it at first sight and didn't care about its condition. Her handiwork while raising their son, Tom Junior, kept her on her toes, identifying honey-do items. Her eye was keen when it came to decorations and upgrades.

Tom supported her vision, which made him quite happy with the results. It was his way of spending family time, including a dating opportunity in between painting or woodwork on stairs or room moldings. He enjoyed recreating the craftsmanship of an older home. Additionally, Tom never left off romance, even on a short budget. He created specific scenes to keep their love alive, and Mary obliged his advances. One-night Tom lit candles on a small table, grabbed two beers, and centered a wooden flower set he had created months ago. He sat them on the center of the table. What made his effort so great was the detail in his art. He painted each rose, lily, and coronation to perfection. She took a double look when she sat down at the table. He turned on the radio and offered her a swing around the room. They danced and laughed throughout the evening.

Tom worked double shifts on most days. He carried the financial load, especially when Tom Junior got into after-school activities. Tom Junior had turned six when tee-ball became his favorite sport. Besides Transformers and superhero dolls, he started to enjoy baseball. It was Mary who taught Tom Junior how to catch and throw. It was Mary's bat that Tom Junior favored. He would swing it with all of his might and connect just enough to make the ball travel fifteen yards. He learned more each week, and Mary was his personal coach. Tom Junior developed well enough to show off his skills; he threw the ball hard for a 6-year-old and understood the game well enough to catch the eye of little league coaches.

Mary was fascinated by teaching her son. She was a sports fanatic because she had brothers who did nothing but play games. She was the tomboy of the two girls. Her little sister was truly the princess.

Mary played tackle football with her brothers and neighbors, and was the first chosen over her brothers because she threw a ball like no other. If her hair wasn't braided, most guys mistook her for a longhaired boy. But her voice added to her feminine stature. She ran after her opponents like the dickens and threw her body into a tackle as hard as most boys. On the days they played baseball, her arm was stronger than half of the boys in the lot. She rarely tossed a baseball to her teammates. They knew to stand by for some fast pitching heat from her throw. It was her baby sister that got her to play tea and tamper with dolls. But, as she matured, she kept playing ball with the neighborhood kids until she no longer out-threw them.

Mary contributed to her son's skill and studied each game according to the season. She learned to ice skate, just to encourage Tom Junior to play hockey. She also took up basketball, as if the sport were another extension of her relationship with Tom Junior.

Tom Senior spent hours with their son, showing him the ropes on woodworking. Junior was highly interested in tools that made loud noises. He loved watching his dad, even when Mary invited him to play another sport. And as Junior developed, he managed to skillfully balance between Tom, Mary, sports, and school.

Chapter 2

Tom and Mary felt great after their workout; it was their routine. He'd stopped having two jobs before Junior attended middle school. His time was balanced, aiding the development of their only son and attending sporting events, where Junior seemed to excel, with Mary.

Family nights were very good in every definition of the word. Tom and Mary created the perfect environment for the three of them. They enjoyed game nights and usually invited Junior's friends over to make a complete team. During backyard cookouts, Tom had neighbors and work friends attend while Junior managed to entertain other teenagers. Their lives were nearly perfect.

Tom flashed to a moment in the shower when his wife yelled for a towel. He ran his eyes over her body with a look of admiration for the woman he loved, a woman he cherished, and was astonished at how she'd managed to keep a youthful figure. She looked good, and most people thought she was decades younger. He grabbed a towel from the linen closet and walked over to her. When she opened the shower door, he wrapped the long towel around her body. He pulled her closer to him and tilted his head left, gently touching the corner of her lips with his. Tom rubbed the towel over her wet spots and leaned his mouth to her ear. "You are so beautiful," he whispered.

Mary giggled. "What's on your mind?"

"Nothing, not anything." Tom chuckled as he stepped back. "You look so damn good - that's all."

"Thank you." Mary blushed. "It isn't like you haven't seen me every day for over twenty years." She glanced at Tom. "And you still think I'm pretty?"

"As beautiful as the day we met."

Mary's face lit up. "I am so happy you think so." She stepped in front of the large mirror with the towel wrapped around her, the cloth covering from her breasts to the middle of her knees. She tucked it in to keep it from falling. "Look at my wrinkles. I don't know what I'm going to do." She touched her eyes and cheeks, stretching her skin.

"You don't have any wrinkles; you're seasoned with beauty."

"Ha ha ha, you've got jokes." Mary walked into the closet and gathered her clothes. She dressed, pulling her panties up first and then dropping the towel. She grabbed a tee shirt, pulled it over her head, and pushed her arms through. She grabbed a pair of jean shorts and put them on. Tom didn't believe her transformation, even though he'd seen her do it a million times. Mary was blessed to look awesome in simple clothes. "You look nothing like a mother whose son is in the Army."

***

Four years earlier, Tom Junior graduated from high school with honor roll grades and enough extracurricular activities to attend any college. Tom and Mary had planned for his college expenses and encouraged him to attend. Junior claimed he wasn't ready for school and didn't want to waste their money. One day, he arrived home with a handful of Army brochures in hand.

"Mom," he yelled. "Can I talk to you for a minute?"

"Sure, I'll be down in a minute."

"No, Mom, I'll come to you." Junior climbed the stairs and went into his parents' room. "Mom, I want to show you these."

He put the brochures and pamphlets on the bed and stood aside. Mary picked up the first brochure and glanced at it. "I thought you'd change your mind about college."

"No, Mom. Besides, with the Army, I get to pay for my own college. You and Dad can use my savings for retirement."

Mary read the brochure and glanced at her only offspring before looking at the list. "It says you can choose any job you like. Do you have one in mind?"

"Well, it's the Army, and you know, I'm a sports fan. The Army has all sorts of sports. You know, Mom, I'm pretty much following Dad's experience, too. He always talked about his Army days, and I want to experience growing up before I go to school."

Mary looked at her son, put the brochure down, and picked up the pamphlet. "I don't know if this is good for you. There is a lot going on, and you do know there's a war happening right now."

"I know, Mom, but the Army is huge, and if I go, I'm okay with it. Besides, it's my civic duty to fight for my country."

"No, it's dangerous right now. I think you should go to school." Mary turned the page.

"Mom, every soldier doesn't get shot at, nor is he always in the zone. My recruiter said my test scores get me into any job I want, even computers and networking. He said those guys don't go to the war zone much."

"Really?" Mary turned another page of the pamphlet.

"Yes, Mom, really."

"You've pretty much made up your mind. I think we'll have to talk to your father before you sign your life away."

"Mom, it's only for four years."

"I know, baby, but it's a lifetime when you have other things to do."

"I have to go to college, and it's a waste of money if I go now."

"I know, and you've said it before. I know you want us to be proud of you." Mary rose from the corner of her bed and approached Tom Junior, putting her arms around him. "Baby, we are very proud of you. Don't ever forget that." She let go and looked him in the eyes. "We have to tell your father of your decision."

"Mom, he'll understand. Remember, he was a soldier too."

"That's all the more reason to tell him."

***

Dinner came like a flash, and Junior made a chart of things he knew about the Army. When Tom sat at the table, young Tom jumped at the opportunity for discussing his decision. "Dad, I'm joining the Army."

"What?" Tom put his fork down and repeated: "You're *what*?"

"I'm joining the Army. Mom and I discussed it earlier, and we feel it's the best thing for me to do."

"Wait." Mary shook her head. "I didn't say you can or can't, but I said we have to tell your father."

"But Mom, I know - but I thought you were in my corner."

"I am, but you want to be a man. So tell your father your decision."

"A man, huh," Tom Senior chuckled. "Okay, you're a man, now. So what's going on, again?"

"I'm joining the Army. It's a good idea, so I don't waste your money for school."

"You do know there is a war going on."

"Yes, of course, Dad. I know there is a war, but the job I choose may not have me going into battle."

"So, there's your risk. I know the Army, and it's not like you think. I know there are different jobs where you may not get in combat, but support roles go too. Don't let the recruiter fool you."

"Mom and I discussed it earlier, Dad." Junior sighed and looked at his father. "You know I have to do this so I don't waste your hard-earned dollars. I'm not ready for college, and I don't want to wait tables. I need to do something."

"But why the Army? I mean, you can work as a construction helper or something."

"Why did you join the Army, Dad?"

Tom frowned at his son, the smart kid with a whip for a tongue. He shook his head from left to right, acknowledging the intelligent kid whom he raised to be independent. "Look, it was different for me when I joined. I had to work hard after school to help my parents make ends meet. There weren't jobs like there are today. I mean, you don't have to join if you don't want to. It's not necessary, and you don't have to follow me."

"What makes following you a bad thing?" Tom stared at his father.

Mary looked at Tom for his answer, realizing the kid had cornered his father. She waited for a response.

"I..." Tom paused. *Damn this kid is a smartass.* He laughed. "Nothing. You can do as I did at your age...but remember, it's not a game. The Army is serious."

"Of course it's serious. Besides, I get to help you and Mom with college money."

"We have your college money set aside."

"Buy yourself a nice car or take a vacation around the world. I'll pay for my own school with the money I get from joining."

"Like everything else, you have this all figured out."

Mary looked at both her son and husband. "I guess we've raised you to be independent."

Junior nodded. "You two did a great job, even if I do say so."

"He's got jokes." They laughed.

Tom rose first from the dinner table and took his plate to the kitchen sink. He returned with two beers, something he hadn't done since little Tom had joined the family. Mary was surprised at the two beers in his hands. He set one in front of Tom Junior. "Okay, young soldier, it's time I broke the ice and started your journey into manhood."

Junior looked at the beer and glanced at his mother before he gripped the can in one hand and pulled the top with the other. "Oh, Mom, you didn't tell him."

"Tell me what?"

"Nothing, dear. Tom is trying to brag about becoming a man." She winked at her son.

Tom laughed. "As if I didn't know that Mom gave you a beer earlier. Kid, we know everything...so toast with me on your decision."

Tom Junior raised his beer can towards his father. "To our first, Dad."

"I hope not the last, Son."

"Why would you say such a thing?" Mary scolded Tom and rose from the table.

"He's a man now, and anything can happen. I don't want this to be our last drink for this century."

"Then you should have said not our last for the next century."

"Babe, you know I don't have any negative intentions."

"Tom, you know I am nervous about Junior joining the Army. He's our only kid. Isn't there something we can do?"

"He's a man now." Tom pointed to Junior, watching him chug his beer. "Yeah, he's going to do well in the Army."

"Don't be so encouraging." Mary returned to the table, grabbing Junior's dinner plate.

"He's made up his mind, so I'm sure, as you know, that he will stick to it like glue."

"Mom, Dad - I'm sitting right here," Junior slurred.

"Yeah, he can handle his beer, too."

"Mom, I think I'm going to bed. Thanks for cooking dinner. Dad, thanks for the beer." Junior smiled, rose from the table, and stumbled towards his room.

"Yeah, he's going to be okay," Tom laughed.

"You're so evil," Mary giggled.

Chapter 3

Mary woke filled with ideas, smiling at her thoughts. She went into the family room and retrieved an album of family photos from when Tom Junior was a toddler. She placed it on the counter and followed the changes with each family portrait. Mary put the pictures next to each other, counting through elementary school to his junior high school year. She went into the bedroom, photos in hand. "It's time we take another portrait before the family breaks up."

"You say that every year. We're still here."

"And Junior is going into the Army."

"So, we'll have a portrait while he's in the Army and even when we have grandkids. We have time for a portrait."

"Why do you always want to break the chain?"

"What do you mean?"

"Every year we take a family portrait. You complain, but we do it anyway." Mary held the pictures up, showing Tom what she meant. "This year is no different. I'm calling the photographer today."

"Yes, do that, so we can get it over with. I'm sure Tom Junior feels the same."

***

It was months after Junior's high school graduation before he attended Army boot camp at Fort Jackson, South Carolina. It was his first summer of doing things he thought were great and exciting - being an adult and feeling free of any curfew his parents set.

Tom Junior met with his love interest, Sheila, who was not quite a high school sweetheart, but the young woman who showed him interest during theater workshops. Junior picked her up from her home, went to a movie, and found a way to drink beer with her.

He became bold in his moves, and his awkward intentions grew after his second beer. His move was made not in the car but after a drive on I-895 near the Casino, upon checking into a motel room. It was his last night before reporting for duty the next day, and Junior gave his idea of going for all or nothing.

Tom Junior returned to the car after receiving a room key, jumped in the driver's seat, and drove to an empty parking space in the parking lot. He looked at Sheila and nodded. She smiled in return and watched him get out of the car and approach her door. He opened it and offered his hand to hers. Sheila was just as interested in this encounter. She had waited long enough to finally get Tom Junior to be the man she thought would respect her the next day.

Junior and Sheila walked through the lobby to the elevators and waited, holding hands as if their affection was foreplay. Neither one had any experience, but they physically knew what was natural and followed the progression to adulthood. They entered the elevator and Junior pushed the floor button. Sheila looked at him with a sparkling gaze in her eyes. She moved closer to Junior and laid her head on his shoulder.

Junior stood firm with Sheila close to him, holding her hand and feeling her breast touch his arm. It wasn't like copping a feel at the junior dance - or was she doing it by accident as she firmly pressed against him, pulling on his arm as though it were a lifesaving cord?

Junior blushed. He looked at Sheila, tilting his head, and smiled. He saw their reflections in the silver walls of the elevator. The bell sounded and the doors opened. Junior moved, signaling Sheila to lift her head and follow him. The room was six doors down, and Junior held his card key, ready to slide the lock. He'd done it a hundred times before with his parents, opening the door to a hotel room. He stopped in front of the door, slid his key in the slot, and pushed the door open. He stepped in and Sheila followed.

Junior had watched a lot of videos and knew exactly what he needed to do. His first motion mimicked the anticipation he saw on an X-rated film he'd once snuck into his room. In his imagination he saw: *Step 1 - grab her shoulders with both hands. Step 2 - lean to the right and stick out your tongue while easing closer to her. Step 3 - lick her from the base of her neck up to her earlobe.* He looked at Sheila standing next to him, and just as he swung his arms open, she took the initiative and laid her lips onto his, opening her mouth and pressing her tongue into his.

Junior was shocked and followed her lead. He was overwhelmed that she knew so much of what to do. Before he knew it, they'd stripped to their underwear and moved underneath the sheets on the bed.

Sheila reached into his underwear and grabbed his erection, gripping it hard, like tugging on the gym rope they'd used for climbing to the gym's ceiling. "Ouch!" Junior raised his head at her pull. "I don't think this is going to work."

"Be still," Sheila commanded, touching his forehead as if she directed his actions. Junior laid back and closed his eyes, remembering what he had watched on another film. He raised his hands towards her breast, feeling her bra at first and then raised the cup on one. "Aren't you going to unhook me?" Shelia asked.

"I think so." Junior used both hands, cautious so as not to

disturb the grip on his melting erection. Sheila rolled, moving on top, and positioned herself by leaning forward and giving a perfect alignment of her lips to his.

Sheila looked at Junior, released his penis, and with both hands, grabbed each side of the pillow and rocked back on his tool, massaging it with her vagina. He pressed back, but before he remembered to grab a condom from his pants pocket, he felt the gush of embarrassment. Junior stopped her from moving. "Um, um..." he paused, "you have to move." Junior rose sharply after she un-straddled him, giving him room to jump out of bed. "What's wrong?" she asked.

"Nothing. I have to use the bathroom." Junior moved with haste, closing the bathroom door behind him. He looked in the mirror after removing his underwear and put the jockey drawers in water, rinsing his semen from the cloth.

"Are you coming out?" Sheila shouted.

"Ah, yeah, be right there." He opened the door to find a nude Sheila on top of the bed.

"This time, we're doing it right."

Junior dropped his wet underwear and approached Sheila. His erection returned and, like clockwork, he picked up his pants and pulled out the condom He remembered the way his mother showed him how to put one on by using a pickle, and his practice paid off as he rolled it, covering his hardened penis with one push. He climbed on top of her, and using the natural process that should have happened earlier, went straight to work.

The radio clock was showing minutes to one by the time they both got dressed. Sheila picked up her phone and sent a text, announcing her late arrival. She looked at Junior. "I have to go, or my parents will be pissed."

"I'm right behind you." Junior zipped his pants and walked in her shadow.

It was nearly 1:15 when he opened the car door for Sheila in front of her home. She quickly kissed him and turned to walk into the house. Within in five steps, she paused and turned, saying, "Don't forget to write," before continuing inside.

Junior got into the car and drove home. He opened the front door with his key and decided to sit in the family room and watch television since it was not worth sleeping for only 3 hours. He expected his recruiter to arrive at 5:30 am for his reporting time to the Military Entrance Processing Station.

Tom woke early, around five, and the aroma of brewed coffee woke Mary. It was earlier than the recruiter's arrival time, and Junior was sitting, staring at the television when Tom walked into the family room. "Are you ready, son?"

Junior broke from his trance and looked at his Dad. "I am excited, but I don't know if I'm ready. I know it's a good move."

"You're ready, then." Tom smiled as he moved closer and placed his hand on Junior's shoulder. "It wasn't doubt I heard in your voice, but you're not sure of what's ahead. Son, no one knows what boot camp is going to be like until they go through it."

"Yeah, it's what I heard from my recruiter. And I watched the boot camp film a few times. I know I can do it."

"You're going to be fine. I know you'll enjoy your job, too."

"Yes, I'm excited about that. I picked one that will get me work after college."

"Good, you chose a perfect field." Tom walked to the coffee pot where he saw Mary pouring two cups. He winked at her and nodded. "It's your time to say goodbye to our young man," he whispered.

Mary walked over to the couch and sat by her son. She put her arm around him, like she'd done a thousand times during his youth. "I love you, and I want you to be safe while becoming the best you can. I'm always here for you." One tear fell from her eye. Mary sniffled. "I know you're all grown up and have a long life ahead of you." She put the coffee cup down and grabbed her son, embracing him as tightly as she could. "You will always be my baby boy."

"I know, Mom." Junior hugged her back, his arms higher than where his dad would hug her, like he was done growing up. "I know. I love you, too."

The doorbell rang, surprising them even though it was expected. Tom Senior walked to the door and Mary grabbed her housecoat, pulling it tightly closed. She rose as Junior jumped up and ran to the bathroom. "He'll be right back, Sergeant," Tom Senior said.

"Good morning, Sir." The Sergeant stood at the door.

"Come in while you wait."

"Yes sir, thank you." The Sergeant entered and stood firm.

"You can have a seat," Mary suggested.

"Good morning, Ma'am. I hope he doesn't take that long. I have a few guys waiting in the car."

"Junior," Mary yelled. "You're not alone, get moving. The Sergeant is waiting."

"Yes, Mom, be right there," Junior responded, and flushed the toilet, providing the sound of his completion. He brushed his teeth, splashed water on his face, and cleaned his groin. He walked out in the same clothes he'd sat in watching television through the wee hours of the morning. He walked to his mother first, hugged her and kissed her on the cheek, and then approached his father. "I'll make you proud, Dad." He extended his hand, and his father took it. "Come home a man, son; come home a man." Tom Senior put his coffee cup down and hugged his son. "I love you, superstar." He smiled. "Do your best."

"Love you too, Dad." Junior looked at the Sergeant. "I'm ready." Junior walked out the door.

The Sergeant followed but looked at Tom Junior's parents behind him. "The Army will take good care of your son."

Tom and Mary looked out of the window as Junior and the others drove off into the early dawn. Mary held her coffee and looked at Tom. "I don't know if he's done the right thing, but I'm not fighting him."

"You have to let him become a man. We didn't expect him to live with us forever. At least, *I* didn't think he would."

"No, dear, not forever - just until he was fifty."

Chapter 4

It was the fifth week of Tom Junior's Army basic training when he called, filled with excitement. He'd called at least three times since leaving home to share his training experience. This time, he explained about his graduation and how he only had the day to spend with them before moving to the next phase of his training.

The Army has a formal boot camp graduation before the soldiers move onto their Advance Individual Training (AIT), and after Military Occupational Specialty School graduation they will have a break long enough to enjoy a vacation for two weeks before going to their assigned posts.

Junior gave Tom the date and time of his boot camp graduation. He encouraged his parents to attend, as he thought it was a huge accomplishment. Tom Senior knew this to be true as he recalled his graduation, the moment that had changed his life. A week later, Tom Junior sent a letter home reminding his parents to come to Boot Camp graduation ceremony.

Tom and Mary sat on the couch with Junior's letter positioned on the table the coffee table in the family room. "I don't think we should fly to Columbia."

"It wouldn't make sense, since it's so close."

"It isn't that close," Tom explained. "It's about a six-hour drive."

"But six hours is still a good drive if we are careful."

"Right, careful." Tom looked at Mary. "We've done a lot more than six hour in one day, you know."

"I want us there early enough to see him for as long as I can.

I miss my son." Mary touched her cheek with her hand and stared at Tom.

"Baby, it's only been a month and a half since he left."

"That's the longest he's been away from home."

"It's the beginning of a beautiful thing. He'll have a wife and kids before we know it."

"Not so fast, Mister! He's still my baby."

"He's a soldier now, and a baby no more." Tom rose from the couch and walked into the kitchen. "You know, we could spend the night in Columbia the day before the graduation. I'd better make reservations now."

"Good idea." Mary sat back. "Good idea."

Two and a half weeks later, Mary and Tom arrived two days early for the graduation. They took the scenic route down the coast, stopping in Myrtle Beach for a day. It was Tom's idea, leaving early to take advantage of a long-awaited opportunity to romance his beloved wife. It had been three years since they'd had time without Tom Junior.

Their afternoon arrival offered a full day of Myrtle Beach activities. Their first stop was Barefoot Landing, just long enough to enjoy the unique shops and lunch at the local seafood buffet restaurant.

Mary was grateful when Tom detoured from the interstate and gave her freedom to enjoy the quaint shops of Myrtle Beach, reminiscing about the roadways of her youth and driving down Highway 17 with her parents as a teen.

When they arrived at the local beachfront hotel, their room was the perfect location with a beach facing deck and immediate access to the pool and beach. Mary didn't hesitate to explore her best friend and lover with a unique gift during sunset. Her aggression surprised and excited Tom. Their walk hand-in-hand along on the beach was the catalyst for a rewarding evening. Their touch and silent conversation increased their desires. Tom didn't hold back his romantic persuasion, softly touching her erogenous pressure points of influence. He turned her towards him and pulled Mary tightly in his arms, swaying left to right and moving in rhythm with the waves as he gently kissed her behind her ears.

Mary followed whatever lead her husband of many years put forth. She pulled him in, touching him where she knew would cause the right reaction. Her response to his kiss was the move that drove her man wild. The swoop of a two-step maneuver put her womanhood exactly onto his sensual zone. The dance lasted long enough to influence ideas of a youthful act, diverting the walk into sitting in the sand where Mary straddled Tom, indulging in kisses as time lapsed into seductive moments. Tom pulled back from Mary and, with darkness now their cover, pressed his luck, tugging at her shorts.

Mary giggled like a schoolgirl on her first date. She leaned forward, blocking his hands from moving. "Are you serious?"

"Why not?"

"We have a perfect room with the right view, you know."

Tom removed his hand. "Let's go. I don't want the mood to change."

"We have all night, dear. All night."

Morning nearly surprised Tom and Mary. They managed to stay up past the bewitching hour before falling asleep, cuddled together like cute little puppies. Tom moved first, going to the bathroom and later making coffee. Mary followed after she watched Tom walk in front of her like many times before, enjoying the view that influenced her to give her all, at any time, within reason.

Mary rose from the bed and grabbed the housecoat the hotel had provided. She waltzed into the bathroom as if the room were filled with classical music. The coffee maker hissed from brewing the morning pot and Tom put on the short pants he'd thrown on the floor the night before. He pulled out two paper cups from the coffee display and made up one the way Mary usually drank her morning caffeine. "Babe, will you be long?"

"I'll be right out."

Tom poured his cup and waited for the bathroom door to open after he heard the toilet flush. Tom handed the cup to his loving companion. He nodded towards the clock on the room desk. "We have time before checkout."

"Yes, but doesn't that have us rushing to Junior's free day?"

"No, babe, the free day is in the afternoon. We'll make it before he's released for visitors."

Mary followed Tom to the deck and sat next to him. They watched the sun rise to its morning glory, blaring the heat of a day usually experienced in mid-afternoon in Baltimore. Mary had finished her coffee and sat the cup on the floor next to the chair.

"I'm showering first. Don't get any ideas, young man," she giggled.

"How can I not follow you?" Tom turned and watched Mary walk. "With an inviting ass like that, I'd follow you to the end of time."

"And time is why you can't." Mary laughed as she closed the

bathroom door.

It was an hour into the drive when Mary reached for the radio's volume knob, turned the music down, and looked at Tom. Recognition tapped Tom's mind as he looked at his wife and noticed her frown, the disappearing bottom lip, and the unique crinkle of her chin. He looked back at the road and waited for the question or comment that usually moved to bigger discussions.

"Will Junior die by being in the Army?" Mary looked at Tom and waited with the same look she'd had before asking.

"Of course not. He'll be fine."

"I mean, if he goes to war, do you think he'll fight?"

"There is a possibility he will go to war, and I'm sure the training he receives will keep him safe. He's a smart kid, and the job he chose is purely technical."

"But some of the techies go, too." Mary paused. "Right?"

"Yes, baby." Tom saw the face, the worried look he knew as the warning for deeper explanations. "But again, it's not like he's walking in the middle of the village with a rifle. He'll support those guys." Tom paused, glancing from the road back to Mary. "He'll be fine."

Mary changed the radio station to 'talk radio' instead of listening to music. She sat back in her seat and stared at the countryside. *He had better be fine.*

Tom followed his path instructions on the way to Fort Jackson. He stopped a few hours north of Florence, South Carolina at the Thunderbird gas station. He looked at Mary. "We don't have far to go, but I need a cup of coffee. Would you like something?"

"Sure. Besides, I need the ladies' room."

Tom set the pump and watched his wife head for the bathroom inside the truck stop. She always grabbed his attention simply because she was the catch of a lifetime. He glanced at the gasoline pump and then watched his wife disappear inside the doors. *She's not really happy with Junior's decision. Maybe this graduation and seeing him will change her mind.* Tom finished pumping gas and followed Mary inside. He looked around and followed his bladder's command to release the pressure. Outside the bathroom, he saw Mary. "I'll be right out."

Mary nodded. "Okay." She walked to the coffee area and prepared a cup for Tom. She knew he'd be right out, and she jumped in line for the cashier. Tom joined her right before it was her turn to pay. "Here, sweetie." She handed the coffee to Tom and stepped aside.

They walked to the car, holding hands. Tom always loved touching her, and Mary had no complaints about Tom's affection. He opened the car door for Mary and closed it once she grabbed her seatbelt. He walked around and jumped behind the driver's wheel. "Okay, this is the last stretch. I hope the hotel is ready for us."

"If not, can we see the base our son just spent eight weeks on?"

"If they let us in, I don't see why not."

"Good." Mary looked out of the car window, watching traffic. "How far is Columbia from here?"

"About ninety miles or so."

Mary settled in for the last leg and talked about their stay at Myrtle Beach. "We should go back to the beach for a week next time. There's a lot going on."

"I read about how people love that area. Maybe it'll be a retirement place for us?"

"Something to think about." Mary smiled. "Something to really think about."

It was an hour and a half later when Tom and Mary arrived at their hotel. The hotel lobby was busy, full of people anxious to get to the Boot Camp graduation. Mary couldn't believe the crowd of people. Tom pulled out the reservation number on his cell phone and waited in line to get to the front desk clerk. He looked at Mary and signaled her to come over. When she arrived, he said, "Once we check in, we still have time to see the base."

"Okay, I would like that." She stepped back into the lobby and sat next to a woman who wore an Army Mom tee shirt. Mary glanced at the woman and saw an opening. "Going to the graduation tomorrow?"

"Yes, I am," the mom responded. "It's my second son who's graduating tomorrow."

"Now you'll have two boys in the Army."

"Yes, and my oldest is stationed in Germany. He couldn't make the graduation."

"Aren't you nervous about both boys being in the Army?"

"Not at all. I think it's great that they're doing something with their lives."

"You are right; they are doing something very worthy."

"You have a kid graduating tomorrow?"

"Yes, our son. He sounded so excited, the last time we talked."

"It's being new to independence. My older son went through it. I was excited for him."

"But what if he's sent to the war?"

"It's not easy, but my oldest went and came back home. So I learned to pray it through. It's what we do."

"Pray it through." Mary nodded and looked to see if Tom had finished checking in. He was at the counter, reaching into his pocket for his wallet. Mary looked at the lady. "Thanks for the chat," she said and gave a polite smile. She walked to Tom just as he put his wallet back into his pocket. "Are we ready? I can use the bathroom to wash up before we go."

"We're ready. Let's go – Room 215."

Chapter 5

It was an easy drive to Fort Jackson's front gate. Tom didn't attend Fort Jackson in his boot camp days - he went through training at Fort Dix, New Jersey - but he knew to stop at the small building at the right of the front entry gate, a small red brick building with large tinted glass windows. It was the visitor's center, where he could register for a visitor's pass and get a map of the base. He pulled into a parking space and grabbed his registration and proof of auto insurance documents from the glove compartment, following the information he read on the sign near the walkway to the building. "You should come inside with me; it can take a while."

He walked in and pulled a number from the little dispenser, just like most county tag offices use to maintain order. Tom pointed at two seats near the far wall and read posters of base rules and regulations. He looked at Mary while they walked abreast towards the chairs. "It hasn't changed. I think every military base has the same rules." He chuckled. They sat in the corner for fifteen minutes.

The solider called his number and waited for Tom's arrival. "Can I help you, sir?" the soldier asked.

"I need a day pass to visit my son in training."

"Yes, sir. Can I have your registration and proof of insurance, please?"

"Sure." Tom handed his documents to the soldier. "Where do you suggest I go to meet my son?"

"Sir, I will give you a map in a moment. It's quite simple."

"Thank you, Specialist."

'Yes, sir, anytime." The Specialist handed the registration and insurance documents back to Tom. "Sir," she said, and took a map from behind the counter and laid it on the counter. "Drive straight through Gate 4 and go down to Hilton Field." She circled the field on the map. "Then park and go inside the visitor's building for the demonstration. It starts at 0900, so you have to arrive earlier to get a seat. Once you receive the briefing, you'll know where to go for training locations and when you'll meet your new soldier."

"That simple?"

"Yes sir, it's that simple. But please take the map, because too many people get lost on the way."

"Really?"

"Yes, sir, really." The Specialist smiled. "Have a great day and enjoy your visit, sir."

'Thank you." Tom smiled, and turned around. He pointed at the door so Mary would follow. "What time did Junior say he'd meet us?"

"I bet we will find out after the briefing," Mary grinned. "That simple."

Tom walked next to Mary towards their car, opened her door and, waited for her to settle in before closing it. The heat of the day was blistering hot, and he understood why the big windows were darkly tinted. South Carolina during summer was hot, humid, and without a breeze. He closed the door and briskly walked to the driver's side, opened the door, and sat down. He put the ignition key in the slot and started the car engine, quickly turning the air conditioning on to full blast. He buckled his seat belt and glanced at Mary. "Are you okay?"

"I'm - we're here. Believe it or not, I'm anxious to see Junior."

"I know you are, sweetie, I know you are. Tomorrow morning we'll be the first in the building for the brief." Tom looked behind and reversed the car, then followed the instructions the Specialist had given him. "You know, it feels like nothing in the military ever changes. The strict rules to do things and look at the speed limit. It's slow - reminds me of 'hurry up and wait' moments." Tom snickered.

"You haven't changed. You rush to do things, still, and you've been out of the Army for nearly thirty years."

Tom looked at Mary and shook his head. "Okay, you win." He laughed because Mary was right. Some of his Army habits hadn't left him and currently were his pet peeves.

The drive around Hilton Field was quick, and Tom managed to see an obstacle course and a platoon of trainees marching in formation. "See, babe, that's how the Army gets around."

"I see." Mary stared at the formation as if she could spot her son from their distance.

"Babe, I don't think that's our son's platoon."

"How would you know?"

"The guidon flag indicates a beginning platoon. Look at the way they march. It's not snappy or sharp, just a bunch of kids walking together." He paused. "Look at the Drill Sergeant."

"Who?"

"The guy with the Smokey Bear hat. He's the Drill Sergeant, and he's yelling like no end."

"Oh, that's where you get your yelling from...Do they yell all of the time?"

"The entire time." Tom laughed. "Yep, the entire time. I'm

sure Junior will have some stories for us."

After touring the training grounds and walking through the post exchange, they got into the car and returned to their hotel. Mary became overly excited and wanted to sit in the Jacuzzi to relax before seeing her son. She had ideas of how Tom Junior would compare to when she saw him last. It had been almost nine weeks since she'd seen him, and this was the longest they had been separated. Tom Junior had gone to summer camp, but it'd only lasted two weeks at the most. When he visited her sister, he'd only stayed a week, tops, and the same with Tom's family. This summer had been a killer for Mary, who was missing her son for the first time in her life.

Tom wasn't overly excited about missing Junior, since he knew Army life. Instead, Senior was excited that his son followed in his footsteps, joining the Army and making a way for himself, being responsible for paying his college tuition. Tom walked with a peppier step when he entered the Jacuzzi. "I'm telling you, Mary, things are going to be okay. Junior is in good hands, and we have time to enjoy the empty nest."

"I'm happy he's out, but I'm still nervous about his future in the Army. I hope he likes it."

"He may not like it much while he's going through things, but once he's out, he'll love his experience."

"How can you be so sure?"

"Because I loved mine, and most military guys remember their time in service and think about it from time to time. It makes us who we are."

"Twisted, Tom; you're twisted."

"Mary, you shouldn't compliment me in front of others like that." Tom laughed loudly. He sat next to Mary and allowed the jets to massage his side. "The only thing missing is a glass of wine."

"You can say that again."

A couple sitting across from them looked over their shoulders. "If you find a cup, I'll share with you." He grabbed a bottle of red wine from behind his head. "I don't mind. We have two more bottles to drink before tomorrow."

"Really kind of you." Tom rose out of the Jacuzzi and went to retrieve some coffee cups.

Mary looked at the woman. "Do you have a son in boot camp?"

"A daughter," she replied.

"Oh my; that's pretty cool." Mary smiled.

"I couldn't talk her out of it." She shook her head.

"I'm glad you didn't," the gentleman added. He offered his hand. "I'm Larry, and this is my wife, Ann."

"Hi, nice to meet you." Mary smiled, shook his hand and then Ann's. "I'm Mary, and he's my husband, Tom."

"Tom," Larry called, "nice meeting you. I'm Larry."

"Thank you for the wine, Larry." Tom stepped into the Jacuzzi and raised his cup for the wine. "Thanks a bunch, you saved the evening."

"Larry and Ann have a daughter in boot camp."

"I'd guess she graduates tomorrow?" Tom raised the second cup. "Maybe she's in the same company as our son."

"Well, it's a possibility. She is so excited." Ann smiled with pride.

"Brainwashed is more like it, if you asked me." Larry

smirked, "She's on her own and that makes me proud." He grinned.

"Did she join out of high school?" Tom tipped his head to the side.

"Yes, she did, and she was in Junior ROTC. Which I think brainwashed her into joining the Army."

"I'm sure she's a great kid, and you taught her well," Mary chimed in.

"Here's to our kids." Tom raised his cup and waited for the others to join. "May their experiences make them into productive adults."

Tom clinked glasses in the center with Larry, Ann, and Mary. They sipped from their glasses and lowered them before continuing their conversation. "Why did your son join the Army?" asked Larry.

"He wanted to pay for college himself," Mary answered.

"It's his way of becoming independent." Tom smiled. "He's always found a way to make things happen, and I'm quite proud of him."

Mary glanced at Tom with a raised eyebrow, as if signaling him to stop building their son's personality like creating a car product. "He is still a boy looking for a challenge in life. At least he's getting a skill out of this as he earns college money."

"Our daughter is going into missiles." Ann giggled. "I'd hope she had interest in the medical field, but she has this idea about missiles being as close as she can get to combat arms."

"Not usual for a girl to want combat-type jobs." Mary nodded her head. "I thought most would do something different. Not to stereotype, as women are doing a lot more these days, but combat jobs..."

"I know...not to take away from my daughter," Ann sipped her wine, "but she's headstrong and always the tomboy."

"Yeah, she's my only son." Larry laughed.

"Well, that explains everything." Tom laughed, too. "Here's to our kids." Tom raised his wine cup, and was met by the others.

***

Early morning came fast, and their anxiety to be at the Hilton Parade Field made Tom and Mary rush out for breakfast at the nearby International House of Pancakes. Mary jumped in the car, looked in the mirror, and applied lipstick all in one motion. Tom barely closed her door and walked to the driver's side.

"Are you ready to see our son?" she asked.

"I'm ready. You okay? It's like you're giving me something to make me jealous. I have never seen you so anxious to see anyone."

"He's my baby, and I missed him...stop messing around, let's go." Mary snapped the seatbelt buckle and relaxed. "My God, it's hot."

"Baby, it's South Carolina in summer. You didn't expect anything different, did you?" Tom pulled out of the parking lot onto the main road to Fort Jackson. They were astonished to see so many people for this family day with new soldiers. Hilton Visitor's Center parking lot was full, and he struggled to find a parking space. When he finally went to open Mary's car door, they heard Drill Sergeants barking cadence, and platoons passed them as if a parade of soldiers in formation were on display. Mary looked into the ranks of each platoon marching

41

in her view. She didn't see her child; not one soldier made her go with her heart. *Everyone looks almost the same. They even walk alike*, she thought. *How am I going to find my baby?*

Tom looked at his wife's expression. Her raised eyebrow and tightened lip indicated an uneasy feeling. "Don't worry, he'll find us."

"I know he will. Let's get inside and check in. I think we have to check in, right?"

"You're right. We have to check in so that he's called, if he doesn't find us first." Tom led Mary towards the building, holding her hand to keep her from running into people while she looked for Junior. "He'll find us, trust me."

"We said we would be here for the graduation, so I know he's expecting us."

"Baby, he'll find us."

In a distance, she heard Tom Junior's voice. "Mom – Dad!"

"Did you hear him?" Tom asked.

"I do, but I don't see him."

"Mom – Dad," Junior shouted while walking towards his parents.

"There, right there!" Mary shouted. "I see him." She broke into tears as her son raced to her. "You look great, Junior." Mom grabbed him and pulled him as tight as her muscled arms allowed. Her mind flashed to his infancy, when she held him tight on days of early bonding. "You're always going to be my baby, you hear me?"

"Yes, Mom, I know," Junior responded. When Mary broke the embrace, he hugged his dad. "I made it, Dad, I made it," he exclaimed with joy.

"It wasn't so bad, now, was it?"

"Not as bad as I expected," Junior laughed. "We have to go here so I can show you around. I mean, sir, that we have to check in."

Mary looked at Tom in surprise. She nodded at his response, directed to his newly found titling of respect. Tom knew what to expect from Junior and smiled. "Yep, the Drill Sergeants got to him." They followed Junior into the building and went straight to the desk, signing the visitor's book. "Okay, let me show you what we did."

"We're following you...Soldier." Tom smiled with pride as he and Mary shadowed Junior to multiple training areas within walking distance of the parade field.

The day was an experience for Mary as she had learned how civilians became soldiers. Her pride ran deep from her son's decision, even though she feared a war where he would leave America to stand in harm's way. His quick education didn't comfort her - instead, it gave her a new understanding of Junior's accomplishment.

It was graduation morning, and Mary sat next to Tom in a crowd of anxious parents, friends, and relatives of those new soldiers. She sat listening to multiple conversations where people discussed where their loved ones were heading next. She wasn't surprised that Tom Junior had a technical job that put him in school for six months to a year. By the time she heard another parent explain the new base and advanced training location, the voice over the loudspeaker broke everyone's attention. It was as if a voice from heaven boomed upon a herd of lambs. "Please rise for the distinguished guest," the speakerphone echoed.

Instructions over the loudspeaker dictated what the crowd should and shouldn't do and pointed out the significance of the coming ceremony. And, like clockwork, once the band played, everything started happening. Movements began from one side to the center. Larger-than-life formations marched in unison, looking picture-perfect in Army uniforms. They moved like organized ants in a column, in step with the rhythm of the band. They looked unique and impressive to a first-time viewer.

Tom smiled as he remembered the day he marched across the parade field, in full dress green uniform. He nodded his head, leaned towards Mary, and whispered, "Watch what they do next."

The large formation with flags unfurled, and all stood in the center of the field. The announcements followed, and after being told to sit, the actions began. The speaker volleyed key comments over the loudspeaker and shared his sentiments about the graduating companies. At the end of his speech, the huge organization marched in front of the viewing stand where Mary was fortunate enough to identify Tom Junior passing in front of her. She screamed, "Tom Stetson Junior!" and jumped while she clapped her hands.

Her excitement took Tom Senior back to the moment when Junior graduated high school. The excitement was overwhelming as tears of joy streamed down Mary's cheeks. Tom Senior glanced at the field and watched his son move through, priding himself on being a new member of the United States Army.

Chapter 6

Tom centered himself in the middle of Junior's bedroom, holding an empty, brown cardboard box. He scanned the room for the trophies Junior had earned and picked up the oldest one, reading its inscription, *2nd Place Soccer*. Tom smiled, believing it was from his toddler's league. He flashed to little Tom's game where he ran the field from end to end and played with grass, tossing it in the air. When the ball passed him, he jumped on it, stopping the ball's travel instead of kicking it.

Tom's soccer trophies, t-ball award, and the miniature medals were staged neatly around the hutch. Tom had additional trophies on the desk and dresser.

It has been six months since Junior's boot camp graduation. He'd visited once since being transferred to his new post, Torri Station, Japan. His furlough was only two weeks long, and he'd barely stayed home during those fourteen days. Yet he kept his activities reasonable and respectful, like he'd learned as a young man.

Mary had been adamant about storing Junior's things. She wasn't sure little Tom would come back to live in their home. Mom walked into little Tom's room and stood next to Tom Senior. "You know we don't have to do this today," Mary explained. "He can do it when he comes home. I'd rather he put his own things away."

"It's not like we're selling his stuff; we're putting it in the attic."

Mary walked to the closet and removed the hanging clothes. "He'll never wear these again." Mary turned to Tom and threw he clothes on the bed. "We can sell these at a consignment shop or give them to the homeless."

"Great idea. We can get something for them. He's a man now. It's not likely he'll come back to take these with him."

Mary nodded in agreement and threw more clothes onto the bed. She cleared his closet, coming across a shoebox. "Look at this."

"What is it?" Tom turned from packing the box he had on the floor. He recognized the shoebox. "Before you look inside, don't be surprised over nude magazines or cut-out pictures of women."

"Why should that surprise me? I taught him all he needed to know." She laughed.

"Only a woman would think so," Tom chuckled. "If only you knew."

Mary lifted the lid and placed it under the box. She picked up a picture and her eyes welled. "Oh my, this is our picture from his Cub Scout day with me."

"He loves his mom, and I don't blame him." Tom smiled before adding another trophy to the box. "Hun, I just had a great idea. You know we're officially empty nesters."

"Yeah, and it's been months since Junior was around. And you haven't noticed he's not here that often?"

"No, dear, that's not what I'm getting at. Cleaning his room means we can make it into an activity room, or..."

"...or?"

"Let's travel a little. We haven't been on a trip since going to his graduation."

"Well, it's not like we have Junior to set things up for anymore." Mary picked up another picture from the box. "I like this one; he's such a good boy."

"Well, what do you think? Are you game?"

Mary sat on the bed with the box in her lap and looked at Tom, who stood at the door. "If it's a place we'll enjoy, I don't see why not."

"Leave everything to me." Tom smiled before leaving the room.

"You left the box," Mary yelled.

"I'll finish it later." Tom went downstairs to his laptop and pushed the 'on' button. He waited for the screen to come alive before his fingers danced on the keyboard. He typed, searching for a Google page on San Francisco. He remembered multiple conversations where had Mary wanted to visit it. She thought her life would be grand, living in a row house near downtown.

Tom clicked on the page showing San Francisco homes for sale. He clicked on pictures of row homes, priced to fit their budget. Click after click and picture after picture, he reviewed homes he thought Mary would love to see. He wrote on a pad and created notes where the list was prioritized as 'hot' to 'warm'.

After thirty-five minutes of reviewing homes, he decided to settle on dates and flight times for their exploration into new territory.

"Mary," he yelled.

"Yes?"

"Can you get away next week?"

"You mean, take vacation days from the job?"

"Yes, can you take vacation days on short notice?"

"Sure." She paused. "Why not?"

"Great, because I'm setting up flights now."

"Where to?"

"Someplace you've always wanted to go."

"That's a lot of places."

"Yeah." Tom laughed. "I know." He went to a travel site and booked flights for them, then selected a hotel near the townhouse locations. He created a schedule and rented a car for the week. *It won't take all week to see these homes,* he thought. *Why not see something else? What's close to San Francisco to see, besides the Wharf?* He returned to Google and searched vacation ideas for San Francisco Bay areas. It seemed magical for Tom when a number of suggestions came up on the webpage. He clicked one after the other and stopped at Napa. "I've always wanted to experience the Napa Valley wineries." He read about the variety of wineries he and Mary could visit. "Uhm, Berringer, Black Stallion, St. Michele, and others..." They started to wet his whistle with ideas.

He looked for hotels around the area, and the idea of romancing his wife came into mind. "If I pull this off?" His mind wondered to their youth, when they'd dated right after he left the Army. He remembered how Mary fell for him when he owned a 1974 Dodge Dart and how she enjoyed cruising along the main drag in his hot rod. She enjoyed his passion for dancing and picnics. Once, he took Mary to a wine tasting before they'd acquired the love of wine. They both had the horrible experience of sour grapes and old fogies. Tom's flashback ended. "She'll love it."

Tom put down the laptop and walked to the kitchen. He grabbed a bottle of wine and walked upstairs. "How are you, dear?"

"I'm doing fine. Are you done playing with travel so you can help me?"

"Yes, but don't get mad if our trip isn't awesome."

"Babe, everything you do is awesome..." Mary looked at the empty box in the hall. "Like filling that box with these clothes."

Tom moved the box from the hall and put the wine on the dresser. "I guess we can open this later."

Mary looked. "I thought we'd have this with dinner. Is there a reason you want to drink it now?"

"Wine while you work, sounds like an old army trick."

"No, you did not drink while working...did you?"

"Of course not, baby...of course not."

The room took shape when Tom moved all the boxes down to the garage. He separated 'keep' and 'discard' so his plan to manage the space in the garage wouldn't block the use of parking cars. Tom moved the last box on the shelf and positioned the discard boxes at the back of the garage where they'd be easy to put into cars. He brushed the dust from his pants and looked at his organizational skills. He imagined his wife of twenty years smiling and wondered how to get her to do it in person. He walked into the house and saw Mary busy cooking dinner.

"We're ready to get those boxes to either Goodwill or some consignment store. Whichever works for you."

"I'll think about which is best." Mary poured something into a mixing bowl and moved the large wooden spoon around in circles. "Dinner won't be ready for another half hour."

"Okay." Tom walked to the laptop, sat down on the couch, and clicked on his last website. "I hope you don't mind me planning our excursion."

"Of course not." Mary walked to the cabinet and retrieved a

square pan. "You know what I like."

"Yes, as if you need to remind me."

"I need to remind you, alright."

Tom surfed the Internet for fifteen minutes before coming across the website for a bed and breakfast in Napa. It hit him hard, the idea to stay in a bed and breakfast where Mary had always shown an interest. *I'd love to stay in a bed and breakfast; they seem so romantic.* He remembered the last time she'd suggested the idea. *Perfect! I'll do just that.*

Tom was impressed with the multiple pictures from the Churchill Manor Bed and Breakfast. He saw the huge late 18th early 19th century mansion and fell in love with its decor. He read the reviews, and they increased his interest. It was the pictures about the inner chambers that made him search further. It was an amazing setting from the living room, high ceilings, and chandeliers to thick oak doors. He saw the detail from earlier builders who focused on wood, the oak and cedar colored to perfection. The door with the crystal glass knob took him to his youthful days of those being the norm. He looked further at the antique furniture setting and knew that Mary would simply sit in that room admiring the multiple dated pieces with their cloth seating and heavy wood, the little twirl at the bottom of the couch's leg a unique design of the times.

Tom flipped the page to individual rooms. They were unique and titled to what he thought was appropriate for the area. He looked at Oak Knoll and saw how the bed, walls, and furniture contributed to the beauty of the escape. He priced it but was not sure about booking it because he hadn't seen the rest of the available rooms. He liked the fact the fireplace was next to a cast-iron tub. He clicked on another room and set his sights on the unique trend in decorations. He imagined throwing rose petals around the room for Mary, adding to the environment and setting a tone. Then he saw the position of the fireplace, facing the bed. It would be perfect simply to lay a fire and let the burning flames influence the ambiance.

By the third room, he'd searched for unique and favorable influences where he could use the décor for romancing Mary. He fell in love with the Radford, an elegant room with a bed high off the floor. A small person would need a stepladder or a running start to jump on top. The iron bathtub was near the corner of the room. It was angled between two windows and flanked the fireplace. Anyone soaking would surely feel the warmth of the fire. Tom smiled at the idea of a big tub for two.

The bathroom was at the other end opposite the room, and it was fitted with a shower built for two. He loved the way the sinks were fitting for the era, yet looked up-to-date with a modern faucet and a toilet made for any sitter. He fell for the room, and without any further searches, clicked on the calendar for booking it. He clicked and verified his entry data and uploaded his credit card number, booked the room, and made plans for how to get Mary to Napa without knowing what he'd set up. Tom closed the laptop, went to the kitchen, and sat at the table where Mary had dinner ready. He opened the bottle of wine Mary suggested they use for dinner and poured two glasses. He sipped from his glass and smiled.

"What are you smiling about?"

"You are going to love our excursion...I know you will love it."

Mary looked at him with a raised eyebrow and tilted head. She placed a dinner plate in front of Tom and set the other place at the position directly across from him. "Are you planning a visit with Junior?"

Chapter 7

Mary's cell phone rang, waking both her and Tom from a deep slumber. She looked at the alarm clock and recognized blaring red single numbers where zeros blared together resembling a superhero's cape.

"It's 2 am, honey; are you expecting a call?"

"Who would call me on your cell phone?" Tom yawned. "Go ahead and answer it."

"Hello," Mary answered.

"Mom, hey."

"Junior!" she shouted. "Are you okay? It's early."

"Yeah, I know, Mom. I had to call today because we're doing exercises and I won't get to call you for a month or so"

"How long did you know about this?"

"It's why I'm calling now. I had to replace a soldier who was supposed to go."

"Oh, really." Mom paused. "Tell me about Japan."

"It's like I told you before, Mom. Okinawa is hot, really hot, and there's a lot to do if you want, or if you simply want to relax, you can visit the beach near my quarters."

"I know you're doing a lot these days. I love the pictures you shared."

"Yeah, but can I call you on Skype? My card is about to expire."

"Sure, I'll be online in a minute."

"Okay, Mom. Is Dad there, too?"

"Yes, he's not traveling."

"Great, I'll chat with you soon." Junior disconnected the call.

Mary jumped out of bed and grabbed her robe. "Junior will Skype with us. Come downstairs."

"You can bring the laptop to bed."

"Stop being lazy and come on."

Tom placed his feet on the floor and picked up his robe before putting his feet in the house shoes he habitually set beside his bed. He walked downstairs only to hear Mary, giggly, talking to Junior about some girl she'd seen in the last picture he'd sent.

"Here's your dad, he finally made it downstairs." Mary moved from the front of the laptop and walked into the kitchen. She grabbed a coffee pot.

"Hi, son, how's it going?"

"Great, Dad. I'm glad to do something more than troubleshooting the network."

"But isn't that your job?"

"It is, but it's not as exciting at times. I mean, I love the technical aspects, but I'm not soldiering."

"Aren't you in the Army?"

"You know what I mean, Dad. I'm not doing a lot of gun training, and technology is supportive. I want to do something more active, so I'm going to the Northern Training Area with the Special Forces."

"Oh, I see. How long will you be out there?"

"I'm told a month, and I won't have any connection with technology to call you guys." Tom Junior waited. "You know, Dad, you have to experience it at least once."

"That's a tough group of guys. Are you sure you want to train with them?" Tom waited for an answer.

"I think so, Dad; it's going to be fun."

"As long as it's training, I don't mind." He paused and scratched his head, "What am I saying?" He shook his head, "I can't tell you what to do, soldier. You have to do what you think is good and fun. But do not deploy with them."

"Yes, sir. No deploying with the Special Forces."

"You got it," Tom laughed. "Have fun, son. You'll be a great member of the force."

"Thanks, Dad." Junior waited. "Is Mom still awake?"

"Yep, I'll get her." Tom walked over to Mary and pointed at the laptop. "He's waiting for you."

"Okay." Mary briskly walked to the laptop and resumed their conversation about his pictures and what Okinawa offered for fun.

"As you know, Mom, the difference here is more than driving on the opposite side of the road. It's a cultural difference, and the beaches are awesome. You and Dad should visit."

"He set a trip for us to go somewhere. He didn't tell me exactly where, but I suspect it's California. Your dad is smiling a lot because we leave in a week."

"California! Mom, it sounds like you two are having a great

time while I'm gone. I mean, California! Dad would never think about taking both of us to California."

"It's about being an empty nester, son. You know, now that you're okay, we can spend your inheritance," Mary chuckled. "I'm sure you don't mind."

"What? No, Mom, go ahead and have fun. I'll be fine... just leave me enough for after college. I may need a little for the transition."

"Ha! Get a job, kid...get a job." Mary laughed at her smart comment.

"Okay, Mom, I gotcha."

"And be careful over there. I'm not ready to be a grandmother."

"No worries from me. I had a great teacher who taught me how to protect myself."

"Good boy." Mom smiled. "Well, it's late, and I still need to work, so we'll catch you when you're back from training. Be safe and remember: Mom loves you."

"I will, Mom, and tell Dad I love him, too."

"I'll whisper that to the old man in the morning; he won't hear me now," Mary giggled. "Be good, son." Mary disconnected from Skype but stayed glued to the screen. She looked at Junior's picture, reminiscing about his childhood.

***

A week passed like the wind blowing on a spring eve in Chicago. Days blew by as if neither had time to take notice until Mary realized their trip was the next day, and she hadn't packed. She wasn't sure how to pack until Tom walked into the bedroom and looked at her suitcase. "You won't need those heavy clothes. It's not too cold during the day in San Francisco."

"I knew we were going to California." Mary looked in her dresser drawer.

"You've always wanted to go, so it's time to see if we'll like it or not."

"And then what? A few days exploring San Francisco, and then what?" She grabbed a sweater and a long-sleeved shirt, placing both on the bed.

"Don't you think San Francisco will be enough? We can visit a lot there, including the famous wharf, the prison in the bay, the immigration park, and we can go through the famous Chinatown."

"Oh, I'm sure we can see that in a few days."

Tom went to his dresser drawer, retrieving a shirt he always enjoyed wearing. "That's enough, right? We haven't talked about nightlife."

"But nightlife can be fun. Why don't we find something to do, then?"

"You can't stay up that late."

"Why not?"

"It's aging, baby; we're not young chickens," Tom chuckled.

"We can take a nap during the day."

"No way, we'll miss a lot if we do…No worries, I have plans for us."

"Plans?"

"Trust me, I have great plans ahead."

The next morning at sunrise, Tom placed their two carry-on bags into the trunk of the car. He returned to the house and waited for Mary in the living room. When he yelled, Mary was already walking downstairs, totally ready to leave. "I checked everything to make sure we have what we need."

"Good." Tom rose from the couch. "It's smart because we don't need to purchase anything while we're traveling."

"Unless it's something I really want."

"Funny, that doesn't bother me." Tom smiled and walked to the door. "I've shut everything down so we're ready for our trip."

"Good, then let's go."

It was twenty-five minutes to I-895 and another twenty minutes to Baltimore–Washington International Parkway. He took the airport exit and made it to the entryway a few miles ahead.

Tom and Mary arrived at Baltimore-Washington International airport's long-term parking lot. They opened the trunk of the car and retrieved the luggage, then walked to the stop where they'd catch the shuttle for Southwest Airlines. It was a half hour before the flight when they finally cleared the security checkpoint. Tom increased his pace and Mary scurried behind him, rushing to get to the terminal.

After boarding the flight and settling down, they pulled out the airline's magazine and thumbed through it. Mary hoped to find something interesting about San Francisco but read an article about San Antonio, Texas. Tom fiddled with a marketing magazine someone had left in the rack. He didn't want to seem too anxious for the surprise he'd put together for the end of their visit.

San Francisco was five hours of airtime, and both Tom and

Mary slept on the flight. They woke at the pilot's announcement of the initial approach. Tom jumped from his seat and went to the toilet at the back while Mary went to the toilet at the front of the plane. It was a routine they'd done many flights before while Junior would normally wait in the middle seat for their return. When they arrived at their seats, Mary had the biggest smile on her face.

"What happened?" Tom inquired.

"Oh, nothing. I remembered when we took Junior on his first flight. He wouldn't move from the window." She slid to her seat.

Tom followed. 'Yeah, I remember. And the year we took him to Mexico...he had a blast, but was sick on the return flight."

"Boys will be boys – he didn't listen to us about the water."

"And he did well during his days there. I don't know why he didn't listen to us on the last day." Tom chuckled.

"He's definitely your son." Mary smiled.

The airplane landed and Tom followed Mary into the terminal. He couldn't believe how well she looked, being in her forties and sexier than the woman he'd first married over twenty years ago. When she arrived at the middle of the terminal, she saw the overhead directions to baggage claim and ground transportation. "I guess we're going to rent a car first."

"Babe, your guess is right." Tom walked abreast of her and kept observing the environment. It was their first time in San Francisco, and he had heard about the seafood, as well as the clam chowder, which was unique to the city. Tom looked at one vendor restaurant. "We haven't had anything to eat since breakfast. What do you think about hitting the Wharf this afternoon?"

"I'm game. It's a great idea. I'm starving." Mary touched her stomach. "It's like we'd forgotten about my stomach." She laughed.

"Not for long, baby, not for long." Tom motioned for Mary to follow him and walked to the side, away from pedestrian traffic. He bent over his carry-on and pulled out a document from the side pocket. Tom unfolded the paper. "It looks like a straight shot from the airport to downtown. We'll pass our hotel on the way."

"There is plenty of time before we do what you have planned, right?"

"Yes, and you're going to love the plan."

"I know I will." Mary touched Tom's arm and gazed at him with loving eyes. "I know I will."

***

Tom adjusted the rearview mirror in their rental car. He kept the printed itinerary available to put the address in the phone's navigation. He pinned the green phone icon and the phone came to life, giving instructions.

Mary looked at the map she'd gotten from the rental car counter. "According to this, Fisherman's Wharf is downtown, about twenty miles from here."

"Perfect, it's right on the path of our next stop and hotel. I think we'll have a great lunch."

"Good." Mary looked out of her window and saw the landscape of San Francisco's airport area for the first time. She liked how the airport was a quick exit to a major interstate. The scenery was fantastic to her: arriving midday was the perfect time to take the views and feel the different atmosphere from Baltimore, and the ocean being nearby made an impact on the ridged banks and valley near the highway. She was especially impressed that the landscape was still green, which she'd hadn't expected.

Tom drove through traffic, following the directions downtown, taking the right exit off of 1-280 merging to King Street, and following King Street for easy access to the Embarcadero. He followed the navigator instructions to a parking deck near the wharf.

"Baby, can you smell it?"

"Yeah, it stinks. What is that?"

"Not clam chowder," Tom laughed. "It's better when we're out in the fresh bay air. It's not like back home. I think it's going to be good."

"No, I'm serious. What on earth is that horrible smell?" Mary covered her mouth with her hand.

"I think it's the trash over there." Tom pointed.

"Oh, I didn't see that. For my first time in San Francisco, I didn't expect such a horrible smell."

"Then you know it's not normal. Come on, let's go before we both get sick and lose our appetites."

The walk to the wharf from the parking lot was simply magical. Crossing Embarcadero was a simple maneuver, and the sidewalk near the pier was amazing. There were street performers, artists, and each warehouse building was more like a mixture of restaurants or coffee shops.

Tom held Mary's hand, as he'd done a million times. This time it was more because of his affection for his wife. This journey to Fisherman's Wharf was something he'd imagined years before, but had not been able to afford a trip including

Tom Junior.

The restaurant Mary chose was known for its clam chowder. They served it in a bud, a backed bowl cut out in the middle and filled with clam chowder. The funny thing was that the taste included potatoes, rice, and all sorts of meat. Tom enjoyed it so much that he ate Mary's bun, once she'd finished. Mary looked at the map on the wall and shared what she liked about the city. "Are you asking about the plan I have for us?"

Mary looked at Tom, giving him the same sign of curiosity or indifference. She folded her lips inward. "I'm talking about places around here."

"We can, but we have an appointment within two hours. I mean, a 3 p.m. appointment."

Chapter 8

Tom parked on the street of row houses not far from Embarcadero Street. He walked around the car to Mary's door and opened it. "What do you think?" He reached out his hand to help her step out of the car.

"Are we buying a house?"

"No, not right this minute. But I thought it wouldn't hurt to explore our options."

"I don't want to leave Baltimore."

"Mary, it's been our home forever. I'm not saying we will leave, but if we ever have a reason to leave, I've always thought about your dream. A San Francisco townhouse would be awesome."

Mary stepped out of the car, with Tom's assistance. "You know I may love this townhouse."

"And if you do, I know what to look for when you decide it's time we spread our wings from the empty nest."

Mary looked at Tom with a raised eyebrow, "You think you're slick." She chuckled.

"I can't get anything by you." Tom led the way up the walk to the door. He raised his hand to ring the doorbell just as the door opened. "Mr. Stetson?" Pamela Winker smiled and extended her hand.

Tom took her hand. "Ms. Winker, this is my wife, Mary," he said and moved aside, allowing Mary to enter the house first. His wife took Pamela's hand and greeted her with a smile. "I don't know what this man has in mind."

"He told me you might like this and a few others."

Mary nodded in agreement. "He does listen." She smiled, and looked at Tom. "Well, lead the way." Mary grabbed Tom's hand and walked behind Ms. Winker, who showed them the foyer and the living room. They walked to the ground floor kitchen, with its stone counter supported by a walnut bar, unique wood that in most new houses would be made of sheetrock.

"They did a lot of upgrades," Mary commented.

"Actually, this is original. It's what makes these homes so beautiful. This was built in the early thirties, and everything is actual woodwork, a craft we don't have anymore."

"Oh my, it's lovely." Mary touched the wood and looked at Tom. "It's what I didn't think about when I told you I love these old homes."

"I know, baby. I see it, too." Tom followed, touching the wood.

The realtor led them to room after room, pointing out the unique features and the remodeling upgrades. The bath was amazing: cobblestone features on the floor, tiled walls, and granite tops, all color coordinated to make the impression one of a kind. The master bedroom had a bay-sitting window and a hutch under the seating, which Mary fell in love with. She looked at Tom with her eyes glazed, nearly crying. "I'm impressed." Mary touched the detail on the windowsill.

Tom released Mary's hand and stepped back for a better observation. He quietly allowed the ladies to move around the house while he trekked upstairs to the other two bedrooms, which were connected by a Jack and Jill bath. He walked through both rooms, imagining how Mary would decorate them if they decided to move to San Francisco, for whatever reason. He looked out into the hall from the main entrance from the bathroom and watched Mary and Ms. Winker walk up the stairs, holding the oak banister, and listened to the creeping sound of the stairs.

"You know, it's like going back into another century when people lived here. I can imagine their joy in a house like this. It's true San Francisco." Ms. Winker commented.

"Yes, I can imagine," Mary agreed. "I can see this being my house."

"Good, I'm glad you like it. Does that mean you don't want to see the others?"

"Others?"

"Yes, I have three others available, not far from here."

Mary looked at Tom on their approach to the bathroom. "More?"

"Well, I thought we'd see what's available," Tom smiled.

"Not all today, right?"

"No, I scheduled this first and the others starting tomorrow morning, unless you want this one." Ms. Winker smiled.

"No, it'll be good to see the others." Mary walked into the bathroom and looked around. She was just as impressed with the upstairs as with the downstairs. "I love the size of each room. You can tell, they didn't hold back on space like they do now."

"It's why we're looking here," Tom admitted. "If we ever decide to make it work, I want you to have the same look and feel of our home."

Mary gently touched Tom's face. "You're a sweetheart."

Tom kissed his wife on the cheek and held her hand as they followed the realtor downstairs. "We will see you tomorrow morning. I have the address."

"Oh, good. We have a strict schedule, as those others are occupied," Ms. Winker reminded him.

"No problem, we'll be there." Tom helped Mary step down from the porch. They waved to Ms. Winker from the passenger side of the car, and Mary entered and buckled up. Tom closed the car door and walked to the driver's side, entered, and put on his seat belt. "If you don't want to see the other houses, I can cancel."

"I don't mind seeing them. I think it's nice and a wonderful idea." Mary looked out of the window at the area. "I like it here. It seems really comforting."

"Yes, I feel the same, and I'm not usually fond of cities where I'm pretty new."

"Come on, you have a lot of adventure in your soul. Remember when we took Junior to Mexico?"

"That was nearly disastrous." Tom laughed, flashing to the memory of Tom Junior sliding down the zipline without a snapped harness. "We nearly lost our kid."

"And he didn't listen not to drink the water...that boy."

"Yeah, our boy is something else."

"A full-grown man now." Mary's eyes teared.

"Don't worry, baby, he's a man now. The Army is good and he's enjoying it."

"I know, but I still worry about him."

***

Tom slammed the trunk of the car after placing their carry-on luggage in the compartment. He opened the driver's side door and buckled in. "Are you ready?"

"Yes." Mary touched his arm. "This has been really nice. I love the feel of San Francisco."

"Well, I want you to see more."

"See more...what do you mean, more?"

Tom turned the car onto the main street. "Sit back, relax, and enjoy the ride." He turned into traffic heading to the Bay Bridge. After fifteen minutes, Mary saw the red steel structure suspended above the waterway below. She rolled down the window, got her phone, and took a picture. "It is amazing up close."

"Yes, and it took some brave people to build it."

"I can see why."

Tom pulled over to the right lane and dove at a slower speed. "Should we stop at the lookout?"

"Yes, stop and let's look at the bay."

"You got it, sweetheart." Tom smiled. He pulled off the highway and found a parking space. He got out and opened the car door for his lovely wife. After she stood, he grabbed her hand and they walked on the sidewalk away from traffic.

Mary pointed to the bay, "Can you imagine the look on Junior's face if he had been with us?"

"He would have loved this. I'll suggest he do this while he's on furlough. Maybe I can tell him about getting stationed here after Japan."

"Then we could visit more often..." She nodded. "I'd like that."

"And when he's married with kids, we'll have a lot to show our grandchildren." Tom grinned. "I hope it's a boy, so I can show him the ropes."

"Oh, no, you don't. I can see him being spoiled rotten already."

They looked over the protection wall from the steep cliff and scanned the beauty of the city skyline as well as the bridge. Mary looked through the binoculars and got a closer look at Alcatraz. "That's a hell of a place to escape from." She pointed at the island.

"It was really a serious prison during that time. I can't imagine how they would survive now."

"We should visit," Mary suggested.

"Sure, one day, when we return." Tom looked at the statue of the sailor. "Have you seen enough?"

"I think so."

Tom took Mary's hand and they walked to the car, got in, and he backed the car out. He drove towards the main traffic on I-580 and merged. He drove northwest, heading to San Rafael and Sausalito. The car went over the mountain ridge, and the beauty of Sausalito by the wharf was like a picture-perfect commercial in a paper magazine. Mary couldn't believe the view. She wanted to snap a picture, but the traffic didn't allow them to pull over.

During the drive northwest, Mary got a chance to guess where they were headed. "Are you taking me to the wine country?"

"Yes, and we have a wonderful time ahead. I have it all planned."

"And you said you weren't adventurous."

Chapter 9

On the flight to Baltimore, Mary couldn't wait to get her hands on the wine she ordered. Tom did his best to show his wife a wonderful time. He managed to time Modavi's visitation at night so they could see an all-male college chorus serenade the visitors. She couldn't believe the experience nor the wine she enjoyed. "Tom," she whispered while their arms were linked together. "Thank you." She placed her head on his shoulder. "This was the best week."

"You are welcome, baby. I can't say how fun life is going to be until we have grandkids. We need to play as much as possible." He pulled the airline magazine from the seat pocket. "See?" He flipped to a destination page. "Our next trip will be a cruise to the Western Caribbean or a riverboat ride through Europe."

"I can't wait. But let's try to include a trip to visit our son."

"Japan...yeah, that works." Tom grinned.

Mary fell asleep on his shoulder. He knew she was tired because he kept her up most nights. They watched movies nearly every evening, took walks through multiple vineyards in the moonlight, and on one evening they had dinner overlooking the winery and listened to a string quartet. Four nights flew by like the wind during spring. Tom barely allowed his wife to enjoy the fluffy bed in the bed & breakfast.

The voice over the intercom announced the initial landing into BWI. Tom gently shook his wife. "Babe, babe."

"I heard." She moved her head from his shoulder and yawned. "I'm up."

"Good, you know the routine."

"Not this time; I can wait."

"Actually, so can I."

The plane arrived at the terminal and debarkation started. Both Mary and Tom grabbed their belongings and followed the crowd to the main terminal. They walked to the nearest bathroom and relieved themselves. Tom waited for Mary when he came out, observing the difference between the people traveling to Baltimore and those in San Francisco. He loved his city, but San Francisco showed him something he'd forgotten since leaving the Army. It was the ease of living, something he realized wasn't the best since they'd become empty nesters.

Mary arrived out of the bathroom and looked at her husband. She noticed the intense look on his face. "What's the matter?"

Tom stared without responding, grabbed his carry-on, and walked towards Mary.

"What's wrong?" Mary touched Tom's shoulder as they walked towards the exit.

"Nothing, just watching people," Tom replied. The walk to the car was silent. Mary was confused as she noted the unusual behavior of her best friend. When they got to the car, Tom opened the trunk and placed the carry-on luggage in the compartment. Mary stood at a distance and watched him. "What's bothering you, honey?"

"It's nothing, baby. I don't have a good feeling, for some reason. Something is bothering me, but I have no idea what."

"Do you think it's too much wine, or was the food bad?"

Tom looked at his wife as he walked to the driver's seat. "No." He shook his head, got in the car, and put the key in the ignition. "It's not my stomach nor my head. It's an eerie feeling."

Mary got in the car and buckled in, then touched Tom's arm. "Whatever it is, I hope it goes away." She looked in her purse and pulled out a roll of Tums. "Just in case, you should chew on this." Mary handed him a Tum. "We ate a lot of rich food last week, and your stomach isn't durable like it once was, dear."

Tom took the Tums and tossed it in his mouth. He chewed on it as he backed the car into the lane and drove towards the exit. "I feel better already."

"Good." Mary looked at her husband and touched his arm, then ran her hand down it. She didn't like the clammy feeling she experienced. "Yeah, you're going to be fine."

It was music and memories during the drive from the airport. Tom commented on Mary's drinking at the Black Stallion Winery and joked about the Berringer's cave they'd visited. "You could have had a barrel at Berringer's. I couldn't believe you stuck to one wine for the entire tasting."

"Babe, it's like most things. You stick to what you find and like."

Tom and Mary simultaneously exited the car once in the garage. They walked to the rear of the vehicle and pulled their carry-on luggage from the trunk. "You can get used to this."

"Cruise the Caribbean next?"

"Yes, dear." He raised an eyebrow, "It's a cruise next."

Tom entered the house first and walked around, checking room after room, and then shouted that everything was fine. Mary got a flashlight from the cupboard drawer and led herself to the postal box with a beam of light. She retrieved a letter and a pink slip announcing her mail. She looked at the unusually-colored letter and was surprised at its return address. Mary opened it and read the letter from Tom Junior. He was excited about the training experience in NTA. It was his first time being in a jungle environment, where soldiering was fun and not boring, like sitting in a Conex-type box in front of a green laptop. He got a chance to climb mountain cliffs, rappel down slopes, hover helicopters, and shoot different types of military weapons. Tom Junior had discovered a new love for that type of unit. Mary walked slowly into the house with the letter in hand. She stopped on the porch and finished it. The last part got her.

I like this so much; I may change my job to this group. I'm really thinking about it because it's a great bunch of soldiers and they are really hardcore. I know it's not much of a future for jobs, but after I'm out, I'll go to college.

Mary dropped the letter and opened the house door to enter. Tom had gotten drinks for them both; one was in his hand, and hers was on the table. When he looked at Mary's flushed face, he asked: "Are you feeling like you need to relieve yourself?"

"Ah," Mary closed the door. "No, I don't...It's this letter from Junior."

"What did it say?"

"He likes being in the jungle with a bunch of guys doing soldier stuff."

"Here, let me read it." Tom met Mary in the living room. "I made you a drink; it's on the counter." Mary gave him the letter and went to retrieve her drink. She stood at the counter while Tom read the letter.

"Babe, he's having fun. I know about this type of stuff. It's like he's full of adrenaline. He'll get over it once he learns how hard it is to become a member of the Special Forces."

"You know Junior. When he gets something on his mind, he'll stop at nothing to make it happen."

"It's what I love about our son. Trust me, he has to be on his second enlistment to get into this bunch. It's not for everyone."

"I understand, and I hope you're right." Mary put her drink down and took the luggage into the bedroom. Tom dropped the letter on the coffee table. *I hope I'm right.*

Two weeks passed before they heard from Tom Junior. He called at a decent hour. "Mom, how are you?"

"I'm good, son. Nice of you to call."

"Yeah, we came back yesterday, and after cleaning up, I wanted to call. It was fun. I mean, a *lot* of fun."

"I read that in your letter. You sounded like this was your new excitement."

"It's like something out of a video game, except that I'm actually doing it."

"Excitement from the time you got there to the time you got back?"

"Well, Mom, it's not to say there wasn't any downtime, but we got to do a lot, and that's what I like about going."

"I am glad you liked your training. That says a lot."

"How's Dad?"

"He's good. He went to work early. He wants to travel more and see some of the world since you aren't home, now...I was thinking that we should visit you."

"I would love that. When do you think you'll come?"

"I don't know, but I wanted to tell you of our idea, first."

"Can't wait to show you around. Okinawa is really a beautiful place. There's a lot to enjoy."

"Good, because I want to see everywhere you went in Japan."

"I haven't done much on the mainland, but on Okinawa there is never a boring moment."

"Okay, we'll see you when we get there."

"Tell Dad I love him."

"I will." Mary waited before disconnecting.

"I love you too, Mom," Junior admitted and disconnected the phone.

Tom Senior met his wife at the gym for their usual routine. He ran on the treadmill while she attended a group workout session. At the end of their cardio, both walked to a weight lifting machine. Tom set up the weights for Mary as she positioned the seat. "Junior called today."

"He did?" Tom pushed in the clip. "What did he say?"

"He was excited about his NTA experience and made me believe that he really wants to do it."

"Don't take that to heart, Mary; he's a kid having fun right now."

"Okay." Mary grabbed the handles on the weight machine, positioning herself to press. "He said it would be nice for us to visit."

"Now you're talking."

Mary pushed and breathed out, extending her arms to full length. She eased them back to the starting position. "He said he'd show us around." She repeated the exercise and breathing.

"I'm sure he'll show us as much as he knows." Tom waited for her to reset. "What do you think, should we go?"

"I thought you wanted a cruise to the Caribbean first?"

"A cruise is cheaper than Japan. But let me look into it."

"Yes, look into it and let's see how we can visit him and still do the cruise."

"Now you're talking." Tom positioned himself in front of Mary and grabbed the handles. "Now, push. You got this."

***

Tom booked their cruise right after scheduling their flight and hotel to Okinawa. It was their first trip abroad that was more than a few hours flight to Mexico. She was excited to see her son. It had been more than seven months since the last time they'd seen each other.

Tom wasn't overly excited about the cruise, but was more excited to see his only son. He knew the trip to Okinawa might be difficult for Mary, especially leaving her son again. But visiting him was for good measure, keeping their relationship intact, like the time before Junior joined the Army. Tom shared his plans with Mary. "We fly from BWI to Detroit, change planes, and land in Narita, then change to a local carrier and go on to Naha, Okinawa. That's eighteen hours of flying to see our son. Are you ready?"

"I'm as ready as one can be. I know he's going to love us being there."

"I'm know right," Tom smiled, "Before we go, we will take the Western Caribbean cruise."

"Are we scheduled for a week or a month later after the cruise?"

"Its a few weeks later and we're off to Okinawa."

"That's a lot of traveling for one month, don't you think?"

"No, I don't. It's time we had a life." He smiled right as she commented

"I thought our lives were perfect?"

"Perfection means that we stay busy and keep moving. We have to enjoy the fruits of our labor."

"I swear," Mary giggled, "you're going back into childhood, and all this free time is like a new toy."

"You got it, a new toy."

One week passed. Tom picked up their suitcase and stored it safely in the trunk of the car. It was another trek to the airport for a flight to Miami and, later, a cab to the port where they were boarding the Celebrity Cruise Line vessel.

Mary's excitement kept her going, since she'd hardly slept the night before. She walked around the house three times, checking to ensure they didn't leave anything they needed. She stopped by Tom Junior's old room and stood at the door, looking in. She pictured the room as it was before she and Tom Senior remodeled. She touched her lips with her hand and placed it on the doorsill as if sharing a goodbye with her second-best friend.

"Mary, baby, are you ready?" Tom shouted from the bottom of the stairs.

"Yes, I'll be right down."

Tom went into the kitchen and ensured everything was off, since they were to be gone for a week. "Gas, water, fridge, coffee maker, toaster - all checked out."

"Why are you unplugging everything?"

"In case there's a short and a fire starts while we're gone."

"Baby, the fridge can stay plugged in, or we'll lose everything in the freezer."

"Oh, yeah, you're right." Tom plugged in the cord for the fridge. "Okay, we're ready."

"Let's go," Mary grabbed her purse on the way out and Tom followed her, holding his set of keys in his hand. He closed the door and locked it. "Do you have your key with you?"

Mary turned from in front of the car. "Yes, I have it."

"Good." Tom took the key from his ring and placed it on top of the doorsill. He walked to the car, got in, and set the process in motion of getting to the airport. "I have our neighbor checking on the house every two days."

"Baby, we're only going for seven, like we did in San Francisco."

"I know, but this time, I'm careful to have us covered. It's a comfort zone, so you can stop looking at me like I'm crazy or old."

"Okay, I'll stop looking." Mary laughed as she turned her head towards the passenger's window.

Their flight was perfect, on time and easy, considering the long travel time from Baltimore. When they arrived at the Miami airport, they found getting a taxi to the pier was as simple as walking to the curb. The ride was as beautiful as their bike ride through Napa Valley. The skyscrapers were buildings of mirrors and reflected the skylight as if assisting the sun in fighting shadows. The multilane roadway was entertaining, cars zooming by with black windows. The nearby bridges and waterways gave Miami a touch of excitement. By the time they approached the pier, Mary had gripped Tom's hand by interlocking their fingers. She held it in the palm of her free hand and breathed easy.

Tom didn't know what to think of his wife's expression, but accepted it as an indicator she was happy to be in Miami. He leaned over to her and whispered, "I love seeing you happy."

Mary turned her lips to his and gently kissed him. "I am. I love you so much."

The cab stopped and the driver jumped out of the car. He went to the trunk and Tom released his wife's hand and pulled out cash for the payment machine. He slid it into the slot and the doors opened. They exited the cab and retrieved their luggage just in time for a luggage handler to approach them. It was like clockwork, the service for the cruise was impeccable, and embarkation went like a Swiss watch's sweeping second hand.

Tom and Mary were amazed at the beauty of the cruise ship. Their stateroom had a balcony right outside of the sliding doors, and the bed was queen-sized, which surprised them because of their presumption there'd be space limitations. Tom hadn't paid attention to the stateroom sizes because he assumed they would get a standard room with full-sized beds, a common size indicated by his research. The bath shower was nicely sized, the sitting couch was a surprise, and the butler service did him in. He never knew cruises offered so much for a seven-day journey.

Mary took Tom to the Lido deck, where they had an elegant lunch and looked at the Miami skyline. They watched passengers board and easily got into conversations with others who were seated nearby. Tom boasted about Junior being a soldier. "Our boy is doing great in Japan. I'm so proud."

Mary looked at Tom's glow and smiled at her husband's gloating. She looked at her fruity drink, picked up the glass, and turned to the skyline. *I hope he's okay. I really hope he's okay,* she thought. She took another sip of her drink before glancing at the woman sitting next to her. The woman nodded as if she understood her worry. "My son went into the service, did his time, and returned. It was an amazing transition for him. Heck, for us, too. He'll be okay." The woman touched her shoulder. "He'll be just fine."

Tom led Mary to the 5th deck for debarkation for their excursion on St Lucia. They walked down the gangway after getting their ship card scanned for security and accountability. Mary hadn't been to a Caribbean island of spices, nor an island of fruit plantations but was surprised at the luscious greenery. It was something she's read about in magazines. Since they were on a ship excursion, they waited with a group, sitting in the same areas for their bus to arrive.

It was minutes within the arrival time window that Tom stood and reached his hand out to encourage his wife to stand. "Come on baby, the bus is here."

"How do you know?" Mary looked left and then right without seeing the large vehicle.

"I heard it and trust me," Tom pointed, "See our guide walk over there?"

Mary walked with Tom to where the guide stood waving others on. They arrived and got on the bus, right in the middle and waited while others boarded. The bus took off and the guide rattled on about the natural herbs and spices of St. Lucia. He talked about the cost of one pound versus the price in stores for simple spices. "You mean the mark up is that great?" Mary whispered to Tom.

"Correct, American capitalism at work." Tom pointed to the natural terrain and the mountain range. He turned to the other side and pointed at the picturesque view of the beach, the ship at the port, and the town structures. Mary picked up her cell phone and snapped a shot.

"Tom, are we taking home sample of the spices?"

"I should say yes." Tom reached into his pocket and retrieved his cash. "You think we can get a few bags with this?" He waved $400 at her.

"Smart ass," Mary giggled.

It was night when the ship pulled out of port for the next island. Tom had jumped into the shower, lathered up, rinsed and called for Mary to join.

"Oh, that's going to work," she laughed. "It's barely enough room for you." She yelled.

Tom laughed finishing the shower, drying and then spraying cologne over his body. He left the bathroom, "It's all yours," he moved to the suitcase and the closet.

Mary followed suit in the bathroom while Tom dressed for the night on the ship. He waited for Mary to get dressed. When she put on the form fitting dress, he sighed, "Oh my," he fanned his face, "My wife is a goddess."

They left the cabin and walked through the entertainment deck, scanned card games at the casino and peeked at the karaoke bar. So much was going on that they nearly missed the stage show. It was a theatrical production in the ship's theater. It's like clockwork where one group can watch the show before dining, and the other dines for a late show. Tom and Mary had late dining. They watched the show, played a hand of black jack, and went to dinner.

It was after her third drink when at the club Mary danced like she didn't have a worry in the world. Tom kept her going with dancing to every song they recognized or had heard one time or another. They danced until the crowd became a small cozy group. That's when Tom decided to serenade her with a special request he made with the disc jockey. She was extremely embarrassed about, but happy he did it. Arriving at the before sunrise, Tom and Mary crashed as if they'd ran a marathon.

The next day they had only a few hours on St. Thomas. Tom and Mary slept through breakfast and lunch, only to get ashore in time to ride the lift to the top of the mountain overlooking the city and bay. The sight was another amazing experience, like that of St. Lucia. Mary took multiple pictures with the idea of enlarging the best for framing. She captured the blue sky, the dark blue water, and the green landscape, all while focusing on the hills right out of the water. The setting sunlight gave the reflective glow, which made the view spectacular. They returned to the ship right before going underway.

They skipped the formal dinner and went to the adult deck aft and sat on the lounging chairs. It was another experience watching the moonlight on the white waves of the ships propulsion. While relaxing on the adult escape deck, Tom was as super attentive and flirtatious as if they were newlyweds. And he didn't pay any attention to onlookers around them. His focus was on Mary, the sexy maiden of his fantasy.

Daybreak found them in bed again, but this time they rose with the sun. Tom quickly dressed and ran to the cafeteria for coffee. He grabbed two cups and returned to the cabin, only to find Mary in the bathroom. Tom opened the sliding door to the deck and sat both cups on the small table between to chairs. Mary joined him.

"Well, tomorrow we're back to Baltimore," Tom reminded Mary. "It's back to the grind."

"Too soon," Mary sighed as she sipped her morning joe. "This was fun and relaxing. I had no idea cruises without Junior could be like this."

"Remember, there's more ahead in our lives. We're old enough to do what we want."

"Old enough to know better." Mary giggled. "You can't keep this pace, young man."

"I'll pay for it all week, but at least," Tom looked around for anyone next door, "you aren't complaining about your action in bed. It's been awesome for me." He grinned like a kid with a lollipop.

"No complaints." Mary touched his thigh. "None at all."

***

Three days after returning from the cruise, Tom woke Mary as usual when he rose from bed. He went downstairs to make coffee, booted up the laptop, and retrieved a cereal box from the cupboard. He grabbed a bowl from the dishwasher and filled it with his favorite brand of cereal. He replaced the box and turned to the laptop. He signed in and went for the milk in the fridge. By the time he completed his breakfast cereal, his laptop had finished its process, and the email notification flashed on the screen.

Tom put the bowl of cereal down and focused on the email. He clicked his link, and the email screen inbox flashed on the page. He scanned it, and an email from Tom Junior was there.

Mom & Dad - Sorry for the email. But I had to tell you to cancel your visit. I'm deploying on short notice. I can't tell you where nor when I'm coming back. OPSEC (Dad, you know what I mean.) I'll be in touch as often as possible. Love always, Junior.

Tom lifted the laptop from the counter and walked to the master bathroom. Mary stood in front of the mirror, brushing her teeth. He looked at her from the door and raised the laptop. "We received an email from Junior. He wants us to cancel our trip to visit him."

Mary spat in the sink and ran water over her hand, sipped some into her mouth, swished, and spat again. "Is he okay?"

"Yeah, he's fine. He is on a mission, and he can't tell us where."

"Mission?" Mary raised her eyebrows. "Is that serious?"

"Well, it could be, or it may be training. But either way, our son is not available for us to meet him. We should cancel until we talk to him. Maybe when he's back."

"When will he return?"

"He didn't say."

"Why didn't he call?"

"He probably couldn't because of what I remember of Operation Security. You know, they're afraid the soldiers will talk too much, so they shut down openings for counterintelligence."

"Counter intelligence?"

"The enemy forces listening to conversations."

"Oh, okay." Mary walked past Tom with a frown on her face,

as if trying to understand Tom's explanation.

Tom noticed her confused look. "It's an Army thing, to keep secrets secret."

"Why didn't you say that?"

Tom smiled. "I thought I did."

Chapter 10

Three weeks passed and there was no word from Tom Junior. Mary started to worry about her son's health and wellbeing. She wondered if everything was fine, or if she was being over-sensitive to the Army's way. Mary looked at her cell phone and scanned her email inbox. To her disappointment, the list of emails didn't hold one letter from Tom Junior.

Tom Sr. explained to Mary that there were times when soldiers couldn't communicate, and said that things would be okay. He reiterated that if something happened, they would be notified. But the nervous fear running through Mary's mind got the best of her. She watched the news for anything about Asia that might involve her son.

It was Thursday morning when the house phone rang. Tom reached over Mary to answer it, a routine he enjoyed simply to involve his wife in his actions.

"Hello," Tom answered.

"Dad, I'm back. Sorry for the inconvenience, but you know I can't control those missions. How are things?"

"Wait." Tom gave Mary the phone.

"Who is it?" Mary frowned.

"You'll see. Answer it."

"Hello."

"Mom, what's up?"

"Hi!" Mary's voice rose in excitement. "I'm glad you called."

"Me too, Mom." Tom Junior paused. "Sorry I didn't get to talk to you guys sooner. I was just telling Dad that we can't control the process or break silence before deploying."

"I get it, I think. Your dad tried to explain."

"It's what we have to do, Mom. Did you like your cruise?"

"Loved it. Your dad is like a teenager."

"I'm not so sure I want to hear where that may go."

"You're an adult now."

"Mom...no," Junior laughed. "If you guys want to come over, I'll take leave days and make sure I'm not deploying."

"That's a good idea."

"Yeah, you and dad will love this island. It's beautiful here."

"I've seen pictures. You'll have to tell me about your adventure."

"I'll write an email. There's so much to tell."

"I'll let you talk to your father. I love you and miss you."

"Love and miss you too, Mom."

Mary handed the phone to Tom and smiled when he took the receiver and started talking to his son. "Your first deployment. How did it go?"

"It was fun, believe it or not. But you know OPSEC. I can't tell you all about it. I'll write you."

"Okay. Try to keep in touch as much as you can, son. Your mom worries about you."

"I will, Dad. I will."

"Love you, Junior, and keep charging."

"Love you too, Dad." Junior ended his call.

Tom rose from bed, placed the phone on its base, and went to the bathroom. Mary followed him, smiling now that her worries about Junior were lifted as if a weighted bar had flown off on her shoulders. "See, babe, he's fine. It's all about training."

"Okay, I get it. But there *is* a war going on."

"He's in Japan; the war is in the Middle East."

"I get it now."

Tom flossed his teeth while Mary brushed hers. She looked at her husband and her face flushed, her smile slipped, and she disrobed in front of Tom. "Hurry up, we have business to do."

Tom looked at Mary's beautiful curves and grabbed a toothbrush and paste. "I'll be right there." He finished within seconds and joined Mary in bed.

After their romp between the sheets, Tom jumped in the shower and Mary followed. "I'm so glad he called."

"I know, baby, I know." Tom turned, handing her the scrubber and soap. "If you don't mind, since you're in here..."

"Not at all," Mary giggled. "You know, I wish we had another kid."

"Mary, are you..."

"No, don't think that way, I'm not, but we should have had another child."

"I am happy with Tom Junior, because it took so much to get pregnant with him."

"I know, but sometimes I wish we'd had another kid."

"I know, and I know how much it hurts you, that we can't."

"I am happy to have Junior...but can't a woman wish?"

Mary turned around after pushing Tom under the flowing water. "Here, your turn." She positioned herself for a back scrub. Tom grabbed the scrubber and put soap on it for the back scrub. "I know you wanted more kids, but we're not capable. Besides, the doctors said..."

"I know what the doctors said. I was just saying it would have been nice having one more at home."

"Oh, yeah." Tom rinsed the scrubber and stepped back from the water. "You're not enjoying the empty nest?"

"I am, and we're doing fine. I'm reflecting on if we had one more at home."

"I guess that's good."

"It's just a reflection." Mary turned the water off and walked past Tom, grabbed a towel, and rubbed her back dry. "You don't have to worry; I'm not trying to get pregnant."

"I know, because you know it won't work."

"That's a reminder!"

Tom exited the shower, toweled off, walked into the bedroom closet, and pulled out his work clothes. He didn't dare to say anything more about having other children. His memory of the conversation with the doctor flashed in his head. "I'm sorry, Mr. & Mrs. Stetson, but there's no way her body..." (he looked at Mary) "will allow another egg to pass. I'm surprised you got pregnant the first time..." Mary's attitude changed after that conversation. She didn't want to discuss alternatives to giving birth, but focused on Tom Junior as her way of being fulfilled.

Tom put on his pants, shirt, and belt before grabbing his socks from the dresser. He sat on the corner of the bed Mary had just made. "Are you okay?"

"I'm fine. I'll meet you at the gym today," Mary responded.

"I... ah...okay. Gym as usual."

"Good." Mary walked downstairs to the kitchen, made coffee, and toasted a bagel. She went upstairs to finish dressing while the bagel toasted. Mary managed to pass Tom on the stairs without saying one word.

"Are you okay?" Tom yelled from the bottom of the stairs.

"Yeah, I'm fine." Mary replaced yoga pants with a pencil skirt, pulled a blouse from the closet, fixed her bra, and opened the blouse exactly where she wanted to show Tom her fine body. She returned to the kitchen and saw Tom with a coffee cup and half of her bagel.

"I hope you don't mind." Tom raised the bagel.

"No, dear, it's fine." Mary poured coffee and grabbed the remaining bagel, opened the fridge, and grabbed the cream cheese spread. She covered the bagel with the cheese and properly returned the ingredients to the fridge. She looked at Tom. "You know I'm over the kid thing, right?"

"I know you are, or you'd complain about my grabbing half of your bagel."

"Is that so?"

"As if you didn't know." Mary sipped coffee, bit her bagel, and chewed. She waited for another comment, but before he opened his mouth, she added, "Junior sounded happy."

"Of course he's happy. He got a chance to do something he's trained to do. In the Army, that's a wonderful thing."

"Are you saying some of them go to school and never do what they're trained to do?"

"Not really, but there's a lot of supporting duties that soldiers do. Something like watch duty, where they keep their eyes open for the barracks, or security."

"Like menial things. That doesn't make sense."

Tom stopped talking about the Army and instead shared, "It's about time for us to go to work." He kissed Mary on the cheek, walked to the living room, and grabbed his briefcase. He turned. "See you tonight," he said and walked through the front door. *Man, sometimes she can really yank my chain. Now I'm missing Junior.*

Chapter 11

Eighteen months later, Specialist Stetson reported to Fort Campbell, Kentucky to the screaming 101st Airborne Division. He was excited to be on the last leg of his enlistment. With less than two years left on his enlistment, he'd began contemplating if staying a soldier was more his dream than going to college full-time to complete his degree. He'd taken college courses during the last year and was able to increase his promotion chances with college credits.

Tom Junior settled in with a unit known for multiple deployments. He did not expect the fast pace of training, nor the aggressive overseas schedule his First Sergeant explained during his processing. A month into his tour and out of the blue, he was called up for a special mission. Junior pulled his gear together, picked up his rifle, and reported like the other soldiers. He wasn't sure where they were headed, but he knew it involved more than training. The air seemed intense, even though the unit was as quiet as a mouse.

In the early dawn hours, Tom Junior climbed the stairs, boarding an Air Force C-141 transport airplane. He took a seat, as directed, beside the load master and settled in. He closed his eyes and waited, just like multiple young soldiers had done when going into the unknown. A voice on the overhead loudspeaker broke the silence: "Hoah, Soldiers, I am Colonel Wes Manheim, commander of the force. You have been called to do America's work, and we're going to do it. Everything is in order for us to make this thirty-day mission a success."

Tom Junior looked at the soldier next to him and asked, "Is this normal?"

"You're in the 101st, dude," Keenan responded.

"You've done this before?"

"Yeah, we do missions all the time..." Keenan offered his hand. "Keenan Williams."

"Tom Stetson." He shook Keenan's hand. "So, we're training for something big."

"Dude, you are *on* something big."

Tom Junior sat back and looked at the back of the seat in front of him.

"No worries, dude. Just do your job and all will be okay. It's not that we're straight legs."

"I know, but it's my first time heading out on a real mission."

"Hang with me. I'll let you know what's up, and I'll get us home."

"Okay, Williams, you got it."

***

Mary took her drink from the fountain after working diligently in the gym. She walked by the full-length mirror and noticed Tom's eyes upon her. She pranced to the other side, giving Tom a silly smile along the way.

Tom whistled. "Hey, baby!"

"Hey, sugar." Mary approached Tom. "Aren't you a good looker?"

"I am?" Tom rose from the workbench and struck a pose, showing off his shoulder muscles. "What do you think?"

"Sexy." Mary smiled.

"I have more to show you." Tom walked closer and

whispered, "It's got to be in a private room. Just the two of us."

"Really?" Mary spoke out loud. "You're going to show me what?"

Tom laughed. "My wife is as loony as the day is long." He shook his head and grabbed his towel from the bench. "Are you ready to go?"

"Yep, I'm done."

"Good." Tom led the way to the car and drove home. When he got to the door, he noticed a yellow slip stuck to it. It was a mail slip from the postman. *Payment due upon receipt.* "Did you order anything?" Tom handed the slip to Mary.

"No, I haven't."

"I'm sure it's from Junior."

"He hardly sends postage due packets."

"Yes, that's strange." Mary went inside and walked to the shower. Tom walked into the kitchen and pulled water from the fridge. *Postage due can only mean one thing, coming from a soldier. He's on another mission, I bet.* Tom poured water into a glass he retrieved from the dishwasher. He emptied the glass with one raise to his lips, gulping the soothing liquid. Tom walked to the shower, stripped, and jumped in, passing Mary, who'd just finished.

"Do you know why Junior would send us a package?" Mary looked at Tom while toweling dry.

"Could be souvenirs from his new deployment location." Tom paused, adjusted the shower water, and stepped in, feeling the thrust of water on his body. "I'll pick it up in the morning."

Mary didn't think much of Junior's short notice travel, though she realized through the few years that it was normal in the Army for soldiers to deploy for training. Junior had multiple training missions where he couldn't communicate right away. He always sent things home that were unique to the location where he trained. Mary slipped on yoga pants and a top and went downstairs to the kitchen to start dinner.

Tom finished his shower, dressed in shorts and a shirt, and followed Mary's lead. He entered the kitchen and went for a beer from the fridge. "You want one?"

"No, not tonight." Mary stirred the contents of the pot while she held the lid in her hand. "What do you think it is this time?"

"Huh?"

"The package?"

"Oh, yeah, I'm not sure, but I'll get it in the morning on the way in."

"Okay. I hope it's something we can put on the mantle instead of hanging another picture or woodwork on the wall. I'm not so sure we have space anymore."

"Yeah, it seems he likes hanging things. I know they're unique, and I'm sure he'll take these down when he moves."

"No, dear, he has the same copies."

"What? He didn't tell me that." Tom popped the bottle top and sipped. "Two of everything. That kid is spending a fortune."

"You know he loves sending us things."

"Well, I'll tell him to hold off the next time he calls."

"Don't say 'hold off', say something like 'save your money.' That sounds better."

During rush hour traffic, Tom detoured to the local post

office and stood in line for the package his son had sent. He stepped to the podium and gave the mail clerk his slip. "I'll be right back," the clerk said and turned to go to the back. Tom looked around at the décor of postage stamps, posters, and rules posted on the walls. He read the FBI's most wanted list and found it bizarre that the posters were inside the post office and not at the entry door. The clerk returned with two large boxes. Their size was surprising, as they barely fit into the back seat of his sedan. Tom gave the clerk his credit card and paid the postage. He shook his head in amazement, as these couldn't be gifts.

Tom managed to get the boxes to the car and opened one, then the other. He found a packing list in one, and a note from Tom Junior.

Sorry, Mom and Dad, for the short notice deployment. It was either put these in a big storage warehouse or ship them to you. I decided to send everything to you and retrieve them when I return. I'm sure I'll get furlough for a month, after this mission. Love much, and I'm sure you understand - Junior.

Tom shook his head and called Mary on his cell. "Babe, it's his clothes and other things, like a radio, Gameboy, and other odds and ends. No gifts, simply his stuff for us to store while he's gone."

"Okay, so we'll put it in the workroom until he's back."

"I'll take it home tonight." Tom took a breath. "I think he's overseas."

"Well, at least he's traveling."

"Yeah, traveling...Love you." Tom disconnected the call and put the phone on the car seat next to him. He backed out of the parking space and headed off to work, driving his routine route. *Traveling, huh...this is a serious mission.*

Tom Junior called from the USO-sponsored call center. Mary answered. "Hello."

"Mom, how are you?"

"Junior, it's nice hearing from you. I'm fine, and how are things with you?"

"I'm okay. It's different this time."

"What do you mean 'different'?"

"I'm in Afghanistan."

"Where?"

"I couldn't tell you at the time because it wasn't a sure thing, but I'm here. It's hot, sandy, dirty, and - well, it's the Army."

"Oh my God, Tom, you have to take care of yourself."

"I am a Network Specialist. I am not doing things like the foot soldiers, going door to door. So no worries."

"You are not worried?" Mary paused. "Then I shouldn't worry either."

"No, Mom, don't worry. I'll be fine. The only thing here in the camp is mortars from time to time... that's what I'm told. So far there hasn't been one here since we landed."

"I'll take your word on that." Mary's eyes teared up. "You have to be careful and come home safely. I've read it's not the best situation."

"You're reading about war?"

"Does that surprise you? I have a son in the Army."

"Oh, right, Mom. You know everything I'm doing... Where's Dad?"

"He's in the garage. I'll get him. "

"No, that's okay. I'll call again. My time is up. Tell him I love him, and I love you too, Mom."

"We love you too, son." Mary placed the house phone on its base, looked around the living room, and saw her son's picture from when he was a young teen. *God, take care of my son.*

Tom entered the house from the garage door. "Hey, sweetie, what's for dinner?"

"I'm baking a potato for you, and there's stew in the pot on the stove. We can have dinner whenever the potato is done."

"Sounds good." He looked at Mary. "What's on your mind?"

"Junior's in Afghanistan."

"He's *where?*"

"Afghanistan. It's where the unit deployed, and he just called. He's doing fine, and he said he loves you."

"Okay." Tom went to the powder room, washed his hands, and looked into the mirror. *My kid is in a war zone.*

He brushed his face with his wet hands. *God, look after my son; send him home safe.* Tom closed his eyes and touched his forehead and then below his heart, followed by touching each shoulder, creating a cross.

"Amen," he whispered.

Chapter 12

Two months had passed, and Tom Junior talked to Tom and Mary on a regular basis. He mentioned how much he had learned working long hours of observing the network, and how much he wished for a break. Tom shared his excitement about his scheduled return to the United States, even though there was a rumor of an involuntary extension.

Tom Junior was on duty with his shift and ran his routine checks on the network. He ensured that every node was in sync with the communication equipment. His job was as important to the unit as was his ability to keep signals flowing from operator to operator. He loved his job, and people relied on his keen ability to keep the network in fine shape.

***

Two months passed, and Mary arrived home first, before Tom. He called and explained that he had to work late on an overseas conference call. She went upstairs to shower, change clothes, and run to Tom's favorite restaurant for takeout. She hustled to make the dinner with her husband a magical evening. Mary picked up her cell phone, dialed a Mexican restaurant, and made the order. She walked downstairs, picked up her purse and keys, and whisked off to make her surprise a reality.

Mary waved at the security guard and tapped on the door. Tom had worked in the company for nearly eighteen years. He'd managed to grow with multiple promotions and even lead a department. The guard recognized Mary as he quickly pushed a button, allowing her to enter. The guard stood. "Good evening, Mrs. Stetson."

"Hi, sir." Mary pointed upward. "He hasn't left yet, right?"

"No, Ma'am, he hasn't according to our log."

"Oh. Good." She reached into the bag and pulled out a burrito.

"I hope you like this." Mary smiled and handed it to the security guard.

"Thank you." The security guard took the container and returned to his post. Mary walked to the elevator, pressed the call button, and walked in when the door opened. She called for the 8th floor. She looked at her image in the shiny steel doors: the tightly-fit dress, her hair pulled to one side, and the earrings, a surprise gift Tom had given her during a casual night out. Mary held onto the bag of his favorite food, and when the elevator stopped, she proudly stepped onto the floor, turned right, and headed to her husband's office. She saw him through the glass window wall and waited until he paused from talking into the speakerphone.

Tom looked up as he slammed a folder onto his desk. "Damn it - why aren't we moving in the right direction?"

"Well, sir, we have a hurdle that's much greater than we expected," a conference member responded.

He looked at the desk phone. "And have you gotten three solutions planned?"

"Ah..." Silence fell from the phone. "We haven't gotten that far."

"I suggest you get me your analysis by tomorrow evening, and we'll reconvene to review it." Tom looked up, saw Mary, and waved her in. "I can't have us lose this account." He pressed the red button to end the call. "What a surprise." Tom smiled.

"I can't let a hardworking man miss dinner." Mary stepped to his desk. "You were hard on that caller. You want to talk about it?"

"No, baby, I'd rather focus on you." He moved from behind the desk and placed the bag on it. "You look marvelous."

"Thank you, baby. I try to make sure my man is happy."

"And this you do."

"Here, let me get dinner out, and we can have dessert later," she smiled.

Tom grabbed his wife's hand and led her to the nearest conference room. He closed the curtain behind them and turned off the lights to allow the glow from the street to enter the room, as if a soft candle was lit in each corner. He grabbed his wife and pressed his lips against hers, squeezing her with his embrace, and lost himself in her arms.

Mary jumped just enough to place her legs around his waist and then held on for whatever Tom had in mind. She was happy she'd worn the crotchless panties she had purchased for just the right moment. Tom turned around and sat on a chair without armrests. His hands roamed his lovely wife's body, and he was surprised at the soft lace he felt. He pushed back from Mary and slid her back just far enough to let his manhood escape the treacherous imprisonment of his pants. He breathed with the release of his erection and positioned his wife to move what he thought was blocking his avenue to destined pleasures. He was surprised when she lifted her dress and his landing zone was as clear as evening sunshine and blue skies in summer.

Tom and Mary wrapped up dinner, took one car, and went to their favorite dance club. He dropped his tie in the car and left his blazer on the back seat. "We haven't been this spontaneous in ages."

"I know," Mary giggled. "It's nice, isn't it?"

"Of course. It's...it's amazing."

Tom held his wife's hand, and together they walked to the club's door. They entered, and hearing good music playing, walked directly to the dance floor.

Mary moved with rhythm, demonstrating where Tom Junior had gotten his dancing ability. Tom moved well enough to keep Mary happy when he danced, but mostly, he watched his wife as if she were the prize of his efforts. At every turn she saw him smiling, and she closed her eyes and tilted her head towards the ceiling, displaying her enjoyment with the music.

They danced for a half hour before leaving the dance floor to find a table. Tom looked at his watch. "What time are you going to the office in the morning?"

"I may call in sick." She winked.

"Call in sick...what a novel idea." Tom waved at a waitress. "I can take my calls from home tomorrow."

Mary sat back on the loveseat next to a coffee table and cuddled right under Tom's arm. She leaned close. "And we can play any time you're off the phone."

Tom kissed her deeply, held her close, and grabbed her butt with his hands. "You are an amazing woman," he whispered. "You and Junior are my world, and I'm so glad I'm with the best thing that ever happened to me."

Mary pulled away to gaze into Tom's eyes. "Baby, our world is exactly as we planned. It's perfection, even with Junior gone. I couldn't love you more..." The music changed, and a slow, melodic melody changed the mood of the dance club. "It's good enough." She rose, pulling Tom up from the loveseat. "Let's go."

Tom jumped to the occasion and followed his beauty to the dance floor. He held his arms wide and Mary moved in, closing the gap between them. She pulled him to her, feeling the connection, she so enjoyed and looked forward to the rest of the night. They danced slowly, touching each other where their connection went beyond the simple press of his groin, where hearts were joined and nothing in the club could become disruptive. They danced, slow, like kids at the prom who didn't want the moment to end. They danced like the moment of their first dance as husband and wife. They danced until the music ended and lights flashed from the ceiling, signaling the club was closing for the night.

Tom kissed his wife while people moved around them, and Mary didn't break the embrace nor stop reciprocating the affection she enjoyed. They kissed until they were the last two on the floor and the waiter touched Tom on his shoulder. "I'm sorry, but it's time you two left."

Tom broke from his wife long enough to respond "Okay." He looked at Mary. "Are you ready to go home?"

"I'm ready for anything in the world with you."

Morning came with a flash as Mary woke, seeing her husband had left the bed. She put her feet on the floor, grabbed her robe, and went into the bathroom. She finished relieving herself and washed her hands and face, brushing her teeth before going downstairs to the kitchen. She was surprised to see Tom using the new office in Junior's bedroom. From his appearance, she could tell he had not slept much. He was on a call, and his laptop was in full view of his face. Tom typed while interacting with whomever was on the call.

Mary continued to the kitchen and made coffee. She decided to make breakfast instead of having the bagel or cereal that was her usual weekday morning routine. She broke two eggs into a bowl, added a little milk, and stirred like a mad woman. She retrieved a skillet from the cupboard, put it over heat on the stove, and touched it with a little oil. She then gathered ingredients: cheese, ham, spinach, and a secret salt mix she always created. She grilled the egg mixture on the skillet and turned to put bread in the toaster, then added four strips of bacon to the mix.

Tom smelled breakfast, and at the end of his call, he left the laptop and walked downstairs. "If I didn't know better, I'd swear you were up to something," he chuckled. "Breakfast smells amazing."

"Baby, we're good. I don't want anything but your joy."

"You got that, baby." Tom poured a cup of coffee. "Can I pour you one, too?" he asked.

"Sure," She flipped the bacon, "I'll call you when breakfast is done."

"I'll be right down as soon as I hear you."

"Okay." Mary kissed him. "Now, go." She smiled and returned to flipping the bacon.

Tom walked upstairs with his coffee in hand and went to the office. He looked at his laptop. *Why am I giving them so much of my time?* he wondered. Fifteen minutes later, Mary called: "Breakfast is ready."

"Be right there." Tom finished typing his email and took his empty coffee cup downstairs. "It looks great." He poured himself a refill of coffee and walked to the breakfast bar. "It's not the weekend, but I could get used to this."

"Sure, you can." Mary sat down with her coffee in front of the plate she'd filled. "As a matter of fact, maybe - just maybe - we should."

"What are you saying?"

"We don't have much to worry about these days.

Between the two of us, we have enough to retire, live smart, and enjoy life. Why work for someone?"

Tom shook his head as he sat in front of the breakfast plate that Mary had created. "I'm...well, you know..." Tom paused. "Maybe you have a point."

The doorbell rang. "Babe, are you expecting someone?"

"Not at all.

Tom rose from the table and walked to the front door. He looked at his watch. It was barely ten in the morning

"Who is it?"

"Sir, it's Captain Calhoun and Sergeant Monarch."

Tom paused and grabbed his face...*no, it can't be.* He grabbed the door handle and turned it slowly, as if the thought would disappear once the bolt cleared the lock connection. He had heard of guys in his unit pulling this type of assignment when he was in the Army. His mind raced to the worst news these soldiers could give and then he thought of the fact that their son could be wounded. Tom opened the door.

"Good morning, Sir, we're here to give you information about your son, Specialist Stetson."

"Captain, Sergeant - please come in."

Mary looked up, pulled her housecoat closed, and stood up from the table. "I'm sorry, I didn't expect company this early. Please forgive my appearance."

"No problem, ma'am," the Sergeant said.

"Sir, Ma'am - can you join me on the couch?"

"Sure." Tom looked at Mary and extended his hand to grab hers as she approached. They sat next to each other and held hands.

"I'm here to inform you that your son, Specialist Stetson, was killed during a mortar attack on his remote base." The Captain touched Tom's shoulder. "The United States and the United States Army offers our greatest condolences for your loss...Sergeant Monarch and I are here to answer any of your questions."

Mary screamed before running upstairs, leaving Tom alone with the two soldiers.

Chapter 13

Tom left the funeral home, holding Mary around the shoulders. They hadn't expected the large turnout for Tom Junior's funeral. Many people who showed up were friends who had grown up with their son, and those who had served who were back from Afghanistan. The procession to the gravesite was two miles long, and it took forty minutes through traffic to arrive as coordinated with the funeral directors and the Army unit.

Mary took Tom's hand to get out of the black stretch limousine. She walked arm in arm with her husband to the gravesite and took a seat at the front, as the funeral director had instructed.

Tom shook the hands of a few soldiers who had known their son. He thanked them for coming, walked over to Mary, and sat next to her. His family was on one side and Mary's extended family sat on the other.

The minister shared a few words, routine for their faith, and ended with the traditional "Dust to dust, ashes to ashes." By the time he said "Amen," soldiers stood at attention and fired weapons into the air three times...BANG! "Aim-Fire!" the Sergeant shouted. BANG! And, repeated for a last time...BANG! A bugler played Taps, and at the end, Captain Calhoun took the flag that was folded on top of Tom Junior's casket, marched to the front, kneeled, and offered it to Mary. "On behalf of the United States and the President, I give this flag in honor of your fallen soldier." He then rose and saluted, made an about face, and marched back to his position near the squad.

"Right, Face. Port Arms...Forward. Hugh!" The soldiers

marched away from the gravesite, and others rose to leave. Mary and Tom stayed behind and watched the gravediggers lower the casket into the ground. Mary was still in tears. She walked over to the grave and tossed one of the roses into it, which landed on top of the casket right above the first shovel of dirt. She watched the grave diggers shovel dirt for five minutes until Tom nudged her to go. "Baby, we have to go. There are people waiting on us."

"Let them wait." She pushed him back and watched the men continue to place dirt on their son's grave. "I'm...I'm..." She broke down in tears again, and fell to her knees. "Oh, my God!" Mary screamed, holding the flag to her chest like it was the young teddy Tom Junior had loved. "OH MY GOD!"

Tom waved at the funeral director to go ahead; they'd catch up. The director left one car and the others were led to the repass.

Mary stood with Tom's aid, stepped back from the completed grave, and sat in the chair under the tent. She didn't talk nor move for another hour. "Mary, baby, I know it's hard, but we've said our goodbyes for now. We can return every day and say them again, but we have to go now. It's getting late."

Mary looked at Tom and nodded. She grabbed his hand and stood. It was Tom's hand that got her to take a step towards the limousine. "Baby, we'll be back tomorrow...I promise."

Mary nodded in agreement and sniffed. "Tomorrow." She wiped her eyes with one hand and held the flag with the other. "Tomorrow," she repeated and took another step towards the limo. Tom stayed by her side with each step to the stretched black funeral home's sedan. "We can make it; we have to. Junior would want us to."

Mary looked at Tom as she sat down in the car. "How the hell would you know what Junior wants now?"

Tom covered his mouth. One hand started shaking and his other hand formed a fist. "Mary, don't say things like that."

"I am right, you know. He's not with us anymore, so how the hell would you know what he wants?"

Tom slammed the car door and walked to the other side, got in, and looked at his loving wife of many years. "I know our son, and I raised him. I know what he likes and dislikes. And, like you, I loved him with all my heart."

Mary wiped the last tear that fell on her cheek. "Tom, let's go home."

"We'll be back tomorrow."

"No, I'll be back tomorrow."

Tom's head tilted as he looked at Mary. "I'll come with you."

"That isn't necessary. I'll be back tomorrow."

Three weeks passed and Mary had visited Tom's grave every day. She made it her routine: wake up, have coffee and a bagel, and drive to Tom's gravesite.

On occasion Tom followed her to be by her side since they hardly conversed anymore. Mary stopped cooking and never gave time to Tom after losing Tom Junior. She kept her focus on Tom Junior and did things he had done during his childhood. She visited his high school, walked into the drama class, and sat in the last seat at the back. She touched his school chair and breezed her fingers across the group picture Tom Junior was in. She walked to the trophy display and stared at the awards he'd helped win. Mary then went to baseball camp where he had played in little league. She sat in the spot she remembered he'd had on the bench. Mary rubbed the wooden space.

Tom followed her for three days, and her routine scared the

drama teacher and shocked the Assistant Principal. The park administrator communicated his concerns to Tom on one of the days he followed her. They were in the living room of their beautiful home when Tom spoke. "Mary, you have to pull yourself together."

"Why are you talking to me? Our son is gone."

"I know he's gone, baby, but we have to find some way to move on." Tom reached for Mary's shoulder, and she moved away to avoid his touch. He looked at her, and his eyes filled with tears as her behavior towards him stabbed his heart. "I'm only trying to help us get through this."

"You're not helping."

"People are worried, and I can't let you continue this way."

"I'm doing fine with my son."

"Mary, are you saying that you see Tom Junior?"

"Every place he's been, I see him."

Tom rubbed his head from front to back and stared at his wife. "Baby, we need to see a doctor. I'm making an appointment for you."

"Whatever." Mary walked upstairs.

Tom dared to follow his wife to the master bedroom. He hadn't been in there since the funeral. Mary didn't see him as Tom Junior's father anymore, let alone let him get close to her in bed. "I'll be in the guest room again tonight. If you want to talk..."

Mary slammed the door and turned all the lights off. It was completely dark in the master bedroom. She modified the window curtains to keep the light from shining through.

In the morning, Tom managed to visit with his Priest and talk about Mary's condition. "Father, I am stumped over what to do."

"You've done what most would do. From what I've heard, you've gone beyond what the average man does for his wife." Father looked at Tom. "God has given you the power so keep influencing her, keep praying for her health, and keep pressing and loving as you've done. It's your blessing to do so, and God will support your efforts." The Priest went silent, looked at the ceiling and back at Tom.

Tom stared at the Priest without blinking and breathed slowly, as if his sentences were a breath of hope. He nodded when the Priest stood.

"One more suggestion," the Priest said. "If you cannot find peace of mind at home, I suggest you think about avoiding places that remind her of Tom Junior."

Tom nodded but not in agreement. "That's about everyplace around Baltimore."

"If not, then seek counseling. I can only help you if she wants to talk, but I'm no psychologist. I think she needs real help."

"Will time be on my side?"

"It can, but from what you shared, I don't think you have much time, as she needs a way to cope with your son's death."

"I see." Tom looked at his open hands. "Father, my hands have known her so much, she who is now a stranger in my home."

"And it's more of a reason to make it your focus to regain your wife and your home."

"I see." Tom stood in front of the desk, offered his hand to the Priest, and said, "I'm sure you're right, Father." The Priest shook Tom's hand. "Go with God, son. Go with God."

"Thank you." Tom turned from the center of Father's desk and walked through the open door. He looked left and then right, hoping that someone would guide his way to a doctor to help his cause. Tom walked through the cathedral, knelt at the altar, and placed his hands together. "Mother Mary, help me touch my lovely wife and aid her return to me. It's your will to take our son, but Lord God, let me have my love, my sanity, my sanctity of home, and return my best friend." Tom touched his forehead, both shoulders, and then his midsection before he rose from his knees. "Amen." He turned to the pews and walked down the center aisle towards the main exit.

Tom arrived home in time for dinner, he'd thought. He managed to enter the house without making a ruckus. "I'm home, baby. Where are you?"

Mary sat in the office and looked at the clothes they hadn't taken to Goodwill in case Junior returned home and wanted something clean to wear. She heard Tom's entry and his call, but when she didn't answer, Tom repeated: "Mary, I'm home - where are you, baby?"

Mary didn't respond, but rose from the seat and pulled a stack of clothes from the closet. "These have to go." She pulled as much as her hands could grab and threw them on the floor. "These have to go." She repeated the process, and her voice rose to a scream. "THESE HAVE TO GO!"

Tom rushed upstairs and walked into the office. "Baby, are you okay?"

"Junior's clothes have to go." She pointed to the pile on the floor. "He'll never be back to wear them...they have to go!"

"We'll get these out today. I'll take them to the drop-off box at the plaza."

"Good." She walked past Tom, heading downstairs for the kitchen. "I didn't cook." She turned to sit in the family room. "I'm not hungry."

"But, I..." Tom stopped shouting and remembered the Priest's advice. He breathed and pounded his chest with his fist, ignoring the shot of pain that ran through his heart. He recalled the woman who never put off fulfilling his desires. "I guess we'll go out."

"You go right ahead."

"Aren't we still an item?"

"Item." Mary looked towards the stairs and nodded, leaning slightly forward and shouted. "Really?"

Tom stripped off his shirt and threw it on the bed, placed a tie around his forehead so the flap dangled in front of his nose, and walked downstairs to Mary. "I can be your dinner." He swung his hips in a circular motion and then moved up and down as if a mating ritual enticing her response. He smiled. "Come on, baby, I'm your dinner."

Mary didn't laugh or shake her head, nor did she say a word. She simply stared and gave him a raised eyebrow, then turned from him and left the room.

Tom went upstairs and changed into running shorts and a tee shirt and put on his jogging shoes. He walked downstairs and, without a word, he opened the front door, went to her car, opened the door, put the key in the ignition, and turned on the engine. He sat in the car for a minute. *She's killing me*, he thought. He turned off the car, closed the door, and took off for the road, to jog down the street. *I will use the priest's advice and do as he suggested.* Tom turned the first corner, headed west. *I can do this. I can get her back to what she was before losing Tom Junior.* Tom turned the corner onto a main artery and jogged, facing traffic. *She needs counseling. How can I get her to see a counselor?* He jogged for another fifteen minutes and his stomach growled. He didn't think to jog for thirty minutes. He grabbed his stomach and turned at the next juncture, heading towards his home. He looked both ways before crossing the intersection and turned down the street on the way to his home.

Mary was sitting in a room without lights when he walked into the house. She had closed all the window curtains, blocking the evening sunlight. Tom flipped a light switch and was startled when he saw Mary sitting on the couch in darkness. "Are you okay?"

"I'm fine." She turned to Tom. "Turn off the lights."

Chapter 14

Tom parked his car in the lot of a strip mall. It was unusual for him not to go to the gym after work. He stepped out of his car, pressed the key lock orb, and walked towards the glass door of the office. He stopped and read the door sign to ensure he was in the right location before entering. By the time he walked in, the receptionist was at the door, a clipboard and pen in hand. "Please take a seat and fill out this form. I'll take your photo identification and give it right back to you. I have to copy it for the file. The doctor said he'll be right out."

"But you don't know who I am."

"No, I don't, but it's the routine. You're not a regular, or I'd have remembered you."

"You know all of his patients?"

"I do. I've been with the doctor for the last decade. I know who's new and who's a regular." The receptionist walked behind her desk and placed his photo on the copier. She pressed the button and the machine lit up.

Tom looked up after completing the first page. "You know, I didn't have an appointment. Is the doctor available?"

"He is, and as soon as I get your documents in order, he'll be right with you."

Tom shook his head and returned to completing the forms. *I know this is crazy. But I have to get some kind of advice.*

The receptionist called Tom and asked for the clipboard and pen. 'The Doctor is ready for you." She rose from behind her desk. "Please follow me." She led the way past a door and into a hallway. The receptionist turned right to open the next door. "Doctor, this is Tom Stetson."

"Thank you," he said, and she moved aside, allowing Tom to enter.

"I'm Doctor Williams." He offered his hand in greetings.

"Nice to meet you, Doctor."

"Please take a seat on the couch."

"Wow, the couch on the first day," Tom laughed.

"Oh, you can sit and not lay down." The Doctor returned behind his desk. He tapped on the keyboard at his computer and asked, "Your full name, please."

"Tom Stetson Senior." Tom looked at his hands. "Well, Tom Stetson - that's my name, now. I had a son."

"I see." Dr. Williams typed. "And are you married?"

"Yes, and that's why I'm here."

The doctor stepped from the computer, grabbed a legal pad of paper, and took a seat on the couch next to Tom. "Marriage is the reason you're here?"

"Yes. See, it's a long story, but I'm here for your help and guidance."

Dr. Williams looked at his watch. "We have about forty-five minutes, so tell me as much as you can."

"Well, Doctor, it all started when Junior joined the Army. I was happy, but my wife Mary was a little uncomfortable about it." Tom swallowed. "I'm a veteran, and having Tom Junior following my footsteps made me proud." Tom scanned the walls of the Doctor's office, reading the awards and degrees from various schools. He turned to the doctor. "And I'm afraid my wife is taking his death hard."

"Death? You mean your son is no longer alive?"

"He died in Afghanistan."

"Oh, I see." The doctor reached for a pen from his coat pocket and wrote 'Family loss' on the pad he held. "Are you here to discuss the death of your son and find a way to cope with it?"

"I'm here to find a way to help my wife cope with it. I need any advice I can get."

"Are you doing okay?"

"I hate that I lost my son. I hate it with a passion, and there is no greater loss than losing your kid. But I'm afraid losing him is driving my wife away from me, too." Tom clasped his hands, interlocking his fingers. "Doctor, I can't lose them both. I don't know how I will function."

"I see." Doc scribbled more on his paper. "And has she sought help?"

"She won't even respond to me, and that's why I'm here."

"Tell me about the relationship you had before losing your son."

Tom spoke of his and Mary's beginning and talked about the journey of their lives. He led the doctor though a sequential list of events and highlighted their recent trips before the news of Tom Junior's death arrived. He talked for thirty minutes without interruption from the doctor. And when he paused, Doctor Williams interjected, "I think you need to come and see me again. I have a picture, now." He paused and looked at his notepad. "I think you should do little things apart from the norm, but give her space as she needs it. Go slow with encouragement, one step at a time, so you see victories as you go. Let's schedule an appointment for next week and assess your progress."

"Okay."

Dr. Williams moved from the couch and went behind his desk. He pulled open a drawer and retrieved a pamphlet. "Read this and take it to heart. I know death is difficult and we all handle it differently, but in this case, this will help you understand what your wife is going through. And I think it's best for you, too."

Tom took the pamphlet and scanned it. "Thanks."

"Oh, there's a list of books in the pamphlet that can also help. But I need you to come back so I can give you my assessment and see how things have changed. I suggest next week and no longer because this is pretty serious, if she's as you say."

"She is, doctor, she is."

Doctor Williams moved from behind the desk and stood in front of Tom. He offered his hand. "We'll work through this," he said, and he shook Tom's hand and led him to the receptionist. "Book him for next week."

"Yes, doctor," she said.

"Tom, remember to read through and try those ideas on the pamphlet. I'll have a plan slated for when you return. Call me any time you need to talk."

"Thanks, and I will call you."

Dr. Williams exited through the door behind the receptionist's desk. Tom watched the door close before giving his attention to the receptionist.

"Mr. Stetson, what time is good for next week?"

"Ah, maybe the same time as today." Tom looked at his cell phone and touched the screen. He activated the calendar application. "Yes, next week is perfect."

"I've got you down for next week, same time, and I'll send you the rest of the forms you need to complete. I have your email address, so please respond with the information. Or bring in it next week."

"I will, thanks." Tom turned from the desk and headed towards the door.

"Mr. Stetson," the receptionist called.

Tom stopped and looked at her. "Yes."

"Sir, you forgot the card." She held the card and extended it forward. Tom walked to her and grabbed it. "Thank you."

"Sure. Have a great day."

Tom left the doctor's office and returned to his car. He sat in the driver's seat and read the business card before dropping it into the passenger's seat, where he placed the pamphlet. He started the car. "How is this going to work?" He pulled out from the parking spot, turned the car down the street, and eased into traffic. He drove to the nearest bookstore and sought those books the doctor had suggested he read. When he arrived home, Tom walked upstairs and saw Mary in Tom Junior's room again, sitting in darkness. "Hey," he greeted her.

Mary looked at him and didn't say a word. She turned to the picture she had thrown on the bed. Tom entered the room and turned on the light. He saw the family portrait that was hung on the wall going up the stairs. "I miss him, too." Tom touched Mary's shoulder.

Chapter 15

Tom arrived at the city library after he left work. He entered the doors, stepped to the assistance counter, looked left and then right, and focused on the lady behind the counter.

"Can I be of assistance?" the librarian asked.

"Sure, I'm looking for anything on depression."

"Let me see." The librarian stepped over to the desktop machine and punched some keys, reading the screen's information. "Depression, depression...are you researching for yourself or someone else? I don't mean to pry, but that makes a difference in the types of books I find."

Tom stared at the librarian with a raised brow, touched his chin with his left hand, and answered, "Someone else."

"Oh, well, that narrows the search." She typed some letters and paused for a moment, her eyes glued to the computer screen. She touched the mouse, rolling the ball that moved the screen. "Here's one available: 100 Questions and Answers about Depression by Alan T. Albrecht." She looked at Tom and watched him nod his head.

"Sounds interesting, for a start. Are there others?"

"Well, yes, there are quite a few books, but you have to narrow your search." The librarian scrolled her mouse down the page, "Here's another. When Someone You Know Has Depression; Words to Say and Things to Do by Susan Noonan is also available. And there are numerous videos available, if you want to watch them."

"Can you print the screen for me, please? I'll go find those books."

"Sure, no problem." She clicked with her mouse and the printer started up. "If you decide on the videos, just ask me, and I'll lead you to them."

"Sure thing, I'll do just that." Tom stood at the counter, waiting for the printout.

The librarian retrieved the printed paper and gave Tom the document. "I'm here if you can't find it. I'm sure it's here, per the system."

"I'll let you know if I can't find it." Tom took the paper. "You've been a great help, thank you." He smiled, turned towards the many rows of books, and mapped his way to the proper aisle. He searched the appropriate column, following the Dewey cataloging numbering system he'd learned as a kid. He pulled the first book and quickly found the second. Books in hand, he settled in a nicely-located chair in the middle of the library. Tom remembered the pamphlet that Dr. Williams gave him, and he went into his pocket, pulled it out, and opened it. He turned to the first page of <u>When Someone You Know Has Depressions; Words to Say and Things to Do</u> and read the Table of Contents, then scanned each chapter. He went directly to 'Finding Professional Help'.[1] He turned to the chapter and began reading.

The chapter brought his mind to angles he'd used and some he'd discovered to be useful. Tom glanced at his watch and saw that his workout hour had passed. He gathered the books and went to the help desk to check out, then scurried to his car. What he didn't want was a break from his routine. Even though Mary wasn't receptive to his interactions, he didn't want her to become suspicious.

*** *

---

[1] From the Table of Contents, Chapter 5, of *When Someone You know has Depression; Words to Say and Things to Do*, by Susan Noonan.

Mary sat in the middle of their bedroom, looking outside her window into the street. She watched middle school kids leave the bus stop, the same one Tom Junior had walked home from. She remembered watching her child carefully cross the street and laugh along the walk home with the kids he played with. Mary's eyes welled with emotions as one tear overflowed. She blinked with the attempt to control her emotions and ran to the bathroom for a tissue. She glanced in the mirror with the tissue in her hand, raised it to her eyes, and found a way of grasping her emotions. She stared into the mirror, hands on the counter, gazed into her eyes, and heard Tom Junior's voice calling for her just like he had through middle school: "Mom, I'm home." Mary looked at the door of the bathroom in hopes of seeing little Tom, the image she remembered, in t-shirt and jeans, sporting the cute haircut she'd had him get at the barbershop next to her beauty salon.

Mary pressed the tissue next to her mouth as she took a deep breath. *Life has to get better. God, show me how; help me.* Mary walked into Tom Junior's room and picked up another box of clothes. She went downstairs and placed the box with the others she had positioned to take out to the car. She repeated the process until there were no boxes left in the room. Mary went back upstairs to Tom's room to look around for anything she thought would aid in her effort to ease those horrible memories of Tom Junior.

She picked up a soccer trophy that Tom Junior had received at age five. Her heartbeat increased and her legs tensed, as stiff as if she'd run ten miles on a rainy day. She held the trophy next to her chest, as if holding little Tom again. She had no tears, yet her gloom carried dark emotions into an unlit prism. Her mind returned to memories, and she pictured her son's casket being lowered into the ground. A noise in the hallway startled her, and she looked at the doorway. There stood Tom Junior, exactly as the last time she'd seen him alive. Mary rubbed her eyes with one hand, still holding the trophy next to her heart. "Oh!" She gasped for breath, blinked again, and the image of her son disappeared.

"Mom," she heard. "Mom, it's going to be okay."

Mary closed her eyes tightly and managed to step back before finding the bed, where she sat. *I know I'm not hearing things.* She opened her eyes and looked towards the bedroom door again. She saw the hallway beyond the door, the pictures on the wall, and the decorative wall colors she'd chosen before Tom Junior's last visit.

"Mom, it's okay. I'm doing fine...Remember, you and Dad have a life to enjoy."

Mary, once again, closed her eyes and held that trophy with both hands against her heart. She didn't move. She hardly breathed and sat on the bed questioning her son's voice. She heard footsteps, and her heart fluttered from fear and excitement. Mary peeked with one eye and turned her head towards the door. Tom appeared, dressed from work. "Babe, are you okay?"

"I'm..." Mary turned to him, moved from the bed, and placed the trophy down on the dresser. She met him at the door and put her arms around Tom. "...I'm scared."

"Scared?" Tom responded, embracing her and putting his lips next to her ear. "You have nothing to fear. I'm always here. We'll get through this."

"I'm not so sure." Her eye closed, and her nose pressed into his shoulder exactly where the butt of a rifle sits before being fired. "I miss our son."

Tom eased a grin, realizing it was the first time in months that she included him in her thoughts of having lost Tom Junior. "Yes, baby. I miss our son, too." He pulled his wife tighter and held her until they breathed in unison. "We have to take one step at a time." Tom remembered the steps he'd read from his research: 'Distract and focus her attention' (Noonan). He released his grasp and looked Mary in the eyes. "We have to find a way to get you back, baby. I've missed you, and I can't live without you."

Mary gazed at the man she'd married, the man she both loved and hated because he'd encouraged their son to join the Army. Yet, she knew he was right, that she wasn't herself. She remembered Tom Junior's voice: "It's going to be okay." Tom didn't push his chances by pressing Mary to seeing a counselor or psychiatrist, but he felt confident that her first embrace including him meant she was on the right path.

Mary released Tom and grabbed his hand, leading him downstairs into the family room. She sat on the couch and pulled him close, using him as her human pillow. She pulled his arm around her and pressed her body next to his, as if losing herself in comfort, secure within a blanket of love and breathing with ease. Mary kept Tom's hand in hers and pulled tighter, ensuring he didn't move, and breathed in rhythm to his chest's rise and fall.

"Baby, I'm here." Tom spoke in a soft voice. "I am here, and we'll get through this."

"I know," Mary sighed. "Don't talk."

They sat for hours in darkness at a time when night filled the earth, then sat in silence where the only noise was the heating and air conditioner regulating the room temperature. Soft lights went through the room from passing cars, and faint glows from outside street lamps kept the room as softly lit as candles. Two hours became four, and when Tom woke from where he'd fallen asleep, Mary was breathing easily.

Tom looked at his wife and gently touched the hair on the

top of her head. He remembered the first time they'd cuddled like this as kids, and flashed to the delivery room where Tom Junior came into the world. He'd touched her hair the same way, on the same spot, using the same pressure of his hand. It was his way of connecting during times of great support. His wife - the woman he adored, admired, and loved with all of his heart - had broken through the tyranny of pain and finally sat next to him for hours. A tear dropped from his eye onto his cheek, and his breathing became faster but shallow.

Mary opened her eyes when a teardrop touched her. She moved, releasing Tom's hand, and sat up from his chest. "It's going to be okay." She looked at Tom. "Junior said it would." She wiped the corner of Tom's right eye. "It's going to be okay."

The sun gleamed through the window, sharing its heat through the glass, touching Tom first. He opened his eyes and moved, sitting up from the couch. Mary changed positions, allowing Tom to fully stand, if he wanted. "Good morning, baby," Tom said, smiling.

"Hey," Mary answered, and sat up. "I'll make coffee."

Tom looked at his love and stood next to her. "Okay, I'll get ready for work." He bent over and kissed her on the lips. "I'll be back in a jiffy."

Mary rose from the couch, wiped her eyes, and went to the kitchen. She grabbed the coffeemaker and followed her routine of preparing the coffee. Her heart beat fast, and her mind lashed to moments she remembered about her Tom, the man who had given her his heart. *Junior is right; he's absolutely right,* she thought. Mary noticed she'd used the last of the coffee grounds. After packing the filter with grounds, she tossed the empty coffee container into the trash. She opened the refrigerator and looked at its scarce shelves - nothing like it had once been. She shook her head. *I have a lot to do.*

Tom looked at his reflection after rinsing the last of the shaving cream from his face. He grabbed a hand towel and dried off with both hands. He reflected on his idea of pressuring Mary to visit a psychiatrist. Tom's mind reviewed the multiple lines he'd read from his research. 'Make her laugh – humor her into forgetting her pain[2].' *Should be easy enough,* he thought. He finished dressing and went to the kitchen, only to find Mary staring into empty cabinets. "I'm sorry, we don't have much for breakfast."

"I usually get something on the way to work these days. I'll do the same this morning."

"I have to go shopping."

"Wait for me to get home from the office, and I'll go with you."

"No, I have to do this." Mary looked at Tom and blinked her eyes twice. "I have to do this if I'm going to work at getting myself back."

"Babe, don't put pressure on yourself." Tom grabbed a coffee cup from the coffee cup tree and retrieved the coffee pot. He poured himself a cup, then returned the pot to the burner. "Do you have a cup?"

"No." Mary watched him repeat the process and nodded her head when he handed her a full cup of coffee. "I won't press it too hard today. But I've got to try."

"If anything..."

"...I'll call you, I promise."

Tom had left hours ago, but Mary hadn't moved beyond the boxes at the front door. She was dressed and well prepared to

---

[2]From the Table of Contents, Chapter 5, of *When Someone You know has Depression; Words to Say and Things to Do,* by Susan Noonan

go out from the house, but it felt like a barrier, an imaginary wall without an escape hatch. She stood at the door with her hand on the door handle, staring at the sunlight shining through the peephole. Mary turned the doorknob and pulled it towards her. When sunlight touched her and the cool breeze of the season whisked against her cheek, she knew it was time to step forward.

She repositioned her hand on the open door and pulled it closed as she made an effort to enter a new life. When the sound of the door broke her concentration, her mind flashed to words she'd heard from Tom Junior: "Mom...it's okay." Mary took another step from the porch. She held her purse tightly and looked at the car in the driveway. It was right where she'd left it months ago, covered with the scattered leaves that had recently fallen from the trees. Mary pulled her keys from her purse and pressed the key fob, unlocking the car doors. She entered the car, put her key in the ignition, and, to her surprise, the engine responded.

***

Tom looked at his cell phone on his desk, just in case he'd received a call from Mary. He looked at his work laptop, scanning a document he'd constructed to ensure the message was clear and concise. At the end of his review, he looked at the cell phone again, picked it up, and touched its sleeping face only to see remnants of a text message he'd kept, from Tom Junior. His mind entered the chamber of memory, recalling the smile he'd had when his son had sent the text. He remembered the hour, the minute, the second, and the last line of his message... 'love you much,' as they had routinely said. Tom snapped from daydreaming when a desk phone rang near his cubicle. He shook his head and placed the cell phone back on the desk. *I hope the car started.* Tom had made it a Saturday routine to run the car engine every week to keep the battery charged and maintain the car so that when she was ready, nothing would keep Mary from the chance to get out of the house.

Tom's cell phone rang, and he quickly answered. "Are you okay?"

"I'm good so far." Mary looked at the road ahead. "Is there anything you want for dinner?"

Surprised at the question, Tom mumbled, "Anything you decide."

"What did you say? I didn't quite hear you."

"I... uh..." Tom remembered the advice from the research he'd done, to be specific. "I think pasta is a good idea. You make the best, and I would love to have pasta tonight."

"Okay, that is a great idea." Mary smiled as she pulled into the parking lot of the local grocer. "Are you working out tonight before coming home?"

"Ah, no, baby." He paused. "I think I'll be home around six at the latest."

"Oh, okay." Mary parked and shut off the engine. "I will have dinner ready by then."

"I can't wait...I love you." Tom waited for a response.

"Love you, too." Mary disconnected the phone and looked into the parking lot. She grabbed the door handle and pushed the car door open. Her leg moved slowly, and her reach for the purse was like pressing the weight of the world with her pinky finger. Mary's hand curled into a fist, and she grasped her purse handles after dropping the car keys into its slight opening. With a second motion, she got out from the car, pushing the car door closed, and glanced at her reflection in the window.

"I can do this," she whispered in a push of confidence, touched her jacket, and turned to the right towards the rear of the car. To her surprise, she saw a billboard, directly in front of her, advertising Army recruiting. Her momentum stopped, and she stood staring at the billboard. Her hand tightened on the purse's handles, squeezing until the blood left her hand. Her eyes filled, and her blinking increased as she did everything she could to control her emotions. She looked to the ground and leaned against the car, her free hand holding her up. *I can do this*, she thought. *I can do this.*

Mary stood without the aid of the car and held her purse higher on her shoulder and under her arm. She clutched it with her hand, securing it from anyone who might snatch it from behind. Her strides became confident as she walked faster than she'd moved since the funeral. At the grocery store's entrance, her free hand grabbed a shopping cart, pulling it from the stack, and, like an ace driver or a one-handed, miraculously talented operator, she whipped the cart right into the store. She controlled it as she'd done for many years, walking down aisle after aisle, picking and pulling items from shelves, her purse hanging from her shoulder and not hindering the motion of her right arm.

Mary saw a neighbor approaching her head on, much as two horse-drawn coaches sharing the same path. She looked at the lady and held her breath in hopes that there wouldn't be anything other than a greeting. Mary dropped her head at five feet of their draw, coming abreast. "Hi, Mary," the neighbor said on approach.

"Hi," Mary responded and glanced at her neighbor. She didn't slow down but pushed forward, towards the end of the aisle. Her neighbor paused and watched her, then turned towards the items and pulled some from the shelf. Mary turned left at the end of the aisle and quickly went to the meat section.

She continued shopping but increased her pace so there was no contact with another neighbor.

***

Tom picked up his cell phone as though a psychic nudge told him she was going to call. He looked at the dark face on his Android phone and touched the screen. The phone's face lit up brighter than a Christmas tree during the holiday season. He scanned it for any activity from Mary. He stood in his booth, phone in hand, and walked to the break room. He looked at the phone before sitting at a table. *I should call. Maybe she didn't go. Maybe she needs my help...No, she'd call if she needed me.* Tom placed the phone on the table and looked up, only to see coworkers - one pouring coffee and another using the microwave. He looked at the blank space on the table. *I'll give her a call in twenty minutes if I don't hear from her.* He looked at his watch, taking in the time.

***

Mary made it to the cashier without waiting and managed to get through the line, without the small talk with the cashier. She focused on the flashing prices of the items. She looked right, at the open space beyond the bagger where little Tom Junior would walk back and forth from the bubble gum machine. Mary fought the urge to hear her son's voice and imagine his playful years. She closed her eyes, breathed slow, and opened them in time to see the final price.

"Ma'am, it's one hundred thirty-two dollars and sixty-four cents," the cashier announced.

"Okay." Mary pulled her purse from her shoulder and pulled out the debt card she hadn't used in months. She swiped it on the machine and an error message appeared: *denied.*

"Do you have another card?" the cashier asked.

"Let me look." Mary grabbed her wallet and retrieved a credit card. She swiped it, completing the transaction.

"Thank you so much for shopping with us." The cashier handed her a receipt and smiled. "Have a wonderful day." She turned to the next customer's items.

Mary put her purse back on her shoulder and pushed the cart with both hands. She walked through the exit and looked for her car. Her pace increased in the sunlight, and she briskly pushed the cart and made it to the car in moments, dodging any interactions. She loaded her groceries in the back seat of the car, closed the door, and pushed the cart into a staging row. Mary returned to the car, entered, and started it, driving home via the most expedient route possible. She reached for her phone and quickly dialed her husband. He answered. "Hi, Tom."

"Hi, babe," Tom exhaled, releasing his anxiety. "I'm so glad you called."

"I finished shopping, and I'm headed home."

"Great." He waited. "Did you see anyone?"

"Was I supposed to?"

"Well, I thought you'd maybe run into someone we know."

"Oh, you mean did I talk to anybody. No, I didn't talk, and that was -" Mary bit the right side of her bottom lip and her voice trembled, "- ah, good." Her eyes swelled. The escape from social interaction was a soft victory.

"I'll see you around six...I love you."

Chapter 16

Tom made his way down on the office building's elevator and managed to escape the crowd that was getting off work within the half hour. He got to his car, jumped in, and headed home as if an automatic chauffer took control. Tom pulled his notepad from his briefcase and held it on his lap during the drive. At the first traffic light, he flipped to one page of his notes and reviewed another advisory step to try with Mary. It seemed that his research was paying off. Her progression was noticeable, and getting her to see a shrink was his next objective.

Tom's stop at the next traffic light gave him time to read his list of advice. He scanned to the middle of the page, pausing as if the words glowed and highlighted places to focus on. 'Get her on a schedule,' (Noonan). Tom read the passage, heard a honk from behind, and looked up, paying attention to the traffic light. He pressed the accelerator, and the car moved through the intersection. *I can tell her, if she's open to a conversation tonight.* He looked at his side-view mirror and eased into the far-left lane. *Lately, it's hit or miss.* He entered the expressway. *She didn't say no when she cooked for the first time in months.* Tom smiled, remembering how they'd cuddled all night on the couch. He recalled the last time he'd made love to his wife, and how close he felt the opportunity was, ahead. The car returned to 'auto chauffer' and, without an incident, he made it to his driveway. Tom placed the papers back into his briefcase and exited the car.

With keys in one hand and briefcase in the other, Tom stood at the door, contemplating how he'd talk to Mary. He rehearsed the passage he'd read on the way home and imagined how he'd manipulate the evening, pressing his points. He entered the house to an amazing aroma. "Oh, my God!" Tom walked through the living room, dropping his briefcase on the couch. "It smells amazing."

"Hi, Tom," Mary greeted him. "I thought you'd like a good dish today."

Tom was taken aback, not expecting to see his wife active, as if he didn't need to manipulate the evening. Unbuttoning his shirt, he stood in the kitchen watching her move from the stove to the counter, preparing a dish she had planned for dinner. "It should be ready in about twenty minutes." Mary glanced at Tom. "Go change."

"Okay." Tom smiled, surprised at Mary's mood and actions. "I'll be damned."

"What's that?"

"Nothing, dear." Tom walked upstairs to the master bedroom and went into the closet. He put the clothes he'd worn in the hamper and pulled out his sweats, changed, and entered the master bathroom, then stopped and stared at the mirror. He gazed into his eyes, which were strong enough to make them appear independent from his face. *God, I am grateful, and I pray this is her path to getting better.* Tom blinked, and his image appeared on the mirror. He bent over the sink, turned on the water, splashed his face, washed his hands, and turned the water off before toweling dry. Tom returned to the kitchen, where he saw Mary setting the table for two. He smiled. "You want me to open a bottle of wine?"

"It's in the fridge. I thought we'd share a glass."

"Awesome." Tom reached into the fridge, retrieved the wine and moved to the cupboard where the wine glasses were kept. He managed to place two on the counter and went for the corkscrew. He twisted the tool into the cork. "Babe, you've been very busy."

"I needed to do something. So, I did." Mary looked at Tom from the dining table. "How was your day?"

"I think..." Tom smiled, "...no, I *know* it was awesome."

"How do you go from thinking to knowing?"

"You made my day." He pulled the cork free from the bottle and poured one glass and then the other. "I'm glad you cooked."

"Yeah, it's been a while since we've eaten together."

"I'm glad we're doing it today." Tom walked to the table and handed Mary a glass of wine. "Here you go." He tilted his glass towards his wife.

She tapped his glass in response. "We'll get back, baby; we will."

The house phone rang. Mary placed her glass on the table. "I'll get that." She walked to the phone. "Hello."

Tom watched her, sipped from his glass, and listened as if he could hear the voice over the speaker next to her ear. A pain shot to his chest as though a medieval arrow wounded him in a fight for his land. He watched Mary fall to her knees and drop the phone. Tom put his glass down and quickly moved to her side on the floor, picking up the phone. "Please call back later."

Mary's body shook violently, and tears ran down her face. She sat back on her heels and raised her hands to cover her crying. "I can't do this."

"Baby, you are doing great."

"I can't do this, Tom; I can't."

Tom comforted Mary, raised her from the floor, and walked her to the couch. "Sit here, baby. Just sit here for a minute." He ran for a tissue, turned off the stove, and returned to his wife. "I'm here." He sat next to her and placed his arm around her shoulders, pulled her close, and didn't say another word. The faint voice he heard on the phone was proof that Mary wasn't ready to face people asking about Tom Junior. He kept his arm around her until she placed her head in his lap. He caressed her, running his fingers through her hair like he'd done a thousand times. She breathed with running tears, wetting his pants, but he sat without making a fuss.

The microwave clock flashed 12:00, indicating midnight's arrival. Tom's legs were bloodless where his circulation had stopped due to Mary's weight. He couldn't move when Mary finally sat up, rose from the couch, and went upstairs.

Tom rubbed his thighs, pressing them for the blood flow to return and feelings to come back to his muscles. *She was so close to rebounding.* Tom's face became stoic as he fought to hold back his tears. He moved his legs from side to side and managed to stand. He walked to the table, picked up his wine glass, went into the kitchen, and retrieved the recently opened bottle of wine. He returned to the couch, placed the bottle on the coffee table, and drank wine. *This calls for drastic measures; forget about the step-by-step method. What should I do?* He gulped the contents of his wine glass and refilled it. *I can't make her go see the psychiatrist, but...* He sipped ... *maybe I should. Maybe my direct approach will shock her into recovery? Maybe.* Tom swallowed the wine and refilled his glass. He sat in the dim light of his house and finished the bottle.

Sunrise arrived with its usual flair, light beaming through the windows and hitting Tom's face. He rubbed his head and looked down to avoid the direct sunrays in his eyes and rose. He walked to the half bathroom down the hall. *Is she up?* he pondered. He splashed water on his face, looked at his reflection in the mirror, and shook his head from left to right.

How will I do it? He leaned against the sink, holding himself up with his hands. His face closer to the mirror, he thought: *I have to do it...I must do it!*

Mary was still in bed when Tom entered the master bedroom. She didn't budge when he opened the door to the bath and turned on the light. That was normally her cue to run downstairs and make coffee, but since Tom Junior's death, she rose late to face the day. Tom had hoped for more, when she'd progressed by shopping and cooking. *That damn phone call.* Tom turned on the shower, grabbed his razor and cream, entered the shower, and lathered his face. He shaved without a mirror and allowed the water to run down his body for a rinse. Tom washed, rinsed, and turned the shower off. He saw Mary walk past the bathroom door. "Good morning, babe."

Mary didn't respond, but closed the toilet room door. Tom heard the lock click. *Damn, that's a signal if I've ever heard one.* He resumed his work preparation routine, dressed, brushed his teeth, and went to the kitchen to make coffee. He stood near the coffeemaker and watched the black liquid drip into the pot. He flashed to a day where Mary would waltz to him and throw her arms around him, placing her lips on his. Tom smiled, staring at the coffee pot. *I miss her so much.* Tom grabbed a travel mug from the cabinet, poured his coffee, and on the way out, grabbed his briefcase. Mary hadn't come down for the morning as she had done many times before. Tom shook his head after he secured the front door, leaving the house for the day.

***

Mary didn't leave the bed for the entire day. She heard Tom's return from the noise of the closing front door. Mary looked at the window and turned over again, as she'd done all day. Her mind raced again, and she heard her son's voice. She opened her eyes and looked to the foot of the bed but didn't see her little boy. She closed them again, slipping back into sleep.

One week of sleeping and not responding was beginning to take a toll on Mary. She hadn't eaten, showered or bathed in days, and Tom kept his distance. She felt weakened from the lack of activities and food. It was noon on the eighth day of hiding from the world when she finally rose from bed. She wobbled to the bathroom, splashed her face, toweled dry, and stumbled downstairs. She was surprised to see a clean house, but grateful there was something in the fridge that didn't require cooking. She grabbed some food, bit into it, shut the refrigerator door, and sat at the counter. She munched until she was done, only to slowly rise for water. She drank from the faucet instead of retrieving a drinking glass from the cupboard.

Mary maneuvered to the couch, sat on the corner facing the window, and felt the sun on her face. *I have to fight back. This sucks; my boy is gone.* She patted her chest, took short spurts of breath, and managed to hold her tears back. Mary mustered her thoughts of returning to the life she'd had before Junior's death. But her legs didn't move when her mind said to get up and get going. Her weakened state made it difficult to respond. She rocked forward, hoping the momentum would help her stand. Mary successfully stood in front of the couch and managed to walk to the kitchen. She leaned against the counter and blanked out before hitting ground zero.

Tom returned home, opened the front door, and found things pretty much the way he'd left them during the morning. He did his normal routine, looking for any sign of a change with Mary. He went to the kitchen and stepped forward to the fridge, and his foot hit something. He looked down and there he saw his wife, on the floor in her pajamas. "Mary!" he called. "Mary!" His volume increased, and he touched her on the shoulder, but there was no response. Tom placed a finger under her nose, paused, and then put his hand on her neck for a pulse. Her breathing and heartbeat was slow, but it frightened him just the same. He picked her up, carried her through the door, and maneuvered her into the car. He ran back inside, collected his keys, and then drove Mary to the emergency room.

Chapter 17

Mary's eyes opened. The first object in her view was a white wall next to a large bay-like window with blinds wide enough to cover it. She turned her head and saw Tom snoozing in the lazy boy chair. Mary pulled herself upright and leaned against the headboard, supported by pillows. "Tom...Tom." She covered her mouth.

"Yes, dear." Tom yawned, rose from the chair, and stretched before moving next to her bedside. "Baby, I'm glad you're up. I was worried."

"What am I doing here? Why is this IV in my arm?"

Tom touched her arm short of the IV. "Baby, you were passed out on the kitchen floor, and you wouldn't respond. I bought you to the hospital. The doctor insisted on the IV because you were dehydrated. I mean, extremely dehydrated."

"I remember falling." She touched her forehead with the back of her left hand. "I was so weak."

"That is the other reason. I couldn't tell them the last time you ate anything. They said you needed proper nourishment, and that's another reason you're on the IV."

Mary moved her fingers to the IV to pull it out. "I don't need this now. I'm feeling better."

"No, not yet. Let's let the doctor see you first."

"Um, I'm okay."

"Babe, it's been a couple days since you fell asleep. So please let him check you before jumping out of bed...Relax, and I'll get the doctor."

Mary watched Tom leave the hospital room, then grabbed the television remote and turned it on. She looked at the window and listened to the voice on television break the room's silence. *A couple of days... hmm, a couple of days.* Mary raised the remote and pressed the button, changing the station. She repeated the process and kept pressing the button, channel surfing without watching. She gazed at the television, remembering she'd not eaten for a week but that one time before passing out in the kitchen. *I stopped crying again.*

Tom returned to the room, followed by a nurse. "Babe, this is Nurse Sutton. She's going to change your IV and check on you. The doctor will visit later this afternoon."

"Hi, Mrs. Stetson. I hope you're feeling better today. Your complexion is returning. That's a great sign." Nurse Sutton smiled.

"I guess," Mary sighed.

"Can you lift your arm, please?"

Mary lifted her arm, and the nurse restarted the IV. Nurse Sutton looked at the machine above, where Mary's head would usually hit the pillow in a prone position. She noted Mary's blood pressure and heart rate. "You really are improving." The nurse smiled.

"I guess so. I don't know why I'm here." Mary rolled her eyes at the nurse. She moved the bed up with the remote and turned the television off. Tom watched her adjust while the nurse continued printing information. "What time did you say the doctor would make his rounds?" Tom sighed, sat in the lazy boy, and waited for an answer.

"I think," Nurse Sutton looked at her watch and dropped the chart to her side, "he'll be here in a half hour or so. Well..." she paused, "that's his usual time, anyway." She looked into the hall through the open door and turned to lock eyes with Mary. "He'll be here." Nurse Sutton then smiled. "Can I get you anything? Maybe order lunch and see if you are up to eating?"

"No, I'm not hungry."

"Maybe I'll order it and you can eat whenever you feel up to it."

Tom interjected, "Yes, that's a great idea."

"Okay, I'll order a meal for you." She wrote on her chart. "It should be here within the hour. Meanwhile, relax, and the doctor will visit on his rounds, as I said."

"Thank you," Tom quickly responded while Mary sat silent. He walked over to his wife and grabbed her hand. "Babe, you gave me a scare. Please, let's do something so you don't get so lost again." He paused. "You're my life, and I'm worried because I think your depression is part of me losing you." Tom looked in her eyes. "And I don't want to lose the best thing in my life now. You have to talk about it with a counselor."

"I..." Mary glanced at Tom. "I was thinking of doing that, actually."

"You were?"

"Yes, because this isn't living." Mary wiped a falling tear away. "And I'm sure Tom Junior would want us to be happy."

"Yes." Tom tightened his grasp. "Yes, baby." He stood without releasing her hand, bent over, and kissed Mary on her lips, then kissed her hand. "It's going to be an awesome journey. The counselor I have in mind is really good."

"The one you have in mind?" Mary's eyebrows rose. "You mean you've been planning my counseling sessions?" She looked at Tom and placed her hand on her cheek. "I guess I'll follow instructions instead of making life difficult."

"I'll be with you."

Mary looked out of the window. "I'd like that. You're there with me, so I don't have to repeat a word. It's important," she swallowed, "and it works."

"Whatever you need, I'm here." Tom released her hand and went outside of the hospital room's door and stood just past the room's threshold. *God I hope she's ready to help herself.* He walked to the Nurses' station. "Is the doctor here?"

"Who's your doctor?" asked a nurse, who looked at a computer screen.

"I'm not sure...you know, I never asked."

"Dr. Pida," Nurse Sutton added. "He's making his rounds. He'll be in your wife's room shortly."

"Thank you." Tom turned in the direction of Mary's hospital room, and then turned back towards the nurses' station. "Is there a psychiatrist here, or do you suggest one?"

"The doctor will make that referral for you. I can't give you that kind of information."

"Okay, I see, but you know that there are some available?"

"Not immediately available, but there are a few in the hospital. We see them all of the time, and they make rounds, too. It's not up to us to refer one for your wife."

"Then," Tom swallowed, "how does it work?"

"The doctor will talk to you about it. Usually that's how you find out who is available."

"Oh, okay - or otherwise, I find my own."

"Yes, you find your own."

"Thank you." Tom turned towards his wife's room where he observed the doctor enter. He scurried to her bedside right as the physician read her chart. "Well, Doctor Pita, is she ready to go home?"

The Doctor turned a page, wrote on the chart, and turned to Tom. "I think she is. She looks physically well. But I suggest we find out why she got to the point she did." He moved to Mary's side. "Ms. Stetson, you had a close call. I think you should talk to someone, and I have a great doctor in mind. I asked him to visit this afternoon. I hope you don't mind."

Mary looked at Tom and nodded her head. "We agreed I'd talk to someone."

"Good, I think that's a start on the path to finding out why this happened." Doctor Pita raised the chart again and wrote a note about her accepting the referral. "Once he's done, I'll release you."

"Sounds like a plan." Mary looked at her IV. "Do I really need this?"

"No, actually, you don't." He moved to the IV and disconnected it, pulled the tube from her elbow, and placed a Band-Aid on her arm. "The nurse will get you ready for discharge."

"Thank you, Doctor Pita." Tom smiled and observed Mary nodding her head.

Mary spoke softly: "Yes, thank you."

Doctor Pita left the room while Mary rose to her feet, moved to the closet, and grabbed her clothes. "I can dress while waiting for the nurse."

"I guess you're right." Tom watched her, as he'd done a thousand times before, as she put her pants on one leg at a time. "You've lost so much weight."

"I'm good."

"Your pants were tighter."

"They're okay." Mary zipped her fly.

"I'm just worried."

"Don't be. I promised to get help." Mary pulled the buttoned blouse over her head.

Tom walked to the window and pulled the blinds back. The sunlight attacked the room, lighting up one side and decreasing darkness on the other. He covered his eyes with his free hand, shading them from the sunlight. Tom sat in the lazy boy again while Mary fully dressed, except for her shoes. She sat at the foot of the hospital bed.

Two hours passed, and both Tom and Mary wondered what was taking so long. Tom stood while Mary watched television. "I'm going to the nurse's station."

"It's taken you long enough." Mary frowned.

A man in a white coat entered the room before Tom got to the door. "Hi, folks." He reached his right hand towards the approaching Tom.

"Hi." Tom accepted the greeting.

"Umm, I'm here to see Mary Stetson, if you don't mind."

"I'm her husband, Tom."

"Nice to meet you. I'm Dr. Nubane, the psychiatrist."

"Psychiatrist?" Mary rose from the bed. "You mean there

isn't a nurse coming?"

"No nurse at the moment, but I'm here for a short visit, and I hope we can have a conversation."

Tom stepped aside and allowed Dr. Nubane to stand at the foot of the bed. "I hope you don't mind, Mary...I can call you Mary, right?"

"Sure, Mary is fine."

"Doctor, do you need me to leave the room?"

Dr. Nubane looked at Tom and nodded. "That would be a good idea." He glanced at Mary. "Can you entertain me for an hour?"

"Tom, we said we're going to do this, so..." Mary gave a slight smile.

"An hour...I can have coffee at the cafeteria."

"Good." Dr. Nubane added, "Please close the door on your way out."

"I can do that." Tom walked to the door and turned back to view Mary's interaction with the doctor. He saw Doctor Nubane hand a clipboard and pen to Mary. Tom closed the door.

Chapter 18

Tom drove Mary home from the hospital. The ride was as silent as the moment their eyes had viewed soldiers at the front door of their home. Their periodic glances at each other gave neither of them a chance to break the cold between them.

"Ah, I saw the psychiatrist give you a clipboard and a pen before I left for the cafeteria."

"Yeah." Mary looked at the buildings on the side of the road. "I had to answer a lot of questions."

"Good." Tom paused, giving his attention to the car ahead. "I think that's good."

"I had to write a lot about our past."

"You mean our relationship?"

Mary nodded. "Yes, our relationship."

"Oh, that must have been a home run answer." Tom smiled.

"Honestly, it was...okay."

Tom tightened his grip on the steering wheel, "I guess it's better than bad. 'Okay' is still a good relationship. What else did you share?"

"You know, family history, drug or alcohol addiction, or habits that may hinder your health or life. Typical questions to see if you inherited or have an electric short in the brain."

"Oh, the survey tries to deduct your behavior and mindset before you talk."

"Yes, I guess so."

Tom turned onto the exit, heading home. "I'm sure you answered it to where the doctor opened your mind and shared his first perception of our situation."

"You mean my situation."

Tom scratched his head and replaced his hand on the steering wheel. "I know, right, your situation."

"Believe it or not, the doctor said he would call you."

"Call me?"

"Yes, he had questions for you to help him understand me."

"Call me." Tom turned the radio knob, and music played in the car. He kept his eyes on the road in front of him, paying attention to the traffic and the roads he needed to drive towards their home. When he pulled the car into the driveway, he put the car in park, unsnapped his seatbelt, and walked around to Mary's door. He pulled it open and offered his hand to her. "I'm confused, but I get it. I need to tell him what I know."

"You know a lot, Tom." Mary rose from the seat, taking Tom's hand and moving beyond the car door. He closed it and trailed Mary's path to the front door. "And don't be afraid to be honest in your responses." Mary turned around, faced Tom, and raised her hand, touching his cheek. "You know I love you."

Tom breathed. It had been months since he'd heard Mary say she loved him. His mind escaped the moment, taking him to a time when Mary said, 'I love you' daily, to a moment in the shower when they'd frolicked like toddlers under a sprinkler during summer. He remembered kitchen moments where she'd let him taste the dish she was cooking and her usual, "I made this because I love you; it's one of your favorites." Tom snapped out of his memories and looked at his wife of many years. "I love you, too."

Morning arrived as easy as a soft wind in summer. The sun peeked through the curtains and hit Mary's eyes. She blinked towards the window, and a silhouette of a child appeared in her view, blocking the direct sunlight just enough to make her squint. Mary sprung to her feet and, rubbing her eyes, walked to the curtains. She opened each side with a whisk of her arms. The sound startled Tom, and he opened his eyes to bright light.

"Get up, Tom, it's morning."

"I see." Tom stood for a moment, stretched, and walked to the bathroom. "I think I'll run, this morning." His urine splashed the toilet water.

"You'll do what?" Mary screamed, standing near the window.

"Run, baby. I'm going for a run this morning."

"Oh, I haven't done that since..." Mary silenced her admission and remembered what Doctor Nubane told her ("Don't stop living. Let the reminders of Tom Junior drive your life and not stop you from doing things you enjoy.") "I'll have to start over. I mean, start from scratch, with running."

"When you're ready, I'll run with you."

"I wouldn't want to hold you back. You're in good shape. That's one of the things I told Dr. Nubane."

"Good shape." Tom pulled his spandex leg up, bending over to repeat the process with the other leg. "I don't mind you running with me. Maybe you can do it in a suit like mine."

Mary pulled a robe down from the back of the bathroom door and put it on. She went downstairs and started coffee. Her position at the table was right over the spot on the floor where she recalled passing out. Mary shook her head. "How can I have been so stubborn?" She grabbed two coffee mugs from the cupboard and placed them near the coffeemaker. "Oh, my God! I nearly killed myself."

"You nearly did," Tom agreed. "I couldn't have that happen. I love you too much."

"I know you do, Tom. I know you do."

The phone rang, and they both looked at it. "I'm not answering yet." Mary pointed at the phone. "You should get it."

Tom moved over to the phone, picked up the receiver, and placed it near his ear. "Hello."

"Mr. Stetson."

"Yes, this is he."

"Dr. Nubane here; how are you?"

"Doing well, Doctor." Tom pointed the phone in Mary's direction. "I'm glad you called."

"So am I." Doctor Nubane paused. "How's is Mrs. Stetson?"

"She's doing swell." Tom smiled. "I can see where your talk has made a difference."

"Great news. Some people respond faster than others. I'm sure that in this case, Mrs. Stetson is eager to get healthy."

"Nice to hear, Doctor; that's nice to hear." Tom grinned, remembering Mary had told him she loved him.

"That brings me to this point. Mr. Stetson, this isn't over by any means. She needs to continue the process. I'm sure you realize the importance of her having sessions."

"I do, and I have a doctor in mind, a Dr. Williams."

"Great choice, we're in the same circle."

Mary waved her forefinger left to right and pointed to the phone. "I started with him."

"Doctor, are you available for another patient?"

"It's why I called, to let you know two things. One is my diagnoses of Mrs. Stetson, and the other is to offer my professional help in getting Mary healthy again."

"Since she's comfortable with you, I think you get the job."

"Fantastic. I'll have my clerk call you with my schedule. I need to see Mrs. Stetson as soon as possible. We'll get on the path to recovery on the next visit."

Mary nodded her head in agreement and poured coffee in one cup. Tom reminded Doctor Nubane, "We'll look for your clerk's call."

"She'll call you shortly."

"Good enough. Thank you, Dr. Nubane."

"Thank you, Mr. Stetson."

Mary sipped her coffee and watched Tom return the phone receiver to its base. "I like the idea of seeing Dr. Nubane."

"I can tell." Tom turned towards the front door.

"It's not that I don't like yours...I mean, I know Dr. Nubane, and he seems okay."

Tom reached for the doorknob and looked at Mary. "I'm glad you are seeing him. I really don't care which one you see, but talk to somebody, and keep doing what you've done in the past few hours. I'm good." Tom left the house.

Mary answered the phone when it rang next and spoke with Dr. Nubane's scheduler. She made the appointment and answered preparatory questions for insurance purposes and was reassured of the doctor's objectives. She walked to the master bedroom, turning right at the top of the stairs. Mary turned around and walked to Tom Junior's bedroom door, which Tom had closed. She touched the doorknob, turned it, and lightly pushed, cracking it just enough to see sunlight through the slit. She stood at the door. *I should go in. No, I can't.* She pushed the door another inch wider than she had, and sunlight struck her face, its glare beaming through uncovered windows. *I can do this...I can do this.* Mary's hand started shaking, her eyes welled, and a tear trailed a path to her chin. One drop of blood fell from her nose. She touched below her nostril, wiped the blood, and looked at her hand. She closed the door and ran to the master bathroom.

Mary grabbed a tissue from the bathroom vanity and wiped her nose. She looked in the mirror. *My eyes are horrible, and my top is really baggy. I liked this top, and now it's so big.* Mary grabbed at her top while looking in the mirror. She wiped her nose and looked at the tissue. *I can't believe I...I can't believe how hard it is to open his door.* She sat on the edge of the bathtub and looked to the sky. *God, help me... this isn't living.*

***

Tom ran beyond his turnaround point and pushed further, where the major traffic intersection stopped him. He waited at the crosswalk and watched cars pass, observing couples laughing and interacting. *We were like that. We always laughed.* Tom scanned his watch and turned around. *We can laugh again. She said she loves me. She said she wants to get better. She will get better, and our lives will return to happier times.* He took off towards home, running the same path he'd trekked from his house. *My baby, my love, my wife, and my life will return. She's the best, and I'm better because of her. I can't let her fight alone.* Tom ran, repeating his thoughts and like rewinding black and white movies of the 1920s. His mind kept him occupied, and when he paused his thoughts, the front door of his home was ahead of him.

He entered the house exactly one hour from his departure. He closed the door and went upstairs to the master bathroom. "Mary, are you okay?"

"I'm..." Mary looked at Tom and returned to staring at the floor. "I'm fine." Her hands were on her thighs and her head slumped.

"But you don't look okay." Tom sat beside her. "Baby, what happened?"

"I can't do it."

"Can't do what?"

"I can't go in there."

Tom placed his arm around Mary, "You will in time. You will in time."

"Are you sure?"

"With the help you're going to get, I'm positive you will." Tom caressed her back. "Did they call?"

"Yes, my first session is tomorrow afternoon."

"I'm taking off work to go with you."

"I'd like that." Mary turned to Tom and hugged him. "I need you to help me."

Tom hugged her. "I'm with you. I'll never leave your side...baby, we'll get better. I know we will."

Morning arrived with the calming sound of birds singing outside of the master bedroom window. Mary placed her feet on the floor and sat up, looking at the clock on the night table.

She stared, and her breathing decreased. She saw the red numbers of the clock become fuzzy, and her hand grabbed the clock. Mary looked at the ceiling. It turned, spinning faster the longer she stared up. Mary released the clock and grabbed her pounding head, falling back onto the bed.

"Mary, Mary, are you okay?" Tom rose from the bed and went to her side. "Baby, say something."

Mary's eyes were closed. "I'm okay; stop yelling."

"Okay." Tom pulled her closer with one arm. "I'm sorry for yelling." He paused. "It's natural to do, since you scared me once."

"I'm okay, no worries." Mary stood. "My appointment is today."

"With the psychiatrist?"

"Yes, with Dr. Nubane. You are going - right?"

"I am definitely going."

"Good." Mary went into the bathroom and ran the shower, disrobed, jumped in under the water, and washed like any other time she'd showered. Tom made a motion towards the shower and disrobed, reaching for the shower door but stopped short of opening it. He pulled the bathrobe from the back of the bathroom door, pulled it on, and walked downstairs. Tom pulled the coffee pot from the coffeemaker and measured the water for several cups. He grabbed the coffee grounds from the cupboard and measured the appropriate amount per cup. *There was a time I'd jump in with her. But now, right now, I'm hopeful for a simple kiss.* He placed the grounds into the filter and closed the lid. He pressed the on button and pulled two coffee mugs from the shelf, placing them near the coffeemaker, and didn't move, staring at the pot. *She used to enjoy us. I hope Dr. Nubane helps her. I miss my wife, her touch, her kiss, her affection.* Tom's eyes welled and tears fell. *I miss Tom Junior, too, just as much as I miss Mary.*

***

Mary stepped out of the shower, toweled dry, and pulled on her robe. She stepped to the vanity mirror and wiped the steam off to see her reflection. She moved her hair from her face, gazing at her foggy image. *I need to do this, get back to my life. I can't let this continue, or I may die.* She grabbed her toothbrush, turned on the water, and rinsed the head. Mary turned off the water and grabbed the toothpaste, placing a small amount on the toothbrush. She brushed her teeth. *I can do this because I have to.* Mary dropped her head above the sink, spat the saliva mix from her mouth, and turned on the water for a rinse. She used her hand as a cup and rinsed her mouth, then spat the water, rinsed the brush, and replaced it.

"Yes, Mom, you have to do this." Tom Junior's image appeared in the mirror next to her. "You have to save Dad."

Mary grabbed the top of her bathrobe and placed it over her mouth. "Yes, son, I have to."

***

Tom stood erect, leaving the kitchen for the master bathroom. He heard water running from the sink and arrived at the door when Mary's head was lowered. He froze, looking at Mary as he'd done a thousand times before, admiring the beauty of his heart. Tom watched her grab the bathrobe.

"You have to do what, Mary?"

Mary looked at Tom. "Didn't you hear him?"

"No, I didn't hear anything other than what you said."

She looked beyond Tom. "Excuse me." Mary walked

153

through the doorway when Tom stepped aside.

"What did he say?"

"Nothing, nothing that you'd understand."

"Mary, please." Tom turned to the vanity with both hands on the counter. "What did he say?"

Mary shook her head and sat at the end of the bed. "To save you."

"Save me?"

"Yes, save you." Mary trembled, dropping her hands into her lap and interlocking her fingers. "Save you." Her eyes blinked, and she lifted her head, focusing her sight on Tom's stature. "I know you don't think I want to, but I want to save us."

"Mary." Tom's eyes connected to hers. "Do you realize it's been nearly a year since you've said you love me?" Tom tightened his robe belt. "You can't imagine how long I've yearned to hear those words." He walked to the door of the bedroom. "And I know you're fighting to come back. I need you to come back. I pray you come back." Tom moved to her side. "I will do anything to help you come back to me." He embraced Mary, and she put her head on his shoulder.

"I will...I'll need your help, but I think I can do it." Mary closed her eyes. "Do you think I will forget Tom Junior?"

"No, no, no - we can't forget our boy. We will never forget our boy." Tom held her tighter. "But we live with his memory." Tom paused and swallowed. "We can't stop living."

Chapter 19

Tom exited the front door of their home, leading the way to the car. He entered, put in the key, started the engine, and watched Mary buckle her seatbelt. She looked at Tom and smirked. "I hope this first meeting is worth it."

"We talked about this." Tom touched her arm. "I think you'll find out a lot today."

"I will?"

"Of course, you will." Tom adjusted the rearview mirror, even though no one else had driven the car. "I don't see why you won't get something from the first conversation in his office."

"Maybe because I don't know what to say."

"Whatever comes to mind will do. I'm sure you'll have plenty to talk about."

"I don't know about that." Mary looked out of her window.

"You are much more of a talker than I can ever imagine being."

Tom shook his head, reaching for the radio, then placed his hand back on the wheel. Ten minutes later, Tom turned the car into the building's parking lot. The building's face bore plantation columns, high like the Roman architecture during Caesar's reign. The entryway was glass, a full, double door type, and anyone could see through to the reception desk. When Tom stopped the car, Mary unbuckled her seat belt and opened the door, easing her way to exit. She closed the door, looked at the building, and glanced at Tom, who stood next to the front of the car. "I think it's cool," Tom pointed out.

"It's for a purpose."

"A purpose?" Tom walked next to Mary, grabbing her hand.

"It's because people need to get in a mindset before walking in."

"Wow," Tom sighed. "I hope you're better when you talk to Dr. Nubane."

After the reception desk, Tom and Mary managed to get to the office, enter, and check in for Mary's appointment. Mary sat at the corner of the waiting room next to an end table. Tom followed and sat on the other side of the table. "Did you get another set of questions to answer?" Tom pointed at the stack of clipboards at the reception desk.

"They didn't tell me to, so I guess I don't." Mary picked up a magazine and thumbed through the pages. Tom scanned the room, not settling on one person but glancing at everyone. He caught some eyes but quickly looked away. He whispered to Mary, "There's a lot of normal-looking folks with problems here."

"Maybe some are just waiting... stop being judgmental."

"Judgmental?" Tom shook his head and picked up an auto magazine from the table. *Oh - judgmental.* He turned the page.

A person from the back opened the doorway to the office. "Mary Stetson."

"Here." Mary rose from her seat, placed the magazine on the table, and looked at Tom. "I'll be back for you."

"I thought..."

"...If the doctor asks, I'll send for you." Mary walked through the open door without a glance at Tom. An assistant, who directed her to an empty office, greeted her: "Please take a seat." The assistant sat behind the desktop computer. Mary glanced at the office decor and concluded it was her office. "I never thought there was a pre-screening for Dr. Nubane."

"Usually there is, but you've seen him once. Right now, I'm retrieving your record."

"Okay." Mary sat, waiting for the data to appear on the computer screen. When the screen print appeared, she looked at the personal information and the insurance data. "Is this correct, Mary?" The assistant pointed to the screen.

"Yes, it is. I don't remember giving this to you..."

"You wouldn't. When Dr. Nubane spoke to you, the hospital shared it. It's their normal process."

"Oh, okay." Mary nodded her head. "What's next, since the record is correct?"

"You see the doctor. I'll take you." The assistant clicked on the mouse, and the computer screen went to a screensaver picture. She rose from the desk and walked to the door. "You can come with me." She opened the door and led the way to Dr. Nubane's office. The assistant knocked on the door. "Doctor, Mrs. Stetson is here."

"Thank you." Dr. Nubane stood from his desk and greeted Mary. "How are you, Mrs. Stetson?"

"I'm here to find out."

Dr. Nubane tilted his head at her answer as he walked to his desk. "Please take a seat and let me get my clipboard."

Mary followed instructions and sat on the chair across from the couch. She watched the doctor move to the couch. "I thought you'd want the chair."

"I believe you should sit wherever it makes you comfortable."

"Okay, I see." Mary shifted in her chair. "I'm pretty comfy here."

"Good, so let's get started." Dr. Nubane flipped a sheet of paper over the top of his clipboard. "The last time we spoke, you were fighting the pain of losing Tom Junior." He paused. "How are you feeling today? Do you still have pain?"

Mary stared at Dr. Nubane, looking beyond his face. "I fight every day, the same as I have since he died. You know, I try not to have reminders."

"Mary you're always going to live with reminders. It's what you do after   that we need focus." He flipped the page and scribbled. "Can you tell me how you feel when you are reminded?"

Mary looked down at her lap and pressed her purse tighter into her stomach. "I cry. I cry until my tears stop falling and my voice changes."

Dr. Nubane scribbled on his clipboard, paused a moment, and then wrote more. "Does every reminder make you respond the same, or is there a difference in how you're reminded that causes you to cry?"

Mary tilted her head and looked at the Doctor. "I cry at anything that reminds me of him."

Dr. Nubane wrote again. "Do you get reminders out of the home"?

Mary clutched her purse. "I do, and they can be from a billboard to a kid's voice."

Dr. Nubane continued writing, flipped a page, and wrote more. He looked at Mrs. Stetson and then returned to writing.

He stopped. "Mary, do you tell your husband about the pain?"

"I do, I usually do. But mostly he knows before I share anything."

"Oh, he's fully aware of your feelings."

"He is." Mary released her grip on her purse. "He knows because he observes my reaction when we're together. Just today, I managed not to break down coming here."

"How did you manage that?"

"I didn't look at billboards and didn't pay attention to buildings that Tom Junior and I visited."

"I see." Dr. Nubane scribbled, and when he stopped writing, he pulled the pages closed over the clipboard. "Mrs. Stetson, we have a challenge ahead of us."

"We do?"

"Yes, we have to get back to being functional in any environment that reminds you of Tom Junior. If we can do that, you'll be on the road to recovery."

"So." Mary looked at her lap and then at Dr. Nubane. "What do you suggest?"

Dr. Nubane walked to his desk and pulled out a folder, retrieved a sheet of printed-paper, and held it up. "This is a list of exercises we should take part in. When you follow one, I'm asking you to take notes on your response. Each one should have a response. I want you to bring it back for the next session."

"Oh, I can do that." Mary walked to the desk and took the printed instructions. "Can I write the responses on a separate sheet of paper?"

"Of course, as long as I know which question is being

answered."

"No problem."

***

Tom watched Mary exit the door most patients entered. He rose from his chair, dropped the magazine, and approached her. "How did it go?"

"It went okay...I think."

Chapter 20

Six days had passed since Mary's session with Dr. Nubane. She wondered what would happen if she didn't complete the assignment. Her eyes were glued to each word on individual sections of the document, scanning for loopholes in the doctor's instructions. *I can lie, can't I?* She placed the paper down on the kitchen counter. *If I don't finish - what can he do?* Mary opened the refrigerator, grabbed vegetables, and placed them on the counter. She grabbed the large cutting knife and cutting board. *If I don't say anything, how can he help me?* The rhythm of the knife chopping veggies sounded like the making of a symphonic ballad. She cut, chopped, and sliced until the colorful mix was completed.

Mary grabbed a pot and frying pan from the bottom cupboard. She rinsed both and retrieved olive oil, measured, and poured it into each. She stepped back from the stove and watched the flame ignite two burners. *Poor kid, I'd scare the crap out of him when those flames blew. It's a wonder he got around to cooking.* Mary chuckled while turning the flames low. She picked up the veggies and placed half in each pot, then added a cup of water to the pots.

Her brand of cooking added flavor through the mixture of multiple spices. She picked up the red pepper, sprinkled it over the pot and frying pan, then added a multiple seasoning mix. *Tom Jr. loved this dish.* She blended the oil and veggies, mixing it over the heat. *Oh, my God! I made this for him, and he's not even here.*

***

Tom stood over the pisser and remembered reading question after question on Dr. Nubane's document. He answered each one and found himself impressed with the outcome of his assessment. *She should answer each one. I know the doctor will get enough to understand her mind.*

Tom got himself together, walked to the sink, looked in the mirror, and washed his hands. His eyes were glued to his features, rescanning his face for imperfections. *She should be okay.* Tom shook the extra water from his hands and grabbed paper towels to finish the job. *She will be okay. I see a difference just from one session.* Tom exited the restroom and returned to his cubicle. He tapped his computer mouse and returned to work. His focus broke when the desk phone rang. "This is Tom."

"I need you to work on this project with me this afternoon," Mike informed him. "It's a client in San Francisco. We're developing a business relationship. You're the guy who can get cozy with them."

"I am?"

"Yes, so met us at five thirty in the west conference room. I'll brief you for the 6:00 p.m. meeting."

"I will be there, Mike." Tom placed the phone on its base. He picked up his cell phone and dialed home. "Babe, I will be late coming home."

"I was cooking dinner. How late?"

"It's a west coast meeting that starts at six, so I guess I'll be there around eight, if traffic is good."

"I'll have dinner waiting for you, so don't eat anything."

"Thanks, baby, I'll be home as soon as it's over." Tom swallowed. "Did you finish the questionnaire?"

"I started it, but I didn't finish."

"Oh, I thought you'd finish in one hour."

"Not today. I didn't get through it all." Mary looked at the ceiling. "We'll talk when you get home." She went to the stove and turned each burner off, covered the pots and pan, and went to the family room. Her stare into the empty room transitioned into a memory of Tom Junior's middle school years, sitting on the couch and asking for help with his homework: "Mom, I don't get it."

"Here, let me look again." Mary moves next to Tom Junior. "This is it. Look at how I'm multiplying the variable." She writes the number under each column. "If you do it this way, it's easier to see. Here, you try." Mary smiled at Tom Junior's attempt. "See, you got it." Her flash of memory disappeared, and her eyes welled, but before a tear dropped, she managed to get up and return to the kitchen. She picked up the questionnaire with the information Dr. Nubane had requested and his instructions. Mary scanned the questions she hadn't answered. *I can do this. I don't need a doctor telling me how to remember my son. Damn it, I remember my son the way I want to.*

***

Tom sat at the center of the conference table across from Mike.

"Are you sure I'm the man for the project? I've never met the customer directly; I'm a backend person."

"If I weren't confident in your ability, you wouldn't be here."

"I appreciate the vote." Tom smiled. "But I'm not sure how I can contribute."

"We're about to discuss that." Mike handed Tom a document. "Follow me on this."

"I think I can." Tom read the document and gave his undivided attention to Mike.

"It's the highlighted account; you saved us with your effort. They were pulling out, and as you know, they were major for our growth this year. I don't know what you really did, but it worked out so well that..." Mike placed his hand over his mouth and coughed, "...excuse me – the director wants you on this account."

"Wow." Tom smiled. "I don't recall doing anything special."

"Maybe you didn't, but the customer likes you. And that's the deciding factor. That account had been in four others' hands. Everyone failed. But your efforts made it grow, and that's why you're on this call. We're introducing you to another tough account."

"You want me to save this account?" Tom reviewed the numbers on the document. "It's pretty dire - um, I mean it's almost in the pit of doom."

"Yes, you can save it."

"I can save it?" Tom wiped his forehead.

"If you aren't up for the challenge..."

"...No, no - I'm up for it." Tom looked at Mike. "I will do my best."

"That's what I like about you, Tom - you give your all on anything coming your way. I can't ask for more."

"Thank you for noticing, Mike."

It was eight thirty when Tom arrived home. He pulled into the driveway and saw a dark house. His heart started to race. *She didn't say she was going anywhere.* He looked at his cell. *She didn't call.* He exited the car and ran to the porch. Tom opened the front door. "Mary! Mary! Are you here?" His heart raced while he turned on the light switch, illuminating the family room. He scanned for Mary on the couch, the floor, and behind the closed curtain. He ran into the kitchen.

"MARY!"

Tom turned on the kitchen lights, saw the pots on the stove, and walked over to them. He put his hand over each one to feel the heat. *Damn, cold as ice. Where the hell is she?* Tom ran upstairs. "MARY!" He turned on the lights in the bedroom and went into the master bath. "Mary, are you here?"

***

Mary turned the corner of the neighborhood block dressed in dark clothes, a walking silhouette against the lighted streets. She paced herself with the rhythm of a night stalker, one step against two heartbeats. Her eyes were mainly on the sidewalk in front of her. She didn't pay attention to passing cars nor did she notice her neighbor walking past. Mid-block, she looked up and observed a teenager walking from the car parked on the street. The girl's voice sparked a vision of Tom Junior's first girlfriend that he'd bought home. Mary stopped in her tracks and watched the girl enter her home and how the young man watched from the car. *Tom would have walked her to the door.*

Mary continued her walk near her house, making it one step closer to the streetlight in front of their driveway. She noticed Tom's car before entering the yard. Mary looked at the house with its lights blaring on every floor. She shook her head, unlocked the front door, and entered right when Tom yelled her name.

"I'M DOWN HERE!" She cried.

Tom ran downstairs to Mary and hugged her tight. "Don't scare me like that."

"What?"

"You left without telling me. I thought you left - I mean, left me or did something I could never digest."

Mary hugged him tighter. "I'm okay; I went for a walk."

Tom pushed back from her embrace, still holding her close. "Let me know the next time you leave." He held her elbows. "Don't let me think of missing you...it's too hard."

"I understand." Mary moved back, pulling her coat sleeve from one arm. "I only went for a walk. I'm not suicidal."

"I..." Tom walked to the kitchen, "...I hope you aren't"

"What is that supposed to mean?"

"I just hope we get through this." Tom turned the stove burners on under the pots. "I know you are fighting." He moved to the counter and looked at Mary. "It's good that you're walking."

"I thought getting out would be good."

"Yeah, a big difference from before."

"Are you insinuating progress?"

Tom grabbed plates from the cupboard. "I had an interesting evening."

"Me too." Mary walked to the master bedroom, sat on the end of the bed, and looked out the far window at night lights shining like fallen stars. *Am I that scary?*

Tom turned the room lights off while walking to the master bedroom. He walked to Mary's side and sat down. "I'm sorry, baby, I overreacted."

"Did you really?"

"I think so. You haven't tried to kill yourself, but I didn't want another surprise."

"I didn't try then, either."

"I know." Tom placed his arm around Mary. "I know you didn't." He kissed her forehead.

"Dinner needs warming." Mary stood. "I'll get it done while you change clothes." She walked to the kitchen, pulled a big spoon from the drawer, and stirred the veggie dishes. *Suicide might be easy.*

Tom didn't waste any time changing clothes; he pulled one jean leg up and hopped to the door while pulling the other on. He zipped and buttoned on the way downstairs. "I wanted to share what happened this evening." Tom entered the kitchen.

"What happened?"

"I got assigned to a west coast customer."

"Oh, is that good?"

"I really don't know, but supposedly it's going to be one of my greater challenges."

"I'm sure they gave you the account because you're good with people."

"That's what Mike said." Tom chuckled. "I can get along with the worst."

"Yeah, you're good at getting people to laugh."

"I haven't heard you laugh in ages."

"I will baby, I will... give me some time."

Tom opened the fridge, retrieved a bottle of juice, and poured a glass. "Did you answer any more of those questions?"

"Nope."

Tom drank from the glass and placed it on the counter. "It's that difficult?"

"It's not difficult; I'm simply taking my time."

Chapter 21

Dr. Nubane read the half-completed form. He looked at Mary, who was sitting in the lounge chair. "I'm surprised you didn't finish."

"I intended to, but I wasn't sure of my answers."

"Let's talk about them." Nubane turned the page. "What do you fear, if you don't remember?"

Mary looked down, frowned, and glanced up towards the doctor. "I'm never going to forget."

"I see, you'll never forget." Dr. Nubane wrote her answer to the question. "How do you think you'll manage your memory of Tom Junior?"

"Manage my memory?"

"Remembering your son is always an option, but since you restrain from everything else when you remember him, it's a struggle." He read from his notes in her chart. "You don't have to fight to remember him. You don't need to stop."

"I wouldn't."

"Get my point. It's about managing your memories so that they aren't controlling your emotions."

Mary shifted in her chair. "Controlling my emotions."

"I read that everything stops when you remember your son. It's about embracing the memory and being active, continuing your life. I mean, it's working through the issue of feeling alone, or feeling as if you can't embrace the memory while living."

"You mean, incorporate his memory so that it's not paralyzing."

"Yes, that's it exactly." Dr. Nubane wrote the answer to the next unanswered question on the document. "Have you done anything to manage your thoughts, lately?"

"I walked around the neighborhood." Mary crossed her ankles and pulled them back towards the chair. "It was dark, so no one noticed me."

"That is wonderful, Mary; you left on your own." Dr. Nubane looked at Mary. "You are strong enough to do it without aid."

"I felt like going."

"Good." Dr. Nubane smiled. "That's huge."

"I guess."

Dr. Nubane wrote another answer to his questionnaire. He scribbled in the file as well. "Do you think you're capable of walking again?"

"If I get in the mood, I think I am."

"So, you're confident that you'll not have reminders of Tom Junior around the neighborhood?"

Mary shook her foot, moving quickly back and forth without tapping the floor. "I managed the other night, even though I remembered him as a teen."

"What was the memory?"

Mary explained the memory on her walk and without leaving out the comparison to the other young man. She contended that her training Tom Junior manners was the most important thing. Dr. Nubane wrote as she talked, answering the empty questions and adding notes to her file. He stopped writing just as she stopped talking. "Mary, you seem to be on the right path. I'm not too worried at the moment. I have one fear, and that's if you don't handle a reminder of Tom Junior well. I think you are on the edge, but lately it's good how you handle the little reminders."

"I think I handle them well."

"I agree, you do. But again, I fear that one lapse and you're back to square one."

"I understand." Mary put her purse on the floor. "Is there something I should do if I experience this?"

"Yes. I want you to read this." Dr. Nubane handed her another document. "This will suggest a process for handling your memories, if they become overpowering. I suggest you practice, once."

"How do you practice?"

"Simply rehearse the process, ask yourself those questions, and sit quietly while you do it."

Mary read the first paragraph of instructions. She glanced at the following steps. "I do this now."

'Yes, it's common; but it's about your control that matters."

Mary turned the page and looked over the contents. "I see."

"If this doesn't work, my next step is to offer you medication. Right now, you're progressing without it." Dr Nubane rose from the couch. "We'll see you next week, Mrs. Stetson." Nubane extended his hand, as always, after their appointment.

Mary shook the doctor's hand. "Yes, next week." She turned to the office door and exited.

***

Tom answered the desk phone: "This is Tom Stetson; how can I help you?"

"Good morning, Tom," Mike greeted. "I'm looking at the screen for the San Francisco account. The condition isn't changing, why is that?"

"It shouldn't change until they finalize their new contract with a company in China."

"Oh, I see." Mike scrolled down the desktop screen. "Where is that information?"

"It's not on the system as a note. We weren't supposed to know."

"Ah, I get it. You're working your magic."

"I don't know about magic, but I'm informed."

"Good. I knew this would work out."

"Thanks, Mike. I'll keep my nose to the grindstone on this one."

"I know you will." Mike disconnected the call.

***

Mary didn't drive directly home after leaving her meeting with Dr. Nubane. *He wants a weekly session now. I wish we were moving for a monthly. Did I say something wrong? Does he see me as being worse than our first meeting in the hospital?* She parked at the local grocery store, got a cart, and walked in. Her first aisle, fresh vegetables and freshly baked breads, was in front of her cart. She picked up a loaf of French bread and placed it in her basket. Her hand loved the feel of fresh fruit: the Granny Smith apples, yellow bananas, and packed grapes. She packed her cart with the idea of creating a tropical evening for Tom. Mary smiled, pushing the grocery cart to the next aisle.

Mary reached for the top shelf, grabbing a box of flavored tea bags. She looked forward after tossing the tea box into the cart.

"Hi, Mary, I haven't seen you in a while." Jeannine smiled.

"Hi, Jeannine, it's been some time." Mary glanced at her. "You look good."

"I've done a few things."

"I see." Mary pulled her cart back. "Whatever it is, keep it up."

"Mary, I hope you're doing better these days. I heard you had a hard time. Losing a child is unbearable."

Mary stopped and dropped her head, staring into the basket. She gripped the car door handle and closed her eyes. Her mind flashed to the instructions Dr. Nubane suggested she follow. Breathe slowly, count to ten, and remember the good thoughts about your loss. Mary opened her eyes. Facing Jeannine, she exhaled slowly. "Yes, it's a painful experience."

"It seems you're handling it well. I would be in shambles."

Mary looked at Jeannine and winked. "There was a time I would be, but..." She walked passed her. "Have a nice day." Down another aisle, Mary grabbed canned goods. She saw one of Tom's high school friends and cringed at the thought of her approach.

"Hi, Mrs. Stetson."

"Hi." Mary smiled. "I don't remember your name, I'm sorry."

"Hilda. Tom and I were..."

"...classmates at high school."

"Yes, you remember."

"I do." Mary gripped the cart, holding it tight.

"I heard about Tom. He was very nice, fun and smart."

"Yes, he was, thank you."

"How did it happen?"

Mary looked at the young lady and tightened her lips then looked in the cart. "It was in the war. He died in the war."

"I never knew he joined the service."

"Yep, he joined the Army."

"Oh, I'm so sorry."

"You said that." She looked at the young lady. "I have to get this done before it gets too late."

"I'm sorry, I didn't mean to hold you up."

"It's okay. Thanks for understanding." Mary whisked past her and grabbed the last can of corn from the shelf. She threw the can into the cart and boogied to the cleaning aisle. Her eyes scanned for anyone who might give her interest and concern. It seemed safe enough to move forward, a natural avoidance of confrontation. Mary sighed, pushed the cart, and looked over the cleaning products. She grabbed one, bent to pick up another, and stood before placing those items in the cart. She didn't recognize the woman standing in front of her, so she murmured, "Excuse me."

"Sure, no problem." The lady moved aside.

"Thank you." Mary pushed her cart without looking back. *I'm so glad she didn't say anything. One more aisle and it's checkout time. I can do this.* It was little Tom who would go for ice cream in the same aisle Mary now strolled. She looked at the freezer and scanned the ice cream brands. Her eyes stopped at the Fudge Royal flavor, and she stood still without reaching for the door. Her cart, filled with items, was reflected in the glass, but her mind saw a carton of Fudge Royal.

"Mom, can we get this?" Tom Junior asked.

"Not today." Mary shook her head. "We have some left at home."

"But, Mom, I'll eat that and then we won't have anymore. If we get this, I can finish that little amount after dinner...please, Mom, please?"

"Well..." Mary looked at his eyes, the dreamy orbs that grabbed her heart. "I guess so."

"Thanks, Mom!" Tom Junior placed the ice cream in the cart.

"I'm sorry, but I need to get that." A customer pointed at the case.

"Oh, oh, yeah, sure." Mary moved aside, looked forward, and pushed her cart to the checkout. She covered her face with her hands, keeping the tears from falling. She picked up a magazine to hide her face. *I nearly blew it,* she breathed, then turned a page and looked at the celebrity's pictures. *I should be so lucky- hiding in a magazine. How embarrassed.*

***

Tom looked at his watch and was surprised he'd called before it was time for his workout routine. He shut down his desktop computer, grabbed his empty lunch kit, went to the break room and rinsed his coffee cup, returned to his cubicle, and ensured that he followed the security procedures. He pushed in his desk chair, put on his jacket, and walked out, following many others to the elevator. He stopped by Mike's office. "I'll see you in the morning."

"You do that...have a great evening, superstar."

"Thanks...you too, Mike." Tom waved and continued his journey. *Superstar? My son would say that when he was young. I miss my boy.* Tom stepped onto the elevator and moved back for others to get on. *Superstar. The kid was a superstar.* Tom looked at his reflection in the elevator's stainless-steel doors. He frowned, noticing the reflection of others staring at his look. Tom's eyes dropped at the exact moment the elevator stopped, and the doors quickly opened. He walked, following the crowd outside into the parking lot, going right to his car. He started his car and allowed the engine to warm. He reached for his seatbelt buckle, snapped it together, and looked ahead, pulling out into the flow of traffic and automatically turning right onto the main street. *Superstar*, Tom wiped his eyes with his right hand, holding the steering wheel with his left. *Superstar...my boy, the superstar.*

***

Mary moved her shopping cart forward, closer to the checkout conveyor. She turned another page, holding the magazine up and masking her face from everyone around her. *I can do this.* Mary peeped, dropping the magazine and raising it up again. She kept her torso on the edge of the cart, and pressed it with her legs, moving slightly forward. *I can do this.*

"Ma'am, do you need help?" The bag person grabbed her cart.

"Oh." Mary dropped the magazine. "No, I can do it. Thanks." She moved in front of the cart and placed items on the conveyor belt. One by one, she put emptied the buggy until the last item was on the belt. "I have coupons." Mary handed a bundle to the cashier. She looked at the cashier with a smile. "I'm so sorry there are so many."

"It's okay, I do this all the time." The cashier scanned and read one at a time.

Mary dared turn around, pulling the cart forward to the bagging person and grabbing her purse. *I can do this.* She grabbed her debit card from her purse and swiped it on the terminal kiosk, then entered her PIN number.

"Thank you, ma'am." The cashier handed Mary the receipt. "Have a nice day." Mary pushed the cart out of the store, only to be stopped at the exit.

"Mary Stetson, how have you been?"

Mary looked at her neighbor of twenty-three years. "Hi, Betty, it's been a long time."

"I am happy you're looking well these days. I like how you've lost weight. What did you do while you were gone?"

"Gone?"

"We thought you were out of town because we only saw Tom at the house."

"I..." Mary paused. "I was not out of..."

"...And I'm so sorry for your loss, we loved Tom Junior."

Mary squeezed the cart handle, and her eyes scanned the tar asphalt below the cart. "Thank you." She pushed forward without looking back at Betty, arrived at the car, loaded the groceries, and rolled the empty cart into the bin. "Damn, I didn't make it." Tears rolled down her face, released from their dam of resistance.

Chapter 22

Six weeks passed as though the winds of time had changed directions. Mary attended doctor appointments with Dr. Nubane, where he confirmed the best thing for Mary to do was to enjoy a vacation. He acknowledged the greatest hindrance to Mary's mental health was her current world. Everything reminded her of Tom Junior, which blocked her recovery.

"I think you should find a new area, either to show you a difference or help you understand that there is life outside of losing your son." Dr. Nubane changed his body position on the chair. "You know, there is a great chance you'll feel better in a different environment. It's the only thing we haven't tried since you've come to me."

Mary's eyes scanned the ceiling. She looked at the light coming through the window, and then took a deep breath. "You are suggesting I leave my home. Did I get that right?" She interlocked her fingers. "Leave my home."

"Not 'leave' as in 'move', but go somewhere outside of Baltimore."

"I get it - maybe visit Fort Jackson where my son's life in the Army began."

Dr. Nubane uncrossed his legs and tapped his foot on the floor, nearly sounding angry. "No, no, no - I mean, maybe to the Caribbean or out west. A simple drive to New York would do."

"I don't want to leave my son." Mary sighed.

"Mary." Dr. Nubane wrote on his notepad. "I guess it's difficult for you to accept it, but you never leave your son."

"He's not here."

"He's inside you. The memory of him never leaves you, and we've accomplished so much through our sessions. Why do I get the feeling you're holding back from a change of scenery?"

"These reminders are all I have left of my son. I don't want to forget him."

"Maybe you'll take some reminders with you, but we need to move in a different direction. It's the last thing we agreed upon in our treatment plan."

Mary sat upright. "Dr. Nubane, I can get through shopping now, go to a movie, and at least cook for my husband without worrying if it's Tom Junior's favorite dish. I think we've come a long way."

"And we have." Dr. Nubane pointed at his clipboard. "I just think we should progress further. A trip down the coast, a journey on an airplane, or anything outside of Baltimore will be a major accomplishment."

Mary picked up her purse from the floor and stood. "I will think about it."

Dr. Nubane rose from his chair and walked to the door. He grabbed the handle and pulled it open. "Please do, and let me know your decision."

***

Mike walked to Tom's cubicle. "Hey, Tom, can we talk for a bit?"

Tom clicked his mouse, closing the document on his screen. "Sure, where should we talk?"

"Let's use the huddle room over there."

Tom rose from his desk and followed Mike. "I hope this isn't serious."

"You're a superstar; why would you have conflict?"

"I hope not." Tom closed the door once he entered and sat across from Mike. "I'm all ears." Tom smiled.

"I didn't want to tell you, but it's my position, even if it means losing you. Our director wants to send you to the west coast."

Tom looked at Mike. "Is this a temporary project, or is it permanent?"

"It's actually a permanent position with a promotion." Mike paused, his eyes fixed on Tom, and he touched his chin with his forefinger. "But I wasn't sure you'd be interested, considering how things are with your wife."

"I see." Tom glanced at the door and returned his eyes to Mike. "I should talk to my wife. I don't know if it's good or not, but maybe." Tom tapped his fingers on the table. "When do I have to give you a decision?"

"Well, by next week at the latest, or we'll have to find someone else to take the job."

"Oh, really? I thought it was specifically made for me."

"As always, it starts with one person in mind, but it turns into headhunters looking for the right candidate. You know the business."

"Yes, I do." Tom rose from the table. "I'll get back to you once I chat with my other half."

Mike rose and pushed his chair back under the table. "I know you'll make the best decision."

Tom opened the door and returned to his desk. He retrieved his desk phone and dialed Mary. "Baby, we need to talk tonight."

"Yes, we do." Mary nodded her head in agreement.

At the end of the day, Tom went to the gym, changed clothing, and walked on the treadmill. His mind shut out all noises and objects, giving him clarity of thought. He contemplated how he was going to share relocating to another city across the country with Mary. *Leaving will devastate her.* Tom adjusted the speed on the treadmill. *She loves Baltimore, and so do I...but...* Tom began to jog. *What will her psychologist say about us moving? What if she doesn't adjust in the new environment? Damn, I'm not so sure about this. Can I focus on the job and also help her with a new life?* Tom kept jogging without answering his questions. He pressed ahead with his workout. *She loved those row houses.* Tom pushed the bar parallel to his shoulder: 2...3..4... *We talked about it before, and it's her second favorite place to live. Her words, not mine.* 5...6...7...8. Tom put the barbell on the floor and set his eyes on the large wall mirror. He stood free of the weights, his hands by his sides. *I know she'll want to visit, but there's no way in hell she'll leave Baltimore.*

***

Mary went upstairs to the master bedroom and sat on corner of the bed. Her eyes scanned from left to right, only to realize that her home was her memory zone. *Tom Junior won't go with us if we leave. Dr. Nubane has to be crazy to think that moving is a great thing.* She took in a breath and slowly released it, collapsing her lungs. *I'm not going. I can't leave my baby. I won't go.* Mary crossed her fingers and rested her hands in her lap. One tear fell from her eye, and she breathed slowly, draining her thoughts of leaving. *I don't care how much I cry; I can't leave because everything of Tom Junior is here.*

He's my son. I can't abandon my son.

***

Tom finished his last set of weightlifting. He placed the weights on the rack, turned for his towel, and walked to the locker room, wiping his face. He walked past people whom he normally greeted and, silent as a mouse, made his way to his locker. *How the hell am I going to convince her to leave Baltimore?* He opened his lock, released the door, and retrieved his bag. Tom unsnapped his keys from the holder and went through the exit door. He made it to the car and sat in the driver's seat. *I think she'll like it when I remind her of how much she liked San Francisco. That's how I'll do it. That's exactly how I'll do it.*

***

Mary walked downstairs to the kitchen. She grabbed vegetables from the refrigerator, placed them on the counter, and grabbed a cutting board. She reached for the large cutting knife and placed it by the board. Mary moved to the sink and ran water, washing the vegetables and placing each on the cutting board. *I shouldn't think about leaving; it's not an option.* She pulled a large pot from the cabinet and placed it near the sink. *He must be out of his mind, telling me to leave my son. That son of a bitch doctor - how dare he suggest something so stupid?* Mary cut, sliced, diced, and dropped the veggies into the pot. She added spices and water before placing the pot on the stove. She grabbed roasted meat from the fridge and minced it, adding it to the veggies in the pot. She covered the pot and went to the wine rack, grabbing a bottle and placing it on the counter. She turned when she heard the front door open.

"Hi, baby," Tom greeted her.

"I'm not going."

"You're not going where?"

"I'm not leaving our son."

Tom dropped his gym bag, "Who says you have to leave our son?"

"Dr. Nubane suggested we move to avoid the reminders of Tom Junior."

Tom dropped his head, grabbing for thoughts to support the doctor's suggestion. *Damn, there goes my idea...maybe not. I think I can do this.* "I'm going to shower." Tom walked past the kitchen and went upstairs.

"Okay. Dinner will be ready in about twenty minutes."

Tom didn't delay his actions; he showered, changed, and returned downstairs. He walked to the photo books, the memories of happier days before Tom Junior passed. He grabbed the latest album with their journey to California and sat on the couch. He opened it and gathered his thoughts.

"Would you like a glass of wine before dinner?" Mary waved a wine glass.

"Yeah, sure, I can use one about now."

"Okay," Mary poured wine in the glass and took it to Tom. "What are you looking at?"

"Just pictures. I was looking at pictures of how much fun we had back then."

"Yeah, I guess."

"Oh, babe, you enjoyed these moments."

Mary handed Tom the wine and returned to the kitchen. She checked on dinner, then grabbed her wine glass and sipped. She leaned on the counter, her wine in hand, and her mind flashed to the picture Tom had pointed out at the couch. "Yeah, California wasn't bad."

"I know," Tom breathed. "I know, because it was a time when we were very happy."

Mary giggled. "Happy, that's something I haven't felt in a long time."

"Don't you want to again?"

Mary put her wine on the counter and walked to the stove, lifting the top on her stew. She waved the fumes towards her nose. "I guess so." She replaced the cover and turned in Tom's direction. "I can barely remember that trip. It wasn't long after that we got word of Tom Junior."

"Yeah, you're right." Tom shook his head left to right. *Damn, she would have to remember that.* "But it was a happier time than right now."

Mary sipped from her glass and put her wine down on the counter. She picked up a cooking spoon and stirred the pot, turning the spoon clockwise and counter clockwise. *I know Tom; he's up to something.* "Tell me why you're looking at the photo album. Why now?"

"I'm glad you asked." Tom closed the book and grabbed his wine glass, walking to the kitchen. "I was going to wait for dinner, but I guess it's a good time now." He sipped from his glass. "I was given a promotion at the job."

"Oh, that's good. It will help with the doctor's bill. He's so damn expensive."

"Yeah, I know," Tom looked over to the stove. "And since it's a pay raise, it comes with a requirement for us to..."

"...A requirement. What kind of requirement?"

"We have to move."

"Move? I'm not moving."

"Baby, we have to; it's for us both. You know, less reminders of Junior and more time to adjust and get better."

"I'm not moving."

"Think about it." Tom touched Mary's shoulder. "You can walk outside and not see a street sign that makes you cry."

"So what? I'm handling it now, a lot better than before."

"Baby, you are, but we can grow from this. We can get back to us, like before."

"We're fine."

Tom dropped his hand and picked up his wine glass. He went into the front room and returned to the couch. He put the wine glass on the coffee table. "I know we are fine, baby, but 'better' is what I want. We have to get better."

Chapter 23

It took three weeks to convince Mary to give San Francisco a try. The final blow was the meltdown she couldn't avoid. A neighbor took her on memory lane by reviewing little Tom's life. She cried for days, avoided Dr. Nubane's appointments like the whale dodging a wave to the beach.

Mary's resolve to leave, coupled with Tom's influence, made the transition a complete healing effort. Tom took every condition into consideration, taking a second chance on the realtor they'd met during their earlier visit. He made an offer on one of the townhouses in the city and mapped the commute to his new office. The decision was finalized, and moving was just as simple. He remembered his Army days of setting things into motion: simply and smoothly, just as he did as a soldier.

The move was completed within two weeks of the decision. They drove across country, sharing moments that reflected the beauty of America. From Baltimore, they drove south I-95 to west I-40 and headed across North Carolina to Tennessee and onto Arkansas. They stopped after eight hours of driving, and Mary didn't mind. Each hotel was one Tom Junior hadn't shared with them, and memories of their loss were less and less. Tom saw Mary returning to normal with each city they passed. By the time they arrived in San Francisco, Mary had a totally new attitude. Her darkness was less than the self-discussion about her latest incident. She remembered her son, but not to the extent of tears.

Tom drove into the garage of their new home: a townhouse, one of the row houses unique to San Francisco's neighborhoods. Its beauty was appealing: hardwood floors, large bedrooms, and a touch of the 19th century modified with 21st century amenities. Tom opened his lovely wife's car door and guided her to the entryway of their new lives. "Watch your step, babe." Tom held her hand, aiding her step up into the house. He raised the switch on the control panel and lights turned on. "I think this is great. I love the change. I like the hooks on the wall for coats and the shoe rack. I'd guess that whoever owned the house before had a policy of no shoes in the house." He giggled.

"I like it, too." Mary smiled and stepped forward, moving beyond the coat room and into the kitchen. "Oh, look, Tom, it's perfect." She viewed the kitchen island, adjusted support the current era and décor. "You know it's going to be nice when you like the kitchen."

"Yes, babe, it's nice, and we'll have a lot of fun cooking together."

"Oh, I didn't say cooking together."

"Why not?"

"I know how you cook," she laughed.

"Don't go there," Tom chuckled. "I have to work tomorrow; can you handle unpacking while I'm at the office?"

"I'll do what I can, but remember, you can't complain about where I put our dishes once I set things up."

"Whatever you do, I'm good with it. Believe me, there's nothing I can change in a woman's kitchen."

"Oh, I'm just some woman now." Mary frowned.

"No, no, baby, you're the greatest."

"Nice comeback - but not nice enough."

It was morning when Tom walked downstairs, striking the many posts supporting the handrail with his hand (*I wonder what kids would do with these*) one after the other - slap, slap,

slap, slap, all the way to the bottom. He went into the kitchen where brewed coffee sat waiting. *I love the coffeemaker's timer feature. Mary knew what she was doing, buying this coffeemaker.* Tom poured his cup, sat at the counter, and paced himself for the morning drive into the office. *I hope it's not like Baltimore. Traffic is not what I'd like for my mornings.*

Tom took to the road with coffee in hand. He drove like every San Franciscan, pulling onto the main roads and winding through traffic lights and onto the highway. Bumper to bumper, he tracked the best route and timed his effort. He saw a bus move past him, steaming way past sitting cars and not stopping, its special lane leading the traffic as if pulling guard on a professional football team.

Tom arrived thirty minutes late after leaving an hour early. He checked in with his director and received the introduction to his new position. Part of their discussion was establishing expectations about the day. By the third day, he figured not driving was his better option.

***

Mary woke at the sound of the closing front door. She put her feet on the floor and sat up, not dropping the blankets from around her, and yawned, stretched, and wiped her mouth with her hand. When she finally rose, her mind went to the many boxes in each room. She went to the bathroom took her meds, performing her morning routine before dressing. Her actions involved grabbing boxes and setting up the house for living. One box was emptied, and her organization skills made each of the three bedrooms a masterpiece of collaboration. She gave her all to support the unique features and décor of the century. On the last bedroom, she decorated it as if Tom Junior might visit, creating a guest room with what was left of his bedroom furniture and decorations. Mary didn't mind, feeling the best way to use furnishing from her son's room was by making it similar to the house they left in Baltimore. But Mary didn't cry, she placed one item after the other without breaking down in tears. "Tom would be proud of me."

***

Tom left his office, walking to the trolley stop that he'd managed to figure out. He jumped on the car and observed passengers who were riding the commuter bus between stops. He'd watch how some people transferred to trains while the others went to parking lots. There were a few people who just caught the city bus going into those unique neighborhoods like the one he now lived in.

One morning he woke early, dressed, and got his coffee. He went to the bus stop and, like any other morning, he greeted people he met. The unique experience was the cute, lively woman who returned his greeting with a smile. *She must be a good person. Maybe Mary would love having a new friend.* Tom made his way onto the bus and spoke to the woman who impressed him. "Hi, I'm Tom, and you are?"

"I'm Tiffany." She looked at his hand. "You must be married."

"I am. Does the ring give it away?" Tom raised his hand, examining it in front of her. "I'm married for sure." He smiled.

"Well, at least you're honest."

"There's no other way to be." Tom looked ahead and wondered if his new acquaintance would be interested in meeting Mary. "How about having lunch with me?"

"I don't date married men," Tiffany responded.

"I didn't think you would, but it's not exactly for me."

"Do you have a friend?"

"Believe me, she's more than a friend."

"I don't think so. I'm not that liberal."

Tom looked down at his lap and stopped talking. At the right moment, he pulled the cord, signaling the driver to stop the bus. He jumped from the bus to the trolley, a typical move of the San Francisco commuter. Tom made it near his office building, downtown, right in front of a Macy's department store. From the trolley stop, he walked two blocks.

One morning he didn't get off the trolley until Tiffany stepped down the stairs for her stop. She walked to the park, adding one block to his trek to the office. Tom didn't approach her but decided to see if she'd have lunch with him. Her many talks with him made him feel confident that Mary would enjoy her company. It was midweek when Tom ventured into Macy's where she worked. He approached her and made it known that he'd enjoy having lunch with her. Before he finished asking, she rejected his invitation: "I don't date married men."

"I know, and it's not dating; it's lunch."

"It's still a date to me," Tiffany responded.

"Well, I only wanted to introduce you to my wife. It's not like I'm working on you for myself." Tom smiled. "I know you don't believe me."

"No, I don't, actually." Tiffany turned behind the counter. "I've heard all types of excuses, and this one is at the top of the chain."

"Okay, maybe we can chat at the bus stop on the way home."

"Yeah, but my answer remains. I don't date married men."

Tom arrived home Friday after his first workweek in the new job. He went to the kitchen, pulled a pitcher of juice from the fridge, and poured a glass. He sipped it while standing by the kitchen counter. Their new home began to feel like a place of comfort. He noticed Mary's touch in decorating the windows, the change in sofas, and the coffee table, which held a different centerpiece than in Baltimore.

Tom smiled before going upstairs to find his wife of many years putting the glass on the counter and briskly walking upstairs. "Mary, baby, where are you?"

"I'm here." Mary looked at the door from her hobby room, the place where Tom Junior may have had space had he lived with them. "I'm in my special place."

"Oh, yeah, the special room." Tom smiled, knowing she had to have something to do other than sit in darkness. "Did you take your meds today?" Tom stopped at the door, looked in, and observed the work on her desk. "That looks interesting," he pointed out.

"Oh, I did." Mary held up a cloth. "I made something from a pattern I picked up for the back wall. I don't think we need to paint."

"Cloth on the wall...hmm."

"It's the latest thing, I read about it in these decorating magazines."

"How many did you read?"

"About a dozen."

Tom stopped short of entering her space and found their conversation much better than those he remembered.

"Would you like to go out for dinner?"

"Ah, well, I didn't think to make dinner. I'm sorry, babe. I got wrapped up in my work."

"It's okay. I don't mind going out or getting takeout."

"I'd like takeout. That way I can finish this."

Tom didn't mind the takeout option, as she was focusing on something other than Tom Junior. Like the doctor had suggested, keeping her mind occupied and having multiple activities aided her progress. "I'll be back in a dash."

Tom went to the Chinese restaurant not far from his house. He walked from block to block, observing the world around him, and noticed Tiffany walking across the street. His mind thought this could be a great time for Mary to meet Tiffany, but he hesitated when he remembered his wife's focus. Tom was on a mission to retrieve dinner.

Chapter 24

Two months passed, and Mary hadn't had a relapse of deep depression. She had managed to decorate the entire house, keeping busy as suggested. Tom began smiling more often, even though Mary's circle of friends was still null. She hadn't left the house without her husband outside of grocery shopping, which she kept short.

Tom got into a routine of going to work, meeting people at the bus stop, riding the trolley to the office, and working with a team that seemed to embrace him. He enjoyed his days and began to entertain Mary a lot better. She would get out with him, going to movies, a music concert, and even listening to chamber quartets from the symphony. Tom was on the upswing but lived with one concern about Mary: "Babe, you should meet people."

"I don't need to."

"But how will you get totally better?" Tom dropped his bag on the floor, something he usually did once he entered the house after his commute. "I mean, don't you think having a friend will give you something more?"

"Look, I'm doing a lot better, and I have to admit that moving was the right option."

"But why limit yourself to the house and me?"

"You're a limit?"

Tom knew it was the wrong way to present his persuasive thoughts and start a conversation. "Well, I'm not any limit." He moved closer to Mary and put his arms around her. "I simply want my wife back."

"And I never left." Mary pushed back.

Tom stood in awe, not believing Mary's point of view. "I didn't mean to be negative, it's just that I remember what you were and how close you are getting to becoming the person I knew. The woman I love. The fun partner I enjoy. It's like there's one missing link, and that's a friend you can have fun with."

"You are my friend." Mary pointed at Tom. "You've been my friend for over twenty-five years."

"I know, baby, but you had friends more than me at one time."

"That is true." Mary moved to the sofa and sat at its corner. "Let me think about it."

"Thinking about it is better than not having a thought at all."

"I said, I'll think about it."

"You got it...Can I suggest something that may help you make friends?"

"You can help me?"

"Come on, Mary, I know you well enough to help you," Tom giggled.

"Okay, help me."

"I will; I'll help you." *Damn, I'll call the doctor and listen to what he suggests.*

Tom walked to the bus stop and spoke to everyone, including Tiffany, who seemed to ignore him. She would usually respond and joke with him about being married and her not dating him. She also engaged in conversations about Mary, thinking he was exaggerating about her depression, his way of gaining her sympathy. "Now, you know there is no way your wife would ever shut you out. She's your wife, and wives don't close doors on their husbands."

"Tiffany, you have no clue. But I never said she intentionally shut me out. She couldn't help it, at the time. She was sick, and it's why I wanted to introduce her to new people around here."

"It's hard to do that when she's not with you."

"Yeah, I know. Trust me, I know how difficult that can be." Tom looked at Tiffany, who sat on the bus across from him. "Why don't you come to my house and meet my wife?"

"How would that look?" Tiffany shook her head. "Really, Tom, really?"

"Since she doesn't go out, what do you suggest I do?"

"There's a community center down the street from the bus stop. Maybe there's a program worth checking out."

"Great idea." Tom smiled. "I'll go first, before she does."

"Why? Why would you do that?" Tiffany shook her head before looking out of the window. "Men. Married, and they have no clue," she muttered. Tiffany looked at Tom. "Go together for the first time. Tell her where you're going, and no surprises. It's not like you're going to force her to attend anything, but at least you'll make her feel comfortable, being there to support her decision."

"Her decision?"

"There you go again, married and clueless."

"I know my wife, Tiffany, and she's a very strong, independent woman."

"So why does she need friends?"

Tom looked at the street and stood. "Here's our stop." Tom stepped aside enough to allow Tiffany to pass first. "You made your point." Tom stepped down, following Tiffany to the street, then caught up with and walked beside her. "I think I'll do that today. Do you remember the name of the center?"

"No, I don't remember the name, but it's just down our street."

"Okay, I'll find it during my research."

Lunch arrived in time to settle the hunger of a new born baby. Tom rose from his desk and tapped his cell phone. He searched community centers and selected the one closest to his address. He then searched available programs and identified a group where Mary would surely find support. He called the center for information about meeting times, how to join, the length of each meeting, and asked for the counselor's name. Tom made notes and then called Dr. Nubane's office. "Doctor Nubane, nice to talk to you again. I won't waste your time, so let me get to the point. I know you told my wife Mary to move. And you know that we did, but I'm looking to get her involved with a support group. What do you think?"

"In Mary's case," Dr. Nubane paused, "I think a group would be helpful, but be careful that it's not one where it's pushy. She's still a delicate person when it comes to Tom Junior."

"Don't I know." Tom took in a breath. "She's improving leaps and bounds, in my book. I know because I'm feeling a difference in her attitudes and actions."

"Good, Tom, that's wonderful. A support group to get her interacting socially can be very helpful." Dr. Nubane added, "No matter what she does socially, right now it's important that she takes her meds until they run out."

"Thanks for the advice, and I'll get her involved pretty soon.

No worries, she's doing great with her medication." Tom disconnected the call and pocketed his phone. He returned to his desk and picked up his work. He didn't stop until the end of his day, walked to the trolley stop, jumped on, and focused on seeing if he passed the community center on his route. He changed to the bus and stood facing the front of the bus where he had vision on both sides. When he saw the center, he noted its cross streets, for his return.

Tom arrived home, entered, and threw his bag on the couch. He went into the kitchen and, like other days, retrieved a drink from the fridge and a glass from the cupboard. He poured a glass of juice and gulped half of its contents. He went to Mary's activity room. She wasn't there. He walked to the bedroom, but he didn't hear a noise. He ran downstairs and looked around each room; she wasn't there. Tom noticed a note on the refrigerator door: 'Grocery shopping, be back soon.'

He grabbed it and looked into the fridge for something he could cook. To his surprise, he grabbed a container of marinated meat, and he placed it on the counter. He grabbed a pan, turned the oven to a set degree, and prepared the dish for dinner. Tom's ability to cook was not a surprise to Mary. There was a time when he'd cooked on odd days while Mary cooked on even days of the month. When Mary entered, she smelled the aroma and smiled.

"I didn't have to call you to put dinner on."

"No, you didn't." Tom smiled and went to the front door, helping Mary with the groceries. "What did you buy?"

"I think I went overboard. I probably bought too much."

"Naw, whatever you did, it's for good reason."

Mary went into the kitchen, dropping her bags on the counter. She organized the groceries in their proper places. Tom gave her a hand but mostly followed her directions. He was glad he did, because it was nothing like the order of their Baltimore home.

"Now, that's done, and we should eat, as I have some-thing to tell you." Mary pulled plates from the cupboard.

"I think I have a suggestion to share, too." Tom took one plate from Mary.

"Sounds like we've been thinking."

"Yes, it sure does." Tom filled his plate with dinner and placed it on the counter. He grabbed Mary's and repeated the process. He took both plates to the table while Mary poured drinks. She went to the dinner table and placed one glass in front of Tom and the other in front of her. "I had an interesting conversation with a neighbor."

"Really, you talked to a neighbor? I think that's wonderful."

"What she said was enlightening."

"Enlightening?"

"I'm so stuck in this house; I need to get out. She told me there's a lot to see in San Francisco that isn't costly."

"Baby, remember coming here before?"

"And that's why we need to do more."

"I see." Tom forked up his dinner and dumped it into his mouth. He chewed, contemplating how to push his agenda. "I guess we can make a list of things to do and plan, then. Let's say, one per week?"

"That's a great idea. I will do that and plan it."

"Yeah, you do that, and I'll follow your lead."

"Good."

Six weeks of visiting events in San Francisco had Tom smiling. He didn't know there was so much to enjoy in the city. He figured he'd visited most of the museums, theaters, and parks that any person could. To his surprise, Mary had transitioned and seemed to be on track, just as the doctor had advised. She hadn't had one breakdown over Tom Junior's death.

On Thursday evening, before going to a local charity concert, Mary walked down the stairs wearing a dress for the evening. Tom watched her approach and covered his mouth, hiding his smile. He shook his head in amazement, startled at the way Mary was dressed and happy she'd taken a chance on looking like the bride he'd married years ago. "You look stunning," Tom complimented her.

"Thank you," Mary smiled. "I thought you would love seeing me in this dress."

"I...I'm surprised. I mean, you look amazing." Tom grabbed Mary's hand and spun her 360 degrees. He looked at his wife, the woman who had nearly killed herself from not eating. The woman had regained her stature and was finally laughing. Tom looked at her with excitement. "Baby, you're back."

"I never left."

"Yeah, you're better than before."

"I am better here, too." She grabbed his groin.

Tom bent forward into the surprise grope. "Now, that's my wife."

Forty minutes later, Tom opened Mary's car door, allowing her to step out. He grabbed her hand and closed the door after she cleared the car. He offered her his arm, and she kindly took it. They walked to the center and entered, showing the tickets Tom had printed. Upon entry, Tom continued walking, with

Mary holding his arm. She stayed by his side until they got to their seats. It was perfect, a night of tender focus. Tom's heart beat with the rhythm, forecasting a night of long-missed passion. Mary gave him the idea, sitting closer to him and rubbing her thighs against his leg. They sat in silence, cuddled as much as they could while in public, and waited for the show.

The show curtains swung open, and out came young men and women in uniforms. Army uniforms, just like the one Tom Junior had worn. Mary's foot tapped faster with her head set straight and staring at the stage, giving it her full attention. Tom felt her heart race. "You want to go?"

"No, we have to watch this."

"Baby, you don't have to; we can do something else."

"No, it's important that I stay."

The play continued and - BOOM, BOOM - the strike of the bass drum gave a thunderous sound. Mary's heart stopped, and her mind snapped to Tom Junior's death. She remembered how Junior's leader had shared his death in a letter. She grabbed her purse and ran out of the show. Tom followed.

It was the doorman who stopped Mary from running into the street. "Ma'am, can I get you a cab?"

"No." Mary stopped at his extended arm. "I have a car."

"Yes, she does," Tom announced. "Babe, are you okay?"

"I don't like that show. It wasn't supposed to be about war."

"I thought you knew."

"I thought it was a romantic drama. Not some conflict our son went through."

"I'm sorry, babe. I'm so sorry I didn't think to tell you."

"I want to go home."

Tom grabbed her arm and walked Mary to their car. He opened the passenger door and snapped her seatbelt for her. He walked around the back, stopped, and looked at Mary from the rear window. *She was so close.* He got into the car and drove home. Neither spoke of the incident nor carried on a conversation. Mary jumped out and ran to the house. She opened the door and ran to the bedroom. Tom followed and went to the house bar, made a drink, and sat on the couch in the dark. He sipped the drink, waiting for Mary to come downstairs.

Morning arrived like a strong wind at the beach on a cloudy day. Tom opened his eyes to the sunlight, in the same position he'd sat in the night before. The kitchen was silent: no coffee, no eggs, no bacon - no activity that he'd become accustomed to for the morning. Tom rose and walked to the master bedroom. "Babe, are you up?" Mary didn't respond even though her silhouette was an outline under the sheets. "Babe, can I get you anything?" Tom sat on the bed and touched her hip. "I'm worried about you. I know it's hard; you were doing so well. I'm sorry about last night."

Mary neither spoke nor moved, except for the rise and fall of her torso with each breath. Tom went into the bathroom and changed for the day. He dressed for work, went downstairs and made coffee, and went out for the bus. He didn't speak to anyone he'd normally greet. Tiffany noticed but didn't want him to be loud like had been times before. She avoided him, standing aside from her normal position on the bus.

Tom made it to the office and, without logging into his desktop, called the community center and revalidated his research information.

It was the end of his day, and he was riding the bus home. Tom's mind was a mass of questions, guessing if, when, and how Mary could work with the group sessions. He went home and walked up to Mary. "You and I need to get some help. You've done well, but last night was a bombshell. We can't afford a relapse."

"I know. I'm so sorry, but that reminded me so much of our son."

"I get reminded of him simply by seeing your smile. But you have to get to where reminders are less hurtful."

"How do you suggest I get there?"

"Community group sessions."

"You mean, share my feelings with a group and a counselor?"

"Yes, exactly. There is a group close to us, that community center down the road."

"We passed it a few times on our way out."

"They have group conversations about addiction, depression, and other health issues."

"I'm not going alone to that meeting."

"Of course not. I'll be there with you...At least, for the first day."

Mary blinked, looked at the ceiling, and back at Tom, "On second thought, you don't have to be there. I'm a big girl."

"Mary, I'm not saying you aren't capable of going alone. I'm saying I will support you from day one."

"Thanks. I'll let you know if I need it."

Chapter 25

On her third session, Mary looked at a young woman who hadn't contributed since she joined. Penny, a mother who lost a child to an auto accident, shared how she added a kicker to her depression medicine. Her emotions would become bearable and life seemingly returned to normal. Mary wanted the same peace.

Mary received a smile from Penny during the time she shared her feelings and talked about her progression through depression. At the end of the meeting, both women found themselves in a conversation. "You looked like you needed a friend."

"You did, too," Mary laughed. "I'm Mary, and you are?"

"Penny."

"Nice to meet you, Penny." Mary extended her hand.

Penny shook Mary's hand and smiled. "You're new to the area. I can tell."

"Practically moved in yesterday. But I thought you were new to the group."

"No, I tend to attend when I feel like I need to release something. It's not often, since I found a way to handle it on my own."

"Yes, handling it on your own is something I haven't quite mastered."

"If you expand your methods, one day you'll find that what I do isn't so bad."

Mary raised her eyebrows. "I don't quite get the picture, but

I'm sure it works for you. I'll find a way."

"If you want to get better, you'll find a way."

After a month of talking, Mary and Penny went sightseeing and explored the great sites of San Francisco. It was different than being with Tom, as Penny shared her insights about several shops, museums, and tennis clubs. At the end of each exploration, Mary gave an in-depth account to Tom. He was elated that his wife was active and working herself out of gloom.

One odd day in the city, Penny stopped talking about her life, opened a small tobacco can and took a pinch of powder, held it to her nose, and sniffed. Mary had never seen anyone actually sniff cocaine, though she'd heard about it and saw folks do it in movies. What Mary observed next was astonishing. Within minutes, Penny's mood improved. She was bubbly, as if by magic. What had seemed like a bad day unfolding for her quickly disappeared. That fast mood swing was exactly what Mary wanted to help her control the pain whenever she faced her worst.

On her son's birthday Mary hit rock bottom, and she called Penny. Mary sobbed like the waterfall in El Yunqi, and though she applied control techniques she had learned in counseling, she couldn't get things back into perspective. Tom went to work as usual and promised to return for lunch because he knew that if things went like recent nineteen months, she would have a terrible day. Though their despair was less dramatic than the first year, it was still hard on Mary. An hour after her call, Penny visited and tried to motivate Mary to handle the pain. She pressed Mary to take her prescription meds and take a dose of Oxycotin, which Penny knew would give her a physical high and make her muscles relax. While she waited for the drugs to kick in, Mary asked, "Does snorting cocaine make the pain disappear? I don't want to hurt so much this time. Is this how you avoid the pain?"

"It makes you mellow, but you stay in control," Penny responded.

"Can you sit with me for a little while?"

"Sure I can, take your time. Sit next to me on the couch so we can chat."

Mary staggered over near Penny and dropped to the couch. It felt like she had lost control of her legs. Penny caught her so she wouldn't fall over and slam her head on the coffee table. She held Mary and listened to her cry and mumble. It was surprising how Mary took those pills during her state of mind, but it seemed she couldn't get it together. They sat in silence after the sobbing stopped, and Penny decided to encourage Mary to get out and appreciate the world.

"We should go somewhere and see something other than these four walls. Come on, Mary, let's go to the Conservatory of Flowers. The flowers and fresh air will do you some good."

"I guess so. I don't know. I miss him so much. He loved being with me. I am proud Junior joined the Army, but I feared his death. I never told him goodbye. I refused to say it, even though I believed his leaving us was important for his growth as a man. You have to let kids grow up and make their own decisions. I knew it was a bad decision. If my baby were here, my heart would be full again."

"Mary, he's in the park waiting for us. Wasn't he a beautiful child? Sure, he was. And the park is where beautiful kids go, so come on. Let's get up." Penny stood, pulled Mary to her feet, and then guided her to the front door. "One step at a time. It gets better."

"I don't think this is a good idea," Mary said.

"You need to move."

"Easier said than done, Penny. I want to go, but my legs aren't moving. I need to sit for a spell. I feel so tired."

"Okay, we'll wait a few minutes. Here, sit on the stoop."

Mary followed directions and passed out as the sun hit her face. Her body became limp like a noodle, and she slumped into a fetal position. Penny couldn't believe Mary's reaction to the Oxycontin when it mixed with her depression meds. She tried lifting her and getting her back into the townhouse, but Mary was heavier, in her relaxed state. Instead, Penny decided they would wait on the stoop until she came to. She went inside to get an umbrella to protect Mary from the sun. Penny sat on the stoop with Mary and watched others stroll along the street. Twenty minutes passed, and Mary eyes were still closed. She hadn't moved from her fetal position. Penny watched Mary's chest to make sure she still breathed and figured that since it was her first time, it might take longer for the drugs to wear off.

Mary was on the stoop for two hours when lunchtime approached. Tom arrived home as planned and saw Mary under the umbrella. *Why would she nap outside on the stairs instead of in our home?* "Mary," Tom said, and waited for a response. "Mary," he repeated. He then leaned over and shouted, "Mary!" Tom repeated her name, and his voice rose in volume each time she did not respond.

"She's okay," yelled Penny. "She's tired and doesn't want to move. She's napping, and I covered her from the sun."

"And who are you? Have we met?"

"I'm Penny, a friend of Mary's from the group."

"I heard about you and I'm glad you're here for my wife. Help me get her inside."

Tom lifted Mary while Penny held the door open and followed. Penny held the flowers Tom had brought with her other hand. "I guess I'll put these in water," Penny said. "She's going to love them. We were headed to the Conservatory of Flowers when she decided to rest on the stoop."

"Why would she sleep in the middle of the day? I told her we would have lunch to celebrate our son's..."

"...Birthday! Yeah, she told me, and said it's the reason she's so depressed."

"What did she do?"

"She took a little something to help her with the depression. Her meds, I presume." Penny dared not share the fact that she had given Mary Oxycontin, the drug that had added to her relaxed state. "Guess she didn't have the motivation to continue. I'll place the vase here. Have her call me when she wakes."

"You're leaving?" said Tom.

"Yes, since you're here. Tell Sunshine I'll see her at the next group session." Penny left the townhouse. Tom sat with his wife and watched her sleep. He couldn't believe how she had checked out since she knew that he would be home for lunch. He gently shook her after two hours and she finally woke up, as groggy as if she'd drunk a fifth of whisky.

"What happened?" Mary asked.

"You've been asleep for the last few hours. Your friend Penny was here. Do you remember?"

"Of course, I remember. We were going to the garden, and at the last minute, I just didn't feel like it." Mary cupped her forehead as if she nursed an excruciating headache.

"So you fell asleep on the stoop?"

"I fell asleep where?"

"Out front, on the stoop."

"Then how did I get on the couch?"

"I carried you there. And we missed lunch," Tom sneered as he walked towards the kitchen.

"Oh, I'm so sorry, Tom. I know how badly you wanted to celebrate Tom Junior's birthday. I guess it shows that I'm still not ready."

"You're using Tom Junior as an excuse not to do what you need to, as a wife."

Stunned at Tom's comment, she stood, only to fall back onto the couch. "How dare you!"

"Whatever you took or drank, it had to be something bad for you. As a matter of fact, what did you do to get such a headache?" Tom got a beer from the refrigerator, and on his return to the living room, he stopped short of the couch. "Well?"

Mary didn't respond. She sat on the couch with her head in her hands and massaged her temples. She thought about Penny's gift and was bewildered about how the pills got Penny through the day. Even though her headache made her feel bad, the slumber did her some good. She couldn't remember a time she'd slept that deep since Tom Junior died. "I took a sleeping pill and probably shouldn't have with my depression meds."

"You've done that before and it never made you sleep that deep. Were they your usual brand?"

Mary slowly rose to her feet and moved to the kitchen. "The usual, but double the dosage. What do you want for dinner?"

"If you're up to it, I thought we'd go out."

"Celebration or not, I don't think I'm up for it with this headache. I can fix you something."

Tom couldn't believe Mary had inquired about dinner. She hadn't felt the motivation to cook since meeting Penny. It surprised him, and he smiled, as if that small question had returned a piece of his Mary. "I'd like anything you throw together." Tom grimaced before he sipped his beer. "You know, it's been a while since you've cooked."

"It's the least I can do for missing our lunch together. Can you forgive me?"

Tom felt excited about his wife's demeanor for the first time in months. She reflected the right attitude; a message indicating that Mary was becoming mentally stable. "I think it's progress - you're in the kitchen, preparing a meal."

"I think so, too. It's the least I can do in celebration of Tom Junior's birthday. I'll cook. If we were in Baltimore, we'd probably be celebrating with a few of his friends. Since being out here, we don't see any of his buddies."

Tom didn't respond. All he had done was follow the doctor's relocation advice. However, it appeased him that she was doing something normal; she'd always loved to cook for her two men.

Later in the evening, Mary did something else that showed she might be returning to normal. She responded to Tom's sexual advance. Not only did she make love to her husband, but she ravaged him in ways he remembered. Like a youthful couple on a Caribbean beach, she had the energy and focus of waves crashing against rocks during high tide. Tom finally experienced the change he needed and figured it was what doctors meant by 'progressive healing'.

One week passed, and it was a terrific time for Tom. He hadn't seen Mary's energy level consistently on the upswing in a long while. He was beginning to feel like life might return to normal. If she kept progressing and doctors agreed that Mary had control of her depression, he thought they might return to

Baltimore.

Three weeks later, after her group counseling session, she purchased a few relaxers to help her mood and received another pack of friendly encouragers from Penny. Those drugs kept her bubbly for Tom. What Penny neglected to tell Mary was that those pills she gave her were an increased Oxycontin dosage. Her doctor had doubled the strength of her prescription at her last appointment.

Mary returned home from the market one day and decided to indulge in her mood enhancer, have a drink, and relax. She crushed and snorted the equivalent of two Oxycontin pills, took one anti-depressant pill, and drank a margarita. Within minutes her muscles relaxed. She lost control and fell off the couch. Slowly and softly, her breathing stopped.

***

After a few weeks of normalcy, Tom was excited about going home. This day, he wanted to do something special. At lunch, he shopped at a few specialty shops, purchased a blue teddy negligee, and bought perfume for his wife. He knew how to make the sparks fly with Mary and thought it would be a treat for them both. His excitement grew during the afternoon after he made reservations at the Ambrose Bierce House Bed and Breakfast and reserved a table for dinner at the Press in St. Helena for Saturday evening. He had hoped they would spend the day exploring the wine country, something he'd wanted to do since their move to San Francisco.

Tom's eager mood took control of his energy. He completed his work and left the office an hour earlier than usual. When he arrived at the townhouse, he wanted to share his surprise with Mary. He entered the living room and saw Mary on the floor in front of the couch.

***

In the ambulance, Tom stared at Mary, holding her hand and rocking as he wondered what had happened and why. The EMT kept checking her vitals and saw her numbers fall along with her slow breathing. He looked at Tom and nodded his head. The EMT took action to keep her awake and responsive, but his efforts failed. Mary wasn't breathing, even after the electric paddles restarted her heart beat.

Tom couldn't believe the situation - his wife had died without the event of bombs, a war, or even a physical conflict. Mary died in route to the emergency room. He dropped his head and tears fell from his eyes. "NO, NO, NO!" he shouted out, holding Mary's hand and kissing her cheek. "Why, baby? We had a chance."

The EMT opened the door and walked to the hospital's emergency room. The doctor on call was informed that she'd expired five minutes before their arrival, and he explained what he diagnosed and how he performed every necessary means to keep her alive. The other EMT helped Tom out of the back and pulled the gurney out of the vehicle. Quickly, he covered Mary from head to toe and pushed her body into the hospital, heading for the morgue.

Tom couldn't believe what had happened. He called a cab and went home. When he got home, he opened the door and sat in the living room in silence. He watched the sun set and observed the arrival of night before closing his eyes.

The morning sun caught him sitting in the same location, realizing that his wife had expired. He waited until nine in the morning before moving from the couch. He picked up the phone, called a mortician, and followed up with his office. He informed the director that his wife Mary had died.

Chapter 26

Tom's last stop on his drive to Baltimore-Washington International (BWI) Airport was to visit his wife and son's graves. When he arrived at the gravesites, he held back tears, as it took the strength of his imaginary army to refrain from breaking down from the loss of his family. He kneeled to place flowers on their graves, and his heart raced, his breathing swelled, and the ability to stand left his legs. Tom buckled onto his knees, and for him, time stood still. Memories swept through his mind - from the first time he saw Mary to the time Tom Junior took his first breath. He remembered what had happened in their lives, all of the events, the laughter, the accomplishments, and the day Tom Junior left for the Army. Tom finally got the strength to return on his journey to San Francisco.

On the way to his rental car, Tom felt the challenge of his life ahead. He recalled conversations with friends and family during his three-week visit. At first, they had encouraged him to stay in Maryland, but when he fell apart at any reminder of his earlier life with his family, they realized that returning to San Francisco was best. They felt obligated to care for Tom and support his transition. Cousins, a brother, and a sister-in-law scheduled visits one after the other. They devised a plan to make sure Tom became emotionally stable without his wife and son.

Tom drove to the airport and traveled the same route he and Mary had driven months earlier. When he got to the rental car exit, he looked at the passenger side and remembered Mary's comment: "Baltimore will always be home; it's where our son lived. We'll return for good after I'm better. I'll miss it, but I have to get better, for us." Tom took the exit and parked at the rental company lot. He remembered how slowly Mary had exited when they'd done so earlier. "I hope it's better, Tom. I really do." Without a pause, Tom grabbed his luggage and the rental receipt and walked to the airport's entrance. Though Tom frequently traveled from BWI for business, it was the first time he felt he was leaving home.

Tom knew life ahead would be difficult, but he thought his mental preparation would get him through. His strategy was to throw himself into his job. He didn't mind San Francisco, but more importantly, he thought that northern California would help bandage his broken heart. He created fond memories of Mary, met a few people, and embraced the quality of living cues that most city dwellers enjoyed. Tom thought well into his life changing strategy and yearned for a quick adjustment period without Mary. He sat at the terminal, waited to board his flight, and remembered what he should do moving forward. He knew that he would have to deal with his grief throughout the transition. But mostly he feared facing the effort to mend his broken heart.

He arrived in San Francisco during the late evening, found his luggage, and took the shuttle to long-term parking to get his car. With less traffic on the road, he drove to his house, entered, and unpacked. Later, Tom sat at his dining room table in silence. His mind returned to the first time he and Mary had entered the townhouse to the last time he saw her. *God give me strength.* He crossed his arms on the table, placed his head on his hands, and fell asleep.

Tom went to his office after three weeks of bereavement leave. Co-workers made an extra effort to make him feel welcome and greeted him like a soldier returning from war. They saw his low energy and made a commitment to help him adjust and return to normal. On occasion, his most interactive associates would stop by his cubicle and chat about sports, jokes, comedy shows, or work projects. During lunch, before the death, Tom would usually partner with a work group or someone who would enjoy his strictly-business conversation. He would even venture to share lunch with someone he'd rode on public transportation with or maybe find a woman he could introduce to Mary, but this first day back on the job, he chose to be alone.

He got a sandwich from the corner deli, walked to the park, and sat in silence, listening to the pains in his heart. He wanted so desperately to call his wife, as he often had. This day in the park, he wanted to tell her of his day and hear about what to expect when he returned to the home she'd created. He wanted to tell her life would have been okay if she had just waited or given them a chance to heal. He felt the world close in around him as if he were deaf, and breathing became a roar with every effort to take in air. He sat on a park bench amid a bustling city and felt isolated in a canyon of loneliness.

Tom sunk into a pit of sadness. He acted the opposite of his usual jolly self, one who joked at every opportunity. He sat there beyond his lunch hour and into the afternoon before he looked at his watch and decided to walk back to his office. Instead of returning to work, he pressed past the work building's entrance doors and ended up at his cable car stop. In late afternoon, he returned to the townhouse, entered it, and walked upstairs to his bedroom. *Life isn't the same without Mary,* he thought as he changed clothes and got into a sweat suit. He never changed clothes before kissing Mary. He could still see her smile and hear her complain about not finding events to enjoy in San Francisco. *She was a soul worth having, worth loving, and we had a great marriage. I loved her so much.* He sat on the side of the bed and cried.

The next morning, Tom started his day with coffee and toast. Mary always made his breakfast, so he hadn't cooked it for years. Instead of looking to create a meal, he opted for simple food items to prepare. He left for the office, just like he'd done for so many mornings. When he arrived at the bus stop, he saw Tiffany and immediately walked past her without saying a word. She saw him and expected his usual smart remark. When she scrutinized Tom, she noticed his lower bearing - a shift in his posture - and was undecided about how to handle the situation. *Should I ask him how he's doing? He looks like he's having a bad day.* When the bus arrived, she boarded and moved to the back. She watched him find a seat and noticed he didn't say a word to anyone, but gazed out of the window instead. *Something is different about Tom.* Tiffany watched Tom until he left the bus and walked to the cable car stop. She decided she had gone long enough without speaking. When she approached, Tom looked her way.

"Hi, Tiffany."

"Hello, Tom. Are you okay?"

"I'm fine."

"No, are you okay? Tom, what's wrong? Are you ill?" Tiffany looked concerned. "You aren't being playful and loud like you usually are."

"You think I'm loud?"

"'Loud' may have been harsh, but today you're something different. You're not the same man I've noticed over the months that we've taken this bus."

"I didn't think you'd noticed."

"Really, Tom, how couldn't I? You nearly asked me out the first time we met. I only stopped you because you're married."

"Well, I'm not asking you out, but I'm not married anymore."

Tiffany gave him a look of surprise and placed her free hand on her hip. "Did you get a divorce?"

"Not at all, I loved my wife. I loved her with all my heart. I was only trying to get you to meet her."

"Loved your wife? Did she leave you?"

"You could say that."

"No wonder you've changed." Tiffany placed her hand on his back.

"Nothing like that, Tiffany. It's not what you think."

"I'm here if you want to talk about it. I won't push you to share, but if ever you need an ear..."

"Thank you, I may take you up on it."

Tom stepped onto the cable car and took a seat in the middle. He didn't say good-bye to Tiffany - he just left. She was shocked at his behavior because he wasn't the gentleman she had seen before. *"Man, that woman sure took his soul."*

Chapter 27

Tom woke earlier than usual with strong hunger pains. He had skipped dinner for three days. His desire was not to have breakfast alone, so he dressed and walked to the nearest diner. He sat in the corner booth far from everyone, even though the receptionist offered him a different location. When the server arrived, he ordered: "Bacon, scrambled eggs, potatoes, and wheat toast, please. Oh, and add water and coffee."

"Sure, sir." The server left and returned with water, a coffee cup, and a carafe of coffee. "Is there anything I can get you before your breakfast comes out?"

"No, thank you." He looked around while he kept his back against the wall and watched folks' faces as they walked in the door. He saw a couple who were near his and Mary's age. He recalled a time in Baltimore with Mary, eating at the Double T Diner. He saw her as clear as day, laughing and sharing a moment, and recalled her taking extra time to read the same menu that she'd read for years. He saw himself preparing her coffee just the way she liked it. Like clockwork, she would drop the menu, take a sip, and then smile, sending a silent thank you kiss to his cheek. Tom snapped back to reality just as his breakfast arrived.

"Is there anything else I can get you?" the server asked while she laid the check on the table.

"I don't think so, but thanks." He finished breakfast and paid his check at the counter. When he walked to the bus stop, Tom saw Tiffany and greeted her. "Hi, Tiffany."

"Good morning, Tom. You came from a different direction."

"I had breakfast before coming to the bus stop."

"If you ever want company for breakfast, just let me know." Tiffany smiled. She wrote her cell number on the back of a business card. "Here, I'm serious. If you ever want company, call me."

"Yeah, next time I may do that." Tom took the card and turned to the street, looking for the bus to arrive. He shared nothing about losing his wife.

Tom caught the next cable car, exited at his stop, and walked into his office. He sat at his cubicle and looked at the workload sitting in his intake basket. Without getting coffee or taking off his coat, he settled into work. He did not converse with any of his fellow employees and spoke only to those he was required to on the phone. Tom worked through lunch and into the evening. He didn't notice the cleaning crew until he heard someone say, "Excuse me, I need your trash can." He silently moved, giving up his space. He looked at the watch, decided he had worked long enough, and headed home.

Tom caught the last cable car for the night and waited longer than usual for the city bus to arrive. It was the latest he'd worked in years. When Mary was alive, he would avoid getting home late. He thought of her on his bus ride and opened his cell phone to call her. *She'd have a fit if I got in this late without calling.* Tom looked at his phone and closed it, reminding himself there was no one to call. He then remembered that Tiffany had given him her number and said to call her anytime. He dialed her number, waited for an answer, and changed his mind after one ring.

Tom arrived home and stopped to retrieve the mail from the box. He entered the townhouse, walked into the kitchen, and opened the refrigerator. Since he hadn't gone grocery shopping, the shelves were bare. The only food left was a partial loaf of wheat bread that he toasted for breakfast. He decided to walk to the corner convenience store and bought a sandwich, chips, and a soda. Tom returned home and munched on them while he watched the late-night news. When he finished, he went upstairs and called it a night.

Morning came like a lightning bolt during a thunderstorm. Tom rose with the sun, went downstairs, and started a pot of coffee. At first, he set the pot for four cups, then remembered to reduce it to two, pouring out the excess water. His heartbeat increased, and his breathing picked up. Tom's hands shook as he put the coffee grounds in the filter. Fortunately, it was the last of the measuring, and only a few grinds hit the counter. Tom closed the lid and pushed the button. He returned to his bedroom, made his bed, and jumped in the shower. He stopped washing himself and stood under the water. His mind roamed between Mary being with him and moments where Tom Junior would enter, watching him shave.

Tom turned the water off, toweled dry, chose his clothes, matching his tie with his socks, and dressed for the day. He went downstairs, toasted bread, and spread it with jelly. He leaned against the counter and drank coffee and enjoyed his breakfast. Tom left heading to the office for the day.

Tom saw Tiffany at the bus stop and greeted her with a smile. "Nice to see you this morning."

"You're in a good mood. Did you find out something about your wife that made you smile?"

"She left, and I'm okay with it."

"That's it?"

"That's enough, Tiffany. I'm okay with it."

"Okay, well, if you need to talk about it, I can have lunch with you."

"Thanks, I'll let you know."

The bus arrived and Tom allowed Tiffany to enter before him. He followed her and found a seat towards the rear. Tiffany sat in the middle of the bus, hoping Tom would sit across from her. She didn't understand why Tom avoided her when before he'd jump to sit next to or across from her. She looked back and then forward, checking on where he'd sat and if there was a space for her. Tiffany decided to stay put, giving Tom his space.

The trolley ride was the same as the bus for the two of them. There was less conversation and more observation from Tiffany. She had no idea how much he avoided her until they stepped off the trolley onto the street at their stop. Tom walked slower than usual, and Tiffany didn't have time to wait for him. She looked over her shoulder, realizing the distance between them had doubled, then tripled, and by the time she arrived at her job, he was not visible.

Tom strolled to the office and didn't think of time. He had little to do with meetings or dealing with customers, as he had done before his promotion. His energy level was like any other day, but his mind was elsewhere. He walked into his office building, went to his desk, and sat in silence. He spoke to the people who'd covered for him during his bereavement and managed to retrieve coffee from the break room. Tom didn't turn on his desktop computer, which was his routine, but sat silently.

"Tom, your phone is ringing." His neighbor pointed to his desk phone. "Are you going to answer?"

"Oh, yeah, thanks." Tom picked up the phone. "Hello."

"Tom, I need to see you in my office. Do you have a minute?"

"Yeah, sure I do. I'll be right there." Tom placed the phone on the hook and walked to the director's office. "You wanted to see me."

"Please have a seat."

"Okay."

"First, I'm sorry that you lost your wife. I had no idea you lost your son, too."

"Yeah, he left us from the war."

"I heard, and it's why I wanted you to talk to you." The director moved from behind his desk to the seat adjacent to Tom. "See, it's a lot to ask of you, but I have to do this for you and the good of the company."

"Are you firing me?"

"No, Tom, no way. You're too valuable to lose.   This conversation isn't about releasing you. But I think you need time to heal."

"I use my work to do that."

"I think you want to use this time to help you heal, but your effort isn't anything like you put out before Mary died."

"Oh, I...honestly, I know. It takes time to get me going."

"I noticed, and since you need time, we're in a position to support you while you take a hiatus."

"You want me to leave my work and do what?"

"Do anything your heart desires and come back like the old Tom. We need you, but we need you at your best."

"Oh, I see. I see." Tom rose and looked at the director. "I'll start today. How long do I have?"

"I've authorized three months."

"Three months...hmm, that's probably long enough."

"Good." The director rose and extended his hand. "Come back as Tom Stetson, the man we promoted from Baltimore."

Tom took his hand and shook it, and the director touched Tom's shoulder. Tom nodded his head. "I'll do my best."

"It's all we ask, Tom; your best is all we ask."

Tom retrieved a box from the supply closet, returned to his cubicle, and cleaned his area of personal items. He picked up his pictures of Mary and Tom Junior, wiped dust from the front, and put them in the box. He followed suit with folders of personal notes. He picked up his coffee cup and sat down. He rolled back and looked at the blank screen of his desktop. Tom sat up, turned on the computer, and finished his coffee. He constructed a thank you note to his team and sent an email blast to his customers asking them to continue interaction with their current contacts. He thanked them for their business.

Tom logged out, shut down his desktop, and went to the break room. He cleaned his coffee cup in the sink, dried it with paper towels, and returned to his box. Four guys met him at his cubicle. "You guys are the best."

"We'll miss you."

"Thanks, but it's for a short period. Nothing to worry about, I'll return."

"We know. It's just that you were awesome with us, and we appreciate it." His cubicle neighbor reached out his hand.

Tom shook his hand and those of the others standing around him. "Thank you, guys, I couldn't have asked for a better group." He unclipped his badge, placed it on the desk, put the coffee cup inside the box, and picked it up. He walked to the exit door without looking back.

Tom stepped off of the bus at his home stop. He carried the

open box in his hands, periodically looking at the contents. Step by step, he paced a path to his front door. He counted up to 798 paces, and then with one hand he grabbed the key from his pocket and placed it in the lock. He firmly grasped the front door handle and twisted it, and the door opened. Tom walked through and put the box on the couch, returned to the door, got his key, and closed it. He stood at the door, staring at the keyhole and waiting - waiting for anything. He waited, listening to his surroundings, as if some message or call would break his thoughts.

An hour later he turned, facing the front room, the couch, and the chairs near the kitchen. The kitchen had a special look, different than in the morning when he'd left. He walked to the stairs and stepped: *one, two, three, four, five...fourteen.* He realized he'd never noticed the number of steps to the next floor. He went into the bedroom and changed clothes, putting on those jeans Mary loved to see him wear. He grabbed his favorite tee shirt and returned downstairs. He picked up a bottle of wine from the few he had left, opened it, got a glass, and poured himself a drink. He sat at the kitchen table, his spot, in his chair, and faced the world he knew. Tom sipped wine, looked around the room, and sipped again. He looked at the furniture and sipped more from his glass.

What should I do now? What should I do? Tom finished the wine. The entire bottle was empty. He rose from the chair, tossed the bottle into the recycling bin, and went to grab another. He finally noticed there was only one bottle left. He picked up his glass, rinsed it, and left it in the sink. He grabbed his wallet and keys, leaving the house for the local grocery store.

Tom arrived at the store and went inside, then selected what he'd like for the coming week. He walked aisle after aisle until he satisfied his mental list. He even grabbed multiple types of wine and set them aside in the cart. When he got to the cashier, he picked up two magazines, one about San Francisco and another national periodical. "Is that it, sir?" the cashier asked.

"I think so." Tom touched his face. "I think so."

"That's one hundred thirty-five dollars and seventy-three cents, sir."

Tom swiped his debit card and entered his pin number. He took the receipt and pushed the cart to his car. When he looked at his watch, he realized that two hours had passed since he left home. Tom put the groceries away and restocked his wine rack. He placed a mat on the table and began to cook his dinner.

At the table, he opened the San Francisco magazine. Tom read page after page, eating dinner as he read. *I should do this*, he thought as he pointed to the museum. *I should do this*, as he noted the symphony. He retrieved a highlighter and marked places that seemed interesting. Before he finished for the night, he'd gathered enough information to create a schedule of events.

The morning came, and Tom was up before the birds. He found a trail near Daly City that allowed him to walk down to the beach. He dressed for the occasion and drove his car to the location. He got himself together, got out of the car, and walked the trail, noticing other people, couples and individuals dodging confrontation. He spoke to some simply because he couldn't avoid eye contact. His first time there, he found the ocean view amazing.

The next day he waited to leave home until the afternoon, dodging the morning rush hour. He went to the train and rode it south, past the airport. He visited a local museum with seafaring, unique items of fishermen and their wives. He walked through each corridor, grasping the idea behind the collection and enjoying the art.

On his third day of activities, he found an ice skating rink. It was something he and Mary had shared with little Tom. He arrived in time to watch the end of kids playing and practicing hockey. It took his mind to a time when little Tom had shared his interest in the sport. His mind imagined his son falling and standing, only to repeat the fall he'd just done. Tom smiled, put on the rented skates, and hit the ice. He spun, twisted, stopped, and skated for hours.

One evening of his new life, he visited the Chamber of the Symphony. He listened to the string quartet and enjoyed the performance so much that he became a supporting member of the orchestra. Tom attended the symphony and chamber performances like the diehard Oriole fan he'd been most of his adult life.

Two weeks of activities filled Tom's schedule, and his life was changing, but it wasn't exactly the transition he'd wanted. He missed Mary, missed her dearly - however, his idea of keeping busy worked.

Chapter 28

Tiffany called him during her lunch break. "Tom, I haven't seen you in a while. Are you okay?"

"I'm doing okay, considering I have time on my hands."

"I need to talk; can we meet today - maybe this evening?"

"Oh sure, I think that's a great idea. I don't have anything to do this evening. Shall I pick you up, or..."

"...I'll come by."

"Give me a call before you get here. Just in case, here's the address." Tom shared his location even though Tiffany had looked him up by his cell number. "Oh, I'm curious: how did you get my number?"

"I figured it out when you called me and hung up."

"You're an investigative spirit," Tom laughed. "See you tonight." He disconnected the call and looked at his watch, seeing that he had time to chill wine, cut cheese, and prepare a fruit dish.

Tom heard the doorbell ring twice. He put down the magazine and walked to the door. "Hi," he greeted Tiffany. "Please come in."

"Such a nice place." Tiffany looked around the living room. "For a single man, you keep a tight ship."

"I try. You know, it's easier when you have things under control."

"You should come and get my place under control like this."

"Yeah, please have a seat." Tom pointed towards the couch.

He walked to the kitchen, pulled out the prepared tray of cheese and fruit from the fridge, grabbed two wine glasses, and went into the living room. He set the tray on the coffee table, and the wine glasses were placed one across from the other and in front of Tiffany. He retrieved the wine from the fridge and poured a half glass for each of them. "I hope you like this."

"I'm sure I will." Tiffany picked up the wine glass and sipped. "Oh, this is good." She looked at the contents of the glass.

"Yeah, my wife chose this brand some time ago. I found it at the local grocer. I had to get a couple of bottles."

"I can see myself drinking a couple of bottles tonight. I'm so confused."

"What do you mean, confused?"

"Well, I like this guy I met, but he lives across the country."

"You mean online."

"Yes, online. And it's been wonderful so far. He's different than most men I've dated, but there's the distance - and we haven't seen each other outside of video chats."

"And you want to take a chance."

"One side of me wants to, but the other side says, 'stay local'."

"But no local man is calling."

"There was this one, but at the time he was occupied."

"Is he still occupied?"

"Things change, and I'm sure if he decided to extend an invitation, I would probably agree to come along."

"Then you should let him know you're available."

Tiffany drank the entire contents of her glass. She placed the glass on the coffee table and stared at Tom, getting his eyes to meet hers. "I just did."

"Oh, I can't be that guy."

"Why not? Things in your life have changed."

"But I don't think I am ready for an immediate relationship. I know my wife left, but it's not like you think."

"She left you, right?"

"Well, sort of. I mean, she left, but it was on good terms."

"What do you mean 'good terms'?"

Tom poured more wine into Tiffany's glass. "Let's just say that we should be friends - good friends - for now."

"Is this a rejection?"

"It's not rejection, but it's what I need at the moment. I can use a good friend."

Tiffany sipped from her wine glass, looked at Tom, and shook her head. "What's a girl got to do to get a man?"

"Let me tell you something. You have an interest in someone who isn't convenient. Love, true love, is never about convenience. The greater reward is from working to achieve it. What's wrong with giving a guy a chance who may be the love of your life?"

"I didn't think of it that way."

"You should." Tom sipped from his wine glass. "What are you doing tomorrow night?"

"Nothing, why do you ask?"

"I have access to the symphony, and there's a string quartet that's awesome. I'd like you to come."

"What time?"

"They start at 7:00 p.m. sharp."

"I work tomorrow, but I get home around three. I can make it. What's the dress code? I've never been to the symphony."

"Casual but nice - let's say, sexy casual."

"Sexy casual?"

"I use to tell Mary that, and she wore a nice dress, not too revealing, but it looked marvelous. I'm sure you have one dress for the occasion."

"I do, and I'll be ready by six."

"Perfect."

The next morning, Tom woke, dressed in gym gear, went to the gym, and worked out as if changing his body image was imperative. He returned home right before midmorning, fixed breakfast, and dressed for his daily routine. He cleaned his house, did laundry, and sat in the front room where he read another of his travel magazines.

At 4:30 p.m. Tom went upstairs and stepped into the closet. He picked out a pair of gabardine slacks, a soft-colored cotton shirt, and a sport blazer. *Hmm.* He lifted a tie from his tie rack. *A tie is too dressy.* He took his clothes to the washroom and set up the ironing board. He ironed his shirt, pressed his pants, and steamed his jacket.

An hour passed from the time he selected his attire to the time he showered and dressed. He grabbed his keys, locked the door, and went to his car, heading for Tiffany's house. He called her in route. "I'm on my way. I hope you're ready."

"I am. I knew you'd be on time."

"I'm usually prompt. I'll see you in a few minutes."

"Okay, I'll be outside waiting."

Tom disconnected the call, and after the traffic light, he arrived at Tiffany's home. She walked down to his car, and Tom jumped out to open her door.

"Such a gentleman."

"It's what men do for beautiful women."

"Flirting, too."

"No, I mean you are a beautiful woman."

"Thank you." Tiffany buckled in and placed her purse in her lap. Tom got in the car, buckled in, and put the car into motion. He drove towards downtown.

"I'm not so sure how to take the string quartet." Tiffany looked at Tom.

"It's a unique experience, one you may never forget."

"What about the people?"

"You see people from all walks of life. Music is something everyone enjoys."

"So it's not like a concert in the park."

Tom glanced at Tiffany with one raised eyebrow. "You have to get out more," he chuckled.

Tom arrived at the hall, pulled into a parking lot, and drove to an open parking spot. He parked, grabbed his jacket, and walked to the other side. Tiffany had opened her door and rose from her seat. Tom locked the car and walked abreast with Tiffany on the way in. They entered the performance chamber, and Tiffany was amazed at its setup. The stage was in the center of the room, an oak wood stage with a reddish-brown floor, very finished, and an impressive half circle. Four chairs were positioned with music stands. The common area floor was carpeted in a combination of maroon and tan; multiple designs made the carpet look like large squares. The ceiling was just as impressive. It was decorated with crystal chandeliers, a sky blue, soft color with floating clouds. On the far side, she saw a bar, and people stood around it. Tom touched her shoulder. "Would you like a glass of wine?"

"Sure." Tiffany walked with him.

Tom ordered two glasses of wine and gave one to Tiffany. He paid the bartender and noticed two of his acquaintances from other times he'd attended the performance. "Hi, how's it going?"

"Ah, Tom, it's nice seeing you again." The gentleman smiled. "You're with a lady tonight."

"Yes. Meet a friend of mine, Tiffany."

"Nice meeting you; this is my wife Carla."

"Hi, Carla." Tiffany shook her hand. "Is this a lovely place or what?"

"It's gorgeous. I love this decoration, and the stage had to have been made in the late eighteenth century."

"I never thought this chamber would be so decorative. I mean, I attended concerts here before, but I never came down to this level."

"Wait until you experience the acoustics." Carla sipped her drink and looked at Tom. "She's charming, kind of different from your deceased wife."

Tom looked at Tiffany, "Yeah, I wanted to introduce them but never got the chance."

"Deceased wife? Tom, I thought she left you."

"She did, but I didn't explain how she left."

Carla and her husband looked at Tom and Tiffany discussing his marriage situation. Tom was a widower, and Tiffany was surprised to know that his wife had died and not left him from a disagreement or irreconcilable differences. "Why didn't you tell me she died?" Tiffany turned to face Tom, ignoring everyone else around them.

"I can explain later; let's listen to the quartet. They're getting ready to start." Tom led Tiffany to a seat on the east side of the stage. Tiffany frowned through the entire performance. She nudged Tom at the end of the first song. "We need to talk."

"Now?"

"Yes, now."

Tom rose and slid his way across to the aisle, and Tiffany followed suit. She grabbed his arm and walked with him to the exit. "Tom, I don't understand why you rejected me yesterday."

"Because it's better that we're friends more than anything else."

"But I thought you were my friend, and that's good for a connection. I mean, even though you're a widower, I don't expect you to jump in with both feet."

"I didn't say I was a widower, and that had nothing to do with my decision." Tom pushed the exit door open and allowed Tiffany to pass first. "I am not ready for anything in the relationship arena." He led the way to his parked car.

"How long ago did it happen?"

"Remember the newspaper article about a wife's overdose?"

"That was your wife?"

"That was Mary."

"I'm so sorry."

"And that's why I didn't tell you. I didn't want sympathy. I'm better off remembering her love and beauty. I don't need the sad eyes."

"Then, I guess..."

"We'll be friends. Here, get in the car." Tom closed the door and entered the driver's side. "I think we'll call it a night." The drive was made in silence, except for the classical music on the radio.

Two weeks passed, and Tom met Tiffany in the park for roller blading. He laughed at how inexperienced Tiffany was at riding line skates. "I thought you said you'd done this before."

"I have, but it's been a long time."

"I think it's like riding a bike; you just get up and do it."

"Bike riding would have been better," Tiffany laughed. She moved one foot slowly in front of the other. Off they went, up and down the paved pathway. Tom stopped at a bench, and Tiffany arrived shortly after. "I guess it's enough for today."

"I thought you'd never stop," Tiffany breathed, then took her roller blade off of her right foot and rubbed the sole of her foot. "I just started getting better, but this foot is so sore."

"Keep rubbing it. I'm sure you'll get the blood circulating again."

"I hope so." Tiffany massaged her foot, looked at Tom, and said, "I have to ask."

"Yeah, ask what?"

"I'm really into this guy in Florida. We talk all of the time. I mean, it's like clockwork. Day in, day out, we spend at least two hours online or video chatting."

"Sounds like it's moving pretty well."

"He asked me to meet him in person."

"Oh, now you're really going in. I think it's great."

"Do you?"

"Of course. You want a real relationship, and here's a chance for you."

"It's long distance."

"How do you feel now? I mean, right this moment."

"Actually, I'm enjoying this."

"I'm sure you'll do the same for years to come."

"Stay online for years?"

"I meant the feeling between you two. When you connect and chat, and do whatever it is that you two do online."

"Yes, it's pretty good. I've gotten used to the attention, and I can't wait to see if he's as genuine in person."

"Where are you two meeting?"

"He's convinced it should be Las Vegas."

"He's probably a smart man for suggesting such a place."

"Why do you say so?"

"He's probably thinking about entertainment value, neutrality, and affordability."

"Funny, it must be a guy thing. You two think the same way."

"I guess you're going."

"I think I am." Tiffany smiled and put her roller blade back on. "I will see you at the car."

Tom rose and followed Tiffany down the slope to meet her at the parking lot. He leaned against the car and removed his roller blades. "You know, I haven't had this much fun since hanging out with my son."

"Really?" Tiffany giggled. "I'll take that as a compliment."

"You should." Tom smiled.

Chapter 29

Tom woke with an idea. He'd read travel magazines for the past month, looking at locations that he would have taken Mary. He sat up in bed, looked at the ceiling, and imagined driving up the coast to Seattle. His idea revolved around visiting Mt. Saint Helen and looking over the beautiful rivers. He wanted to see the trees in his drive through Oregon.

Tom got out of bed, made it up, and ran downstairs to make coffee. He grabbed the travel magazine, and retrieved his laptop before returning to his bedroom. He sat on the bed and booted up his machine.

Tom turned the page on the travel magazine to the Great Northwest. He typed the location in his map application and plotted the course he'd take, heading north. It was an hour later and over three cups of coffee that he finalized his plan. He'd moved to the kitchen table with the laptop and magazine in hand after reading the first two articles. Tom folded the page of interest and noted the travel route between locations. He finished his mapping and looked at his agenda for the coming week. He ran upstairs and packed for the trip. He put the right clothing in his luggage for inclement weather and he added casual wear for the nights for dinner. Before he closed the suitcase, Tom grabbed his desktop's framed family portrait - the one Mary had insisted they take before Tom Junior left for the Army. He stared at it, rubbed its face, kissed his family, and put it in the suitcase's side pocket.

His first intentional travel stop was to visit Jedediah Smith Redwood State Park, what he thought would be a breathtaking experience. Seeing those huge trees would have made his Mary sparkle from excitement. He mapped a path to Redding,

California to enjoy nature the way he once had loved to do before marriage. Then he took a path to see the monstrous gifts - the redwoods.

With his first destination in mind and a better idea of his journey, Tom revised his packing. He made sure that the clothes he chose were easy to clean, quick to fix, and somewhat impressive. He prepared for any situation. He grabbed his toiletries travel kit, pushed it in the suitcase, and secured it.

Tom picked up his suitcase and placed it near the front door. He returned to the kitchen and rebooted the laptop. He set his mark for a hotel in Redding, made reservations, and selected a couple of activities he'd do there. He decided to spend hours enjoying the city and visit the giants of nature the following morning.

His third sightseeing idea was just as remarkable. Eugene, Oregon had a write-up on the town. He was excited about trying a few restaurants and frequenting the nightclubs he'd read about, as well as sampling the museums and some of the finest people you could ever run across. Tom's excitement rose as he fantasized about his upcoming road trip.

The next earmarked page in the magazine took him to Portland, a city full of unique thrills, from donuts to coffee, jazz to a mansion, and a Japanese Garden. Portland offered a grand idea of a visit, based on the redwood he'd see once he got there. Again, he dog-eared the corner of the page he read before turning to his next interest. He pinpointed a hotel within walking distance from most attractions and planned his stay. He wanted two days in Portland, enough time to enjoy the sights at his leisure.

From a city of jazz to the northwest city of Peugeot Sound, Tom remembered how he wanted to see everything the west coast offered. He enjoyed the arts, and Seattle was a place that offered a tremendous amount of entertainment, sites, unique sounds, and great food. His joy over San Francisco's wharf made him interested in comparing it with Seattle's famous wharf. Besides, he'd grown up in Baltimore eating the best crabs in the world. And since there was a difference in cooking styles, he couldn't wait to experience their taste.

He planned the sightseeing and scheduled activities to keep his mind busy, enjoying whatever the area offered and seeing things he'd only read about. Tom closed the last page of the travel magazine. He snapped his fingers and went to his car. His military mind instructed him to perform preventive maintenance on his car for the long drive ahead. Like every good maintenance guy, he pulled the oil stick, measured and adjusted liquids, checked tire pressure, and opened the trunk to ensure that he traveled with a complete emergency kit (cables, small tools, flashlight, water, tie downs, and a can of fix-a-flat).

Tom, being a perfectionist, drove to the local gas station, filled his tank, adjusted tire pressures, and bought a can of oil. He rode to the car wash and cleaned his luxury buggy. When he finished, he went to the grocery store and purchased fruits, water, chips, and sandwich meat with cheese.

By the time Tom finished his preparations, he'd managed to skip lunch. His stomach reminded him he hadn't eaten. He called his friend Tiffany and asked if she'd enjoy dinner. Tom offered to cook when she accepted.

Tom opened the front door, and the aroma hit Tiffany's nose, attacking her taste buds. "Oh, my goodness." Tiffany smiled. "I hope I'm not too late. It smells wonderful."

"You're right on time. Dinner is about ready."

"Did you cook for your family?"

"I did, at times. We had a system, every other day."

"No wonder you're a man who knows how to maneuver around the kitchen."

"I can hold my own." Tom walked in front of the stove.

"I may have cooked too much. You'll have to take some home with you."

Tiffany took in a deep breath. "Oh, I'll be glad to." She smiled. "Why did you cook so much for the two of us?"

"I'm going on a trip, and I hate throwing good food away."

"You're leaving?"

"I'm going north, kind of exploring the northwest. I'm going to places Mary and I once discussed." Tom grinned. "I expect it will be awesome."

"I know it will."

Dinner went off like magic at a circus. Tiffany practically inhaled her food. Tom paced himself, maintaining small talk. "How's the long-distance relationship going?"

"A couple months more, and I'm in Las Vegas."

"That is the destination."

"Again, it's what we think is best for us."

"I agree; it is perfect." Tom smiled and raised his glass of wine. "I wish you the best time ever."

"I'm sure we'll have one. I can't wait to see him." Tiffany smiled and tapped his glass with hers.

Tom placed the glass on the table. "I can get you more, if you'd like."

"No, I had enough. But since you're leaving, I'll take as much as you're willing to share." Tiffany rose from the table with her plate in hand. She put the dish and silverware in the sink and returned to the table. "If you want, I'll wash the dinner plates."

"No, it's okay. I got it." Tom finished his dinner and went to the kitchen sink, filling it with water and soap. "I'll get you the leftovers."

"Okay, thanks." Tiffany drank from her wine glass. "I need to ask a favor."

"Yeah, what is it?"

"Can you go with me to my friend Valerie's party? Her boyfriend is giving her a birthday bash."

"I don't mind...sure."

"Great. I'll give you the date as soon as I find out."

"Okay, but I hope it's not during my travel."

"Probably not, since he asked me to help him plan it."

"Good deal. I know you'll give her a birthday party to remember."

"That's the plan."

After Tom put leftovers in containers, they cleaned the kitchen. Tiffany thanked him for a splendid dinner and conversation. She also smiled at the great cooking he gave her for later. Tom settled in for the night right after securing the front door when Tiffany left. He crashed, anxious to hit the road in the early morning.

The alarm went off before sunrise. Tom jumped out of bed and got himself together. He made his bed as always, already preparing for his return. His glance around the room gave him satisfaction that things were all in place and that he was ready for his trip. Tom ran downstairs, grabbed his traveling coffee cup, unplugged his counter appliances, went to the house water control, and turned it off. He grabbed his gear and went to the car.

At the car, Tom secured his mountain bike, put his suitcase away, placed the icebox of fruit and a case of water on the back seat, got behind the driver's wheel, and put the coffee cup in the cup holder. He started the engine, waited until the revs subsided to 8,000 rpms, and secured his seatbelt. He turned the radio on and off as he drove, heading to the interstate. Tom was happy he'd prepared a travel plan, mapped out his routes, and put the magazines in the front seat the night before. His only stop during the morning was at the local Citgo for coffee. He hit the road with nice tunes blaring, facing minimal traffic.

It was three hours into his journey when he arrived at the exit for Jedehia Smith Redwood States Park. He smiled, applying his brakes and slowing down. He was amazed at the presentation. The overpowering view of trees, bigger than a kid's imaginary giant, overtook him. He stopped at the entrance and, with his camera phone, snapped a few pictures of the park sign. *Oh, my God, how beautiful.*

Tom followed the road around the curve and parked on the side of the road, doing his best not to obstruct traffic. He stepped out and looked up. As far as the eye could see, upward to cloudland, there were limbs green with leaves. He snapped another shot and returned to the car, driving to the visitor's center.

Minutes after parking, he sat in the car and looked left and into the back seat. He saw Mary and Tom Junior at a time when they would drive through parks and sightseeing destinations. He rubbed his eyes, fighting tears, and dropped his head on the steering wheel, closing his eyes. *I miss my wife and son. This may not have been a good idea. God, what was I thinking?*

He lifted his head and saw the visitor's center, where he noticed a lot of people migrating in and out. His breathing strengthened, and he managed to open the door, step out, and close it. His fingers pressed the key fob and locked the doors. When he put the keys in his pocket, he dodged a man who parked next to him. Tom nodded in greeting.

"You're in for a special treat."

"I bet." Tom smiled.

"If you were a kid and liked playing in the park, this would be your gift from God."

"I can believe it. I was actually that kid."

"Then enjoy." The gentleman entered his car and sat behind the driver's wheel. He dipped his head and didn't move a muscle. Tom looked at the back of his head while he walked past the end of the car. *Strange.* When he turned right onto the sidewalk, he passed an elderly couple walking to the parking lot. He figured the gentleman was waiting for the couple to arrive. Tom spoke greeted them and kept moving, walking behind a young couple who seemed excited about their upcoming exploration of the park.

Tom walked into the center, looked around, and followed the wall map of the park, highlighting tree locations, the roads, and the area's unique life forms. Tom took in everything, noting the trails.

Tom returned to his car, took his bike from the back hook, and prepared for his ride. He went into the trunk, pulled out his backpack, filled it with water and fruit, and secured it once he was done. It was the first time in what he considered to be forever since he'd rode his bike. Mary would accompany him on rides through parks or, in Baltimore, would ride with him to the local grocer. They would laugh about their journey. Tom threw his backpack over his head, put his arms through the straps, and lifted his leg, settling on the bike seat as if he were mounting a horse. He put his foot on the pedal and pushed, riding into the motion.

Tom pressed and lifted in simultaneous motion. His bike moved down the trail, dodging cars on the path and stopping at a patch barely large enough for two vehicles. He looked at the trees and the brush and waved at the people in cars who were surprised at the view, like him. Each pedal bought him to another monster of nature. The shade from the scattered clouds only allowed pockets of sunlight to pierce through the canopy. Tom stopped again, looking towards the sky and admiring how nearly every redwood was as high as the eye could see. He kicked the bike stand down, dismounted, stood the bike on the stand, and walked to one tree. He spread his arms as far as he could, only to fully extend his hands, looking like a cartoon character against a flat wall. Tom chuckled. *Mary would have laughed.*

After another great distance, Tom stopped at the path signs leading him on the Stout loop and River Trace. The high road north in the path in the shadows of giants, shaded from the sunlight, gave him a cool ride on an otherwise-hot, sunny day. The brush was just as impressive; he noticed the sword ferns and the green shrubbery as well as large tree limbs that seemed like mascots of ancient statues. Tom peddled right along, only stopping when pedestrians passed him, asking to take a photo of them next to a tree. He looked at the picture and imagined prehistoric dinosaurs walking like puppies in a gigantic forest against the immense size of the redwoods. His imagination returned to a time when he could have impressed Tom Junior with the story he'd told him for his third-grade science project, 'The Giants Who Roamed the Earth.'

Before arriving at the river, Tom parked his bike and walked through fallen limbs that made gates, bridges, or obstacle-like structures, yet there was a clear path to maneuver through them. He stood on the wood, looked up, and couldn't believe the size of the fallen tree. It was a natural crossbeam column, offering accents in a way the Native Americans may have embraced as a spiritual icon.

Tom walked with his bike towards the river. He observed the roots of the monstrous fallen trees. Amazed at their size, he stopped at one and touched it, feeling the reality of nature. He shook his head in disbelief at the amazing trees and ecosystem that supported them. He stared at the roots and connected his emotions to his wife and son, the family he once had. His tears welled and one fell, rolling down his cheek. *I miss Mary. I miss Junior. I miss my life.* He wiped the tears from his eyes and mounted his bike. He looked at the path ahead and pedaled further.

When he arrived at the river, he stood on a crest slightly higher than the riverbank. Tom got off the bike, parked it safely, and pulled his backpack off. He pulled out fruit and water, then watched the river while he ate. The blue water was refreshing, like the memory of his family. He finished the fruit, took a swig of water, and put the water bottle back in the pack. He pulled the backpack on and climbed down to the bank. He looked into the water, observing his reflection. Mary and Junior flanked his image. He shook his head and wiped his eyes, but his wife and son were still there. He turned his head left, and then right, looking at nothing. He wiped his eyes again and there, waving in the water's reflection, were members of his family. He didn't move again, staring in the river until their images faded.

Lonz Cook

Chapter 30

Tom made it to Redding within two hours of leaving the state park. He found the Hampton Inn off the main drag. It was exactly as presented online. Tom checked in with his gear and looked around the room. He turned on the television and explored the local channel covering Redding. Before the hour, he'd compared his plans to the interesting sites the television advertised. He checked and rearranged sites he'd enjoy for the afternoon and evening.

Tom walked his bike to the elevator, got on, and went down to the lobby floor. He exited the hotel and mounted the bike, heading to the first site he'd read about. The Sun Dial Bridge was his first objective, a short ride from the hotel. He started his journey dodging traffic, contending with roadways that weren't bike friendly. Tom relied on his keen ability to dodge in and out of traffic without causing himself a heart attack. He wasn't sure if his antics riding on the side of the road were acceptable for oncoming cars.

The bridge stood as beautiful as its shadow. The design reminded him of a stick in the middle of the circle, but with the flair of the Golden Gate Bridge. He was surprised at how the bridge shared its shadow, like he saw as a child placing a stick in the middle of a circle in sunlight. He looked at his watch to see if the shadow matched the current hour. Tom giggled at himself doing things a kid would do.

He rode across the bridge, avoiding oncoming bikes and pedestrians until he encountered one woman who stood in his way. "Excuse me." Tom pressed his brakes.

"Sorry." The blonde woman moved closer to the rail. "I didn't see you."

245

"It's okay." Tom pedaled forward towards the end of the bridge. He stopped at the overlook for the Sacramento River. The view was interesting, more so for the reflection of the bridge on the water, and extremely interesting to the woman he passed. He turned around, and she had arrived in front of him. "I'm sorry for startling you back there."

"It's okay." She continued walking on the paved path.

Tom mounted his bike and rode back in the direction he'd started in. He approached the blonde woman. "I'm behind you!" He dodged oncoming folks and waved his hand, indicating 'thank you'. He moved to a seat in the park nearly a mile from where he'd crossed the bridge. He took in the countryside, the trees, and, most of all, he admired the families who walked the trails.

Tom rode until he left the mass of people behind him, scattered with short distances between them. He was nearly the only person around for at least a hundred yards in either direction. His heartbeat increased, and he pedaled as fast as he could across the dirt trail, going into the unknown. His skills increased as he turned short curves and dodged loose rocks as if they were street cones. His mind focused on the road. *Come on, Mary, keep up.*

Tom slowed and looked behind him. *Habits - habits are hard to break.* He allowed the bike to roll to a stop, put his foot on the ground for balance, and kept the other on the pedal. He leaned on his grounded foot. *I wish she were here. This could have been a great ride with her.* He mounted the bike and turned around, pedaling at a slow pace and making the bike move as smoothly as it could on a dirt path. He arrived where he started, only to recognize the blonde woman sitting on a bench near the paved path.

"You are safe from me now." Tom smiled.

"I'd say you're right."

Tom stopped his bike in front of the woman. "Where can a guy enjoy a good dinner and maybe a glass of wine?"

"It depends on what you call good."

"I mean something a non-tourist would enjoy. I've learned that the locals know best."

"You're visiting?"

"Yes, I am. I came up to get away from some difficulties in life."

The blonde smiled. "You came to Redding to get away. I'm curious, from where did you come?"

"San Francisco."

"You'd leave San Fran for this place? It must have been something awful, for you to leave."

"You can say that. I think I've endured enough awful things in my life."

"Okay, well, I think that if you like Italian, you will enjoy Gironda's. The pizza is like Chicago's style, and the small plates are perfect."

"That sounds interesting enough. I like Italian."

"If you like Mexican, I suggest Conquista. It's the best."

"Maybe a margarita for dinner," Tom giggled. "Like I need one of those. How about a local mom and pop? Sometimes those are the best."

"We have Clearie's, and its cozy." She looked to the ground. "It's kind of like Cheers, where people talk and aren't afraid to mingle." Her eyes caught Tom's. "For a visitor who's alone, it's what I call being 'one of the locals'. You won't feel like you're by yourself."

"Sounds good. I think I'll ask my hotel clerk for directions."

"It's pretty easy for all of them; just hit the main street, and you'll find yourself within walking distance of all three."

"Oh, that's perfect. I don't have to drive."

"That's one good thing about Redding." She smiled and stood. "Enjoy your dinner." She walked forward on the paved trail.

"Thanks so much. Have a great walk." Tom pedaled to the main road to the hotel. He walked his bike inside and approached the counter. "Excuse me. I don't want to bother you, but I heard of a few restaurants that are supposed to be pretty good."

"Yes sir, I can help you with that."

"I like local cuisine. Fish, locally caught or American style."

"Clearie's, and it's really good."

"I heard that from a lady in the park. Is it far?"

"About three minutes driving time and about a ten-minute walk."

"Walking it is." Tom smiled. "Thank you."

"You're welcome."

Tom arrived at his room, opened the door, and picked out his cell phone from his pocket. He typed in his code and pulled up the pictures he'd taken. He'd captured the image of the blonde on the bridge. He enlarged the screen on the phone and enhanced the picture. He nodded his head in admiration. *She's no Mary, but she is pretty good-looking.* He placed the camera on the desk and disrobed, walked to the bathroom, turned on the shower, and waited for the water to warm. *Let's see what this town offers.* Tom showered clean, toweled dry, and went to his suitcase. He gathered his clothes for the night. As a unique habit, Tom put on his underwear before pressing his pants and tennis shirt. He laid his ironed perfections on the foot of the bed and returned to the bath.

A dash of this and a splash of that cologne went on his face and chest. *I don't want to scare anyone off, but at least I can smell good.* He laughed, returning to the foot of the bed and dressing for the occasion. He put on his loafers without socks. Tom stood in the mirror and looked himself over. He knew it was important to look his best, a habit he'd never let go from his younger days.

He arrived at Clearie's just as directed. He opened the door and was greeted with a kind smile. The waitress said, "Anywhere is fine."

"Thank you." Tom walked to one of the high tables across from the long bar. He scanned the place, remembering bars of yesterday - early 1900s with a long brown wooden bar, stools spaced appropriately, and a large mirror on the wall overlooking the liquor. It seemed to make the place look larger. The blonde woman he met at the park was right; it seemed like an alternate location for Cheers, the television show of the eighties. Tom looked around, watching people mingle and take seats at the bar. "Hey," a guy spoke. "How are you?"

"I'm doing okay." Tom smiled. "How are you?"

"What a day. I didn't catch a damn thing."

"Is that unusual for here?"

"Pretty much, but sometimes the river doesn't give you a gift."

"At least you had fun."

"I love it."

"Yeah, I can see." Tom took the menu from the waitress who walked to his table. "Thank you."

"I haven't seen you here before."

"I'm passing through."

The bartender approached the gentleman. "What are you having today, Dave?"

"I need a beer, draft. I can't do the hard stuff today," he laughed.

"Gotcha, so that means you didn't do well on the river."

"Yep, you know it." Dave frowned. "I used my best bait, too."

"What are you having, sir?"

"I'm more of a wine guy. Red wine is good."

"Coming right up." The bartender poured the beer from the tap and grabbed a bottle of red wine. He poured the wine in a red wine glass. He placed the mug of beer in front of Dave and walked to Tom's table with the wine. "I can take your order, too."

"Thanks." Tom took a sip of his wine and placed the glass back on the table. "What do you suggest?"

Dave turned towards Tom. "The rainbow trout is awesome here."

"Is this what you do when you don't have a great fishing day?"

"You know, it's always good to have an alternate plan." Dave sipped his beer. "Besides, even on my best days, I come here."

"Says a lot about the chef."

"He's a great cook. Let me say this; there isn't a bad meal on the menu."

"Are you boasting again?" Sam, a regular, walked in and sat at the bar. "You can't believe everything this guy says," Sam laughed. "How ya doing, Dave?"

"Oh, I didn't catch a damn thing today."

"The retired life. All you have to do is fish. Must be nice."

"It's my job." Dave tapped Sam on the shoulder.

The bartender walked up. "The usual?"

"Yep." Sam pulled out a money clip and placed a twenty-dollar bill on the bar. "This is my limit."

"Sure it is," Dave laughed. "You can't trust what this guy says; he'll drink until your twenty dollars is included in his tab."

"Aren't that what friends are for?" Tom laughed.

"Sam, he's passing through...I'm sorry, I didn't catch your name."

"Tom." Tom rose from his chair, stepped towards the bar, and offered his hand.

"I'm Dave, and this is Sam." Dave shook Tom's hand, and Sam followed suit.

"Nice meeting you."

"Same here."

"What brought you through Redding?"

"I'm exploring, driving to Seattle from San Fran. I wanted to stop for the night and see the sights."

"If you like the outdoors, there is no other place in California like Redding."

"I see." Tom nodded. "I went to the bridge, and at the end of the trail, I got to see the mountain."

"When you drive north, you'll get a better look," Dave advised.

"Yeah, if you leave early enough, you can detour and see it close up. A nice experience."

"I may do that."

The bartender walked to Tom's table. "What can I get you?"

"I'll take the trout."

"Great selection." Dave drank his beer.

"You're going to love it," Sam encouraged.

"I heard." Tom gave the bartender his menu and sipped his wine. "What else is there to do in Redding?"

"Well, besides this bar, there's a lot to do depending on the season."

"Did I miss the right season?"

"No, right now there are music concerts in the park, and swimming, fishing, and, of course, hiking."

"If you're a museum guy, there's one here, but it's nothing like San Francisco."

"Yeah, San Francisco's bigger." Sam took a swig of his whiskey.

"You right about that, Sam."

"I find that by seeing museums, you learn more about the

area. But I'm on the road early tomorrow."

"I traveled and saw a few museums while I was in the Army." Sam drank more whiskey. "It was fun, but nothing like chasing skirts."

"Oh, yeah, you did that a lot." Dave sipped his beer. "I bet you didn't catch any, just like your fishing." He laughed.

"What? I caught plenty," Sam laughed.

Tom laughed with Sam and Dave, and he looked at them. "You two were in the Army?"

"I'm the vet." Sam pointed at Dave. "He was smart enough to keep his plant job."

"I served in the Army, too. I was with the 101st logistics."

"I was a straight leg, walked a lot back then."

"He didn't score well on his test," Dave said. "I told him to be serious."

"There's smart guys in infantry, you know."

"I'd say so."

The gentlemen talked about their military days without excluding Dave. Tom explained his experiences and talked about how Dave would have enjoyed being deployed to Germany. Sam talked about Korea and how intense their duties were. Dave pulled both veterans to current day situations.

"You mean, the country is losing jobs, and people here are hurting too."

"It's the same across the country." Sam tapped the counter for his third whiskey.

Tom's dinner arrived, and he focused on every bite while

talking to Sam and Dave. At the end, he looked up, and to his surprise, the blonde woman from the park walked in. "Hi, Dave, Sam."

"Hi, Tracey," they both responded.

She looked at Tom. "You took my advice."

"Yes, and it was great." Tom smiled.

"Good. I knew you'd like either one."

"Are you a regular?"

"You can say that."

"She works here," Dave said.

"I would have never known," Tom responded.

"How would you? We didn't get that far," Tracy said.

"You met Tracey?" Sam asked.

"Forgive him, he's a little slow," Dave laughed.

"Yeah, we met in the park by the bridge earlier today."

"Tracey's a doll of a bartender."

"I'm not giving free drinks, Sam."

"It's okay, Tracey, I still think you're the best."

"Don't mind him; he's such a flirt."

Tracey replenished Tom's red wine and served both Sam and Dave. Since the restaurant and bar had gotten busier, she focused on customers and wait staff, filling their orders. Tracey took Tom's plate from the table, moving briskly to the back. She reappeared with a menu in hand and walked to Tom's table. "Dessert?"

"Oh, no, I can't, but thanks."

"Okay."

"You should have the checkerboard mousse. It's a dish you'll never forget."

"Thanks, but I'm not much on sweet stuff." Tom sipped his wine. "Besides, I'm off early tomorrow. That sugar would keep me awake."

Tracey walked behind the bar and returned to her profession. She flowed from one end of the bar to the other, and Tom noticed she moved with grace. He looked at her in motion, her mirrored reflection, and took out his phone, comparing what he'd seen at the park to her ballerina-like control of everything behind the bar. He watched in amazement as though a show had captured his attention. Tracey slowed as the crowd decreased. Sam and Dave had tallied up and vacated their regular spots at the bar. Tom sat with the bill in hand, waiting to give Tracey his credit card. She didn't come to him, so instead, Tom walked to the bar. "Here you go." He placed the bill and credit card on the bar.

"I'll be right there."

"Take your time, I don't have much to do, and it's only ten. Does it always empty out before ten?"

"On weeknights, pretty much."

"I can understand."

"Yeah, most people work early around here, so it's in and out, except on Friday and Saturday nights." Tracey grabbed his credit card and check, walked to the register, and performed the transaction. She walked down the bar and back to Tom. "You can't get most people to leave unless you call their wives."

"I bet." Tom smiled. "And they must make passes at you."

"Just the old guys," Tracey giggled. "They mean no harm."

"Good 'ole guys," Tom nodded. "Well, I'm out. I have to get up and drive in the morning."

"Why don't you stay and we'll have coffee?"

"I appreciate the offer, but I'm not quite sure I can."

"Your wife wouldn't mind."

"I don't have one of those." Tom shook his head. "Not anymore."

"Divorced?" Tracey poured another glass of wine. "It's on me."

"Thank you, but I'm not so sure..."

"Sure you can." Tracey pushed the wine in front of Tom.

"You walked here, right??

"Yes, I did."

"I'll give you a lift."

Tom looked at the wine and peeked at his watch. He imagined leaving at dawn for Seattle. *Since I don't have a schedule - why not?* He sat at the bar and sipped his glass of red wine. "Okay," Tom said when Tracey stood in front of him. "You're my ride to the hotel."

"Good." Tracey smiled. "Where are you from?"

"Originally, from Baltimore, but I moved to San Francisco not long ago."

"Do you like it?"

"Yeah, pretty much. It's an interesting city."

"I go there sometimes. You know; do the tourist thing from time to time. Fisherman's Wharf is not bad."

"No, it isn't. I like it there, too." Tom looked at the bar and back at Tracey. "I don't go as often these days."

"Why not?"

"It's more fun when you're with someone than going alone."

"I agree." Tracey looked down the bar. "I'll be right back."

"Okay, take your time." Tom looked at the wine glass and measured its quantity. He knew he could finish it in five minutes. His eyes rose to the mirror and Tracey's reflection. Her beauty got his attention, and he was surprised to note the effect in his jeans. It had been months since Mary died, and not once had he thought of a sexual encounter. When Tracey returned, Tom's attention went to her features. Her wavy blonde hair met her shoulders and danced when she swung in a direction. He noticed her lips, full, where a cherry would be a perfect fit if she puckered them. She had perky breasts showing through her black tennis shirt working attire. And her bottom was just enough to keep a man smiling at night. Tom nodded.

"Are you okay?"

"With the thoughts I'm having, I'm doing fine."

"What thought is that?"

"Well, I don't know where to start. It's been a long time since I've spoken to a woman about this."

Tracey looked to her left. "Hold that thought. I'll be right back." She helped a customer and then returned to Tom. "You know, I never got your name."

"Tom, Tom Stetson."

"Nice to meet you, Tom Stetson. I'm Tracey Jergens."

"My pleasure, Ms. Jergens."

"Call me Tracey, please."

"And I'm Tom...no formalities."

"Huh?"

"Nothing...what time are you off?"

"In about ten minutes. Can I take your glass?"

"Of course." Tom killed the last of the wine. He gave her the glass and observed what she did behind the bar. Tom watched her close shop, clean the bar, and set things up for the next day. After thirty minutes, she walked from behind the bar. "I'm ready."

"Okay." Tom followed her out of the front door, and they walked abreast to her car. "Are you sure it's okay to take me to the hotel?"

"I invited you, of course I'm sure. Get in."

Chapter 31

Tom looked at the hotel's bed. He had no idea how much of a risk he may have taken. He remembered driving to the hotel and talking to Tracey in the car for hours. He shared his feeling of being lost but held back the depth of his emotions, missing his wife and son.

Tracey had everything a man would find interesting and entertaining. Her mind was as witty as her body was inviting. She had the right mix, and her age was not far off from his. She had divorced a few years earlier, had one son in his last year of high school, and didn't have the good luck of finding available men in Redding. She explained how she crapped out, as she called it, with guys early on in their attempts for a relationship.

The night had gotten the best of them, and Tom found himself amused. He flashed to moments in the car before she walked to his room. He hadn't kissed a woman since Mary left. He wasn't sure that such was appropriate, being a new widower, but his loins were calling for play. Tom moved like a young man, and his prowess took control of the fair maiden. Before he knew it, he'd encouraged her to be in his bed, naked between the sheets, awaiting his arrival.

Tom shook his head in disbelief, walked to the shower, and turned on the water. He jumped in, realizing he'd slept past his departure time for Seattle. Tom stood under the showerhead, feeling the warmth of the water run down his body. He flashed back to last night, feeling her skin next to his, and how he'd enjoyed the moment. He grabbed soap and a washcloth, washing his body. Tom's mind returned to her lips, which had started at his shoulders and moved down his body as he lay in the center of the bed. Her kisses were tender like he experienced a lifetime ago with his wife. Tracey took her time, which he loved, because it was something he enjoyed. She kissed his waist and his inner thighs and explored around the world, touching his nerve endings with her tongue. He jumped a few times, simply by her lips engaging his erogenous zone.

Tom threw the washcloth over his shoulder, holding one end and grabbing the other. He scrubbed his back and looked at the bottom of the tub. The image of Tracey's body appeared like a picture upon a theater's movie screen: lifelike, full-sized, and as beautiful as the picture he'd taken in the park. She moved in front of him, turning the morning after into the morning of. The cloth dropped to the bottom of the tub, and he grabbed the soap bar. Tom washed his loins to an erection. His mind didn't stop the feeling Tracey had laid upon him. He turned around, facing the showerhead. Water hit his erection, and Tom closed his eyes, allowing the water spray to take his feeling down a notch. He got back in control and turned the water off.

Tom toweled dry, stepped out of the tub, and looked into the misted mirror. He again saw Tracey at the moment she'd ridden him like the lost horse of a cowgirl. She bounced up and down, making her perky breasts dance and shake. He hadn't seen that since Mary was youthful. His mind kept going, moving up and down, her curves embedded in the picture. His flashback changed like the wind pushing white sheets on the clothesline. Tracey had her back on the bed with legs bent, inviting Tom's lips to kiss her tender spots. Her hips bucked when his tongue entered her like a snake smelling danger. She bucked again when he focused on her button, pressing and caressing, giving her a tongue lashing and taking her on an out-of-body journey. Tom touched his lips, remembering her smell and hearing her scream of pleasure.

Tom shook his head, escaping the memory and gaining

control. He dropped the towel and went to the chair where he'd thrown his clothes, grabbed his underwear, pants, and shirt, and then dressed. He went downstairs for breakfast and chose his meal carefully, understanding how much he ate the night before. His selection was full of nutrition and without hurtful carbohydrates, something healthy in the long run. He selected a table in the corner of the dining area, got his coffee and juice, and returned. Tom watched people as he ate breakfast. He saw an elderly couple sit across from him. Like his reflective thought in San Francisco, he remembered how he wanted Mary to be with him to the end.

He bit the banana and took a spoonful of oatmeal, sipped coffee, and repeated. It wasn't until the oatmeal was finished that he thought of last night. He couldn't believe it had happened. His frown became real, bringing tears to his eyes, because he saw the couple and wished that Mary had been that woman instead of Tracey. He closed his eyes, remembering the touch of a million years, which led his heart to a painful message of breaking faith. Tom had shattered the dream of Mary, failing his obligation to his beloved wife and carrying his faithful condition as if she were alive. He wiped the corner of his eyes with the napkin and threw it into the paper bowl that held oatmeal. He finished the juice and looked into his coffee cup, drinking it until it was emptied. Tom stood, grabbed the paper trash, and walked to the trashcan. He tossed it, throwing the filthy disgust from last night with it.

Tom arrived in his hotel room after walking twenty yards from the elevators. He looked at the door and flashed to kissing Tracey before tapping the key card into the lock. *Damn, damn, damn. I can't stop remembering.* He entered the room and packed the suitcase. He looked on the table and saw that Tracey had written him a note.

Last night was what I needed. You came just in time, and I hope it's not the last we see of each other. No pressures :), but a phone call could make tomorrow a nice reality.

Tracey

(530) 211-1113

Tom folded and pocketed the note. He didn't think he would call, but then again, a friend could be helpful for lonely days and nights. Tom put his backpack on, grabbed the suitcase, and rolled his bike out of the room to the elevators. He pressed the button, boarded the elevator, and pushed the button for the first floor. At the counter, he gave the clerk the keys and waited for his receipt.

At the car, he put things in order like he'd done many times before. His started his car and warmed the engine, ready to take off on the journey to Seattle. He backed out and pulled into traffic, heading north. He looked in the rearview mirror, expecting to see buildings disappear. *A town to remember!*

Tom entered Interstate 5 and headed north. His plan had him at the next city by early afternoon. That was before Tracey had kept him up so late. His delayed departure got him on the road at the time he was supposed to have traveled halfway to his destination. By Tom's estimate, he'd reach Eugene by around 4:00 p.m., still in time for his hotel check-in.

Tom drove with caution, like he drove from San Francisco. This time he didn't want to stop, but got to Eugene, Oregon at a decent time. He figured he'd arrive with at least three to three and a half hours of sunlight left. That gave him a little time to see the town before it got dark (which made any city look totally different).

He looked left at passing cars where couples were traveling together, and at cars with single occupants. His mind kept churning with the effort of forgiveness. Though Mary had died nearly a year ago, he hadn't been able to open up to a woman's advances, or so he thought. *Mary's gone, and I didn't cheat. If anything, she cheated me out of our future. I don't see why I feel so guilty.*

Two and a half hours into the drive, Tom let go of his grief and focused on the ride, observing the terrain. He compared it to the green landscape of the east coast and the partial green and desert look of California. The mountains were beautiful and breathtaking. He noticed every friend of nature: the rising rocks to the sky and the curving roadways that bypassed each monument.

Four hours passed, and his gas indicator was below the halfway point. He never wanted to push his chances going into the unknown. He took the next exit and stopped at a Shell gas station. He filled up, got some water, made a bathroom stop, and got back on the road. He was proud he'd done all that in less than twenty minutes. He returned to the interstate, refreshed for the next two hours to Eugene.

Oregon came up like a wizard with magical trees, poof out of nowhere. The green trees were a reflection in people's eyes to every passing car. He admired the landscape simply because it reminded him of home. Maryland was full of trees, but they didn't have the desert feel to them. *Oregon has a unique feel to it.* He rolled his window an inch down, simply to smell the fresh air. It impressed him and made his body respond, like the bike ride in the park.

Tom imagined what it had been like when the first settlers arrived. *My God, it's beautiful.* He could see the passing of history right before his eyes. The impressive greenery, rolling hills, and thick atmosphere grabbed his senses and shook them. He looked as he drove, exiting the interstate at the first exit into Eugene.

At the stop sign, he looked for a gas station and came across one within a mile. He pulled over, parked, and took out the pamphlet with the location of the hotel he'd chosen. It was interesting to him how drivers weaved from one side to the other, avoiding close calls within inches. He became extra defensive with his driving.

At the hotel, he checked in, went to his room, and unloaded his things. He took his bike downstairs for a ride around town. To his surprise, the city was bike friendly. He credited it to the University of Oregon's campus, which was located within the mile. His admiration of the town grew as he imagined circumstances if Tom Junior had attended college here. The busy streets and stores were unique in their own right. He glanced at the corner intersection and saw Vodoo Doughnuts, a specialty pastry shop offering weird baked good combinations. Tom parked his bike, locked it, and entered the shop. He couldn't believe his eyes when he saw the decor. From weird icons to mixed messages of donut consumption, the display was as unique as the duck mascot for the college.

His order was quick and easy. Black coffee, hot with no sugar or room for cream, came as quickly as he ordered it. He sat by the window with a view of the door, watching people enter and leave. He glanced outside, watching anything he could grab at that was interesting, but nothing seemed to capture his mind. Tom looked at the coffee before taking a sip. His heart felt a sharp, dagger-like piercing pain. He hit his chest with his fist, causing him to cough, clearing any congestion. He picked up his coffee, sipped, and put it down on the table, seeing his reflection in the black swirl reflecting the light above. Tom stared at the coffee, held his chest, and closed his eyes after a few minutes of evaluating what he'd seen. He stood from the table, leaving the coffee cup, and went to his bike. He pedaled to the hotel, walked in, and went to his room. His eyes welled while he sat on the end of the bed. One tear fell and then another followed. He didn't try to control his emotional burst of sadness. He lay back on the bed and covered his eyes with his hands.

Thunder woke him after hours of sleeping. His eyes were dry, and he hadn't cleaned up from the day before. He went to the bathroom and relieved himself, turned on the shower, undressed, and jumped in. Tom stood under the shower, feeling the stream of water hit his body. He put his head on the tile wall and allowed the water to run down every part of him. Before he moved, he made the water warm enough to make a difference on his body, setting the dial right where he remembered Mary's preferred temperature. His face felt the heat while his body turned a shade darker, responding to the change. He washed while steam built up, waiting for Mary's voice to instruct him to change the temperature. He turned the water off after his last rinse, toweled dry, and dressed. His day started upon checkout.

Tom drove north as he'd planned, picking up scenic views while driving the twisting and winding road along the way. He saw the coast highway and rocks in the water, which were bigger than a house on a deserted island. He parked in the scenic parking area, got out of his car, and walked to the rail. He took out his phone and watched the ocean waves crash against huge boulders, water dancing up the wall of stone overhead like a movie he'd seen a hundred times before. He caught his breath and snapped a picture, timing the photo for when the wave hit against the rocks.

Tom arrived at the Sea Lion Cave, a unique area holding what he thought of as 'swash-buckler history'. Tom laughed at the idea of a galleon parked in the shadow of sea lions, hiding some big treasure. He stopped at the park, paid his entry fee, and took his phone on the walk. He went down some stairs and saw something remarkable, a cave of sea lions. It seemed like a hundred were scattered on the rocks in the middle of the cave and barely shared the catwalk to the sand. He stopped his adventure and wiped a tear from his eye. *Mary would have loved this.* Tom dropped his chin and stumbled backwards until the wall held him upright. His heart pounded like a thunderous cloud burst, and Tom's thought flashed to the woman he had dearly loved who he believed had mistakenly taken her life.

Tom gathered himself and returned upstairs, getting into his car before a flood of tears fell from his eyes. He beat the steering wheel with his hand and shook his head. *Why, baby? Why, why, why?*

It was an hour later when he finally pulled out from the parking lot. He drove north and continued his journey to the next picturesque view – the waterfalls.

Horsetail Falls didn't disappoint; it was as beautiful as the time he'd spent with Mary in the Napa Valley. He watched the water run over the cliff in the shape of a horse's tail (thus its name). He moved on, following the winding road near the Pacific Ocean north to Portland. He drove nonstop, avoiding the scenic sights and paying close attention to traffic ahead.

Portland was embracive, simple from the sight of the city and perfect for easy navigation. He maneuvered through traffic to his hotel, offloaded his bike and luggage, and checked into his room. Tom sat at the desk, looked out of the window, and scanned the area. He opened the local magazine and retrieved his agenda. His planning centered around his idea of exploring the city and what it offered. Tom looked at the magazine, scanned his list, and breathed, feeling the rigors of his journey. What he set out to do was not in sync with his spirit. Seattle became less attractive as a destination, and Portland had just reminded him of the reason he'd gotten bored with San Francisco. He closed the window blinds, turned on the television, and watched the news.

At seven, Tom went down to the hotel's restaurant, ordered dinner, had a glass of wine, and returned to his room. He crashed with the television blaring and lights burning as bright as the sun. In his slumber, he tossed and turned, waking to the light and the television. Tom clicked the light switch and grabbed the television remote, turning both off, and darkness hit the room, reminding him it was still night. He closed his eyes to silence and breathed with ease.

Chapter 32

A month passed, and Tom found himself getting into running, cycling, and swimming after he returned to San Francisco. He followed a routine of physical challenges, going from one event to another. He joined a runner's club, taking to its members like a new kid on the block seeking new friends. He ran a minimum of eight times a week, logging an average of eight miles per run. Tom ran early mornings and later in the evening, making his longest run in the morning and ending with a short spurt later in the day.

When Tom wasn't running, he biked across the Golden Gate Bridge and returned home. Some days he rode miles with a bicycling group he had joined. The group would ride to Santa Cruz and back, facing grueling hills and dodging weekend traffic. He found solitude in his riding, focusing on the riders around him, and saw things he'd never thought he would experience.

Tom logged miles of running, biking, and riding his way into physical perfection. He'd become the fittest of the fit, and at his age, he looked younger than many of his new biking and running group friends. He was ready to take the plunge and enter the San Francisco Mini Triathlon.

He found himself in the middle of a biking group on a road trip to Half Moon Bay, which offered a good day of riding and road challenges. Tom enjoyed the ride, especially since he'd found companions with whom to share the experience. His biking wasn't as advanced as many of the group members, but he managed to stay in the middle of the pack. It sounded like an easy ride of thirty miles one way, and yet, it was difficult because of the hills.

When they arrived at the bay, they took stopped at a point overlooking the bay. He stared at the view, drinking water and stretching his legs for the ride back to San Francisco. He'd become acquainted with Mike and Briana, a couple who took riding very seriously. They rode over a hundred miles over a weekend and were definitely strong riders. They stopped at the Half Moon Bay Wine & Cheese Company, stood at the bar, and ordered a glass of wine. During the break, they talked about different biking routes and traveling up the coast to Seattle, seeing unique sights along the way. Tom expressed his impression of the Sea Lion Cave and how his wife would have loved the experience. Briana nodded her head at his comment. "You aren't married?"

"No, I'm a widow." Tom sipped his wine.

"I have a few friends I can introduce you to." Briana smiled. "I'm sure you'll impress them."

"He didn't say he was interested in finding someone, Briana." Mike shook his head. "Forgive the matchmaker." He looked at his wife and shook his head again.

"You never know. I'm open to new friends. I'm not exactly trying to start a new family." Tom laughed. "But you know, sometimes it can get lonely."

"I can help," Briana giggled.

"Stop, just stop - how do you know he will like the woman you're introducing?"

"No worries, Mike. I'm pretty quick at assessing characteristics."

"Man, you're asking for it. I wouldn't do it."

"Mike, you know my friends are sweet women."

"Yeah, based on a woman's perspective." Mike laughed and finished his wine. He looked around and saw other bikers leaving. "Hey, it's time got back on our bikes."

Tom thought about Brianna's offer to introduce him to her friends, or a friend. *So what if it doesn't work? It's one night I'm not alone, and I can use another friend.* He pedaled faster, pushing himself to stay in the middle of the crowd and not fall behind. His training was paying off, as he made it back without feeling too winded or with muscle fatigue.

Tom made it home, put his bike away, and charged upstairs. He'd given Mike and Brianna his cell phone number to stay in touch. He dared ask for theirs, as he didn't want any misunderstandings. Tom dressed for the evening and walked down the street to the local Italian restaurant. He took the corner table, with his back against the wall. He hadn't noticed anyone around him but heard his name.

"Tom, what a coincidence."

He looked up, and there was Mike and Brianna. "Hey, guys, I'm surprised myself." He rose from his chair. "I'm alone. Join me, I don't mind." Tom waved his arm to the empty seats. The waiter pulled out the seat for Brianna and handed them menus before leaving.

"I didn't know you came here," Mike said.

"Yes, I'm within walking distance from here."

"We love this place; it's so good," Brianna said, looking at the menu. "I'm having the Presto Pasta." She put the menu on the table. "I have to carb up for the next ride tomorrow."

"Wow, you're at it again?"

"Man, it's the only thing we do on the weekends, and since it's our best time together, we seem to have that biking high."

"It's how we date," Brianna giggled.

"Mary and I used to work out a lot together."

"Mary, your late wife?"

"Yeah, I am sorry; I never told you her name."

"You seem to be doing well after losing your wife," Mike commented.

"It's been nearly two years now, so I'm finally adjusting...I guess."

"Time heals, and also living helps you continue."

"Continue living." Tom smiled. "I guess this is where you introduce me to your friends."

"You know it. They want a good man in their lives." Brianna waved for the waiter.

"I am not so sure I'm that good man. But I'm open to making new friends."

"Stop trying to marry him off." Mike frowned.

"It's okay, Mike, I can handle not getting married," Tom laughed.

The waiter arrived, took their orders, and left the table. Mike looked at Tom. "You're in great shape. I know you ride with us, but aren't you working on an event or something?"

"Yes, I am, actually. I took a chance and trained for the mini-marathon that's coming up soon." Tom tapped the table. "I don't know if I'll make it, but I've done everything possible to at least finish."

"Wow, that's why you were pushing hard on the ride." Mike paused and glanced at Brianna. "Brianna and I noticed how you hung in there with our speed, and we were especially surprised that you're new to biking."

"You guys, I joined after working on it, but thanks to the group, I've managed to get better and build the right muscles. I don't know how it's going to feel, running after the bike ride. Man, I'm feeling it now, just walking here."

"It's all about training," Mike said.

"What are you going to do after the race? I mean, what's next for your excitement?" Brianna asked.

"I'm not sure. I've been pretty busy with training and focusing on living," Tom paused, "As you said earlier today."

"Living, yes, that's good." Brianna touched Mike's arm. "We should suggest a vacation spot so he can continue living."

"Don't suggest one of your girls to be his guide."

"Oh, I wouldn't do that. You have to at least know someone before traveling with them."

"Amen to that," Tom laughed. "I can tell you a horrible story about that."

The waiter interrupted and placed water and a bottle of wine on the table. He poured three glasses before leaving.

"You had experience with a bad companion?" Brianna nodded her head.

"It's a long story, but I'd rather not tell it now. Just know that it was not fun."

"Brianna, are you still digging for something to share with your girls?"

"No, I'm just curious."

"Tom, you have to excuse my wife. Once she gets things in her head, it's hard to let them go."

"It's okay. I don't mind."

"Well, if you're up to it after your race, I think you should relax in warm waters."

"Warm waters?" Tom sipped his water. "You mean, some place further south than here?"

"Yes, quite a distance from here," Mike responded.

"Where?"

"We love Cancun." Brianna smiled. "It's a lot of fun."

"Have you been there?"

"Never."

"If you go, you're in for a treat. I mean, it's relaxing and exciting all in one. It's different enough, and the people are awesome, friendly, and practically everyone speaks English."

"How's the water?" Tom asked.

"It's the Caribbean, and the water is pretty clear. Besides, in the summer it's pretty warm, but the environment is hot. Not like the desert, but it is the Caribbean."

Tom looked at Mike and Brianna. "I get the picture. You two love it quite a bit."

"We do, because it's like relaxing and fun. It's adventurous and soothing. The food is fantastic, and the history is full of surprises. And, oh, the money exchange is usually in your favor. It varies, but it's always good for the dollar."

"Now you're grabbing my attention," Tom laughed. "Cancun. I'll look into it."

Chapter 33

Tom arrived home and wondered about the dinner conversation. "Cancun, Mexico," he said, and repeated: "Cancun, Mexico - someplace Mary and I had on our radar." Tom booted up his laptop and searched for information on Cancun. He pulled up YouTube videos, web links, and Travelocity reviews. The more he read, the greater his interest became. Three hours later, he'd selected the hotel, airline, and planned a trip down to the hour of his return flight to San Francisco.

Two weeks had passed, and he'd worked hard, training for the mini-triathlon. He carbed up the night before and ate a small breakfast. Within two hours, he arrived at the check-in point. "Tom Stetson," he reported to the authority, and received his sensor for his shoes and his number to wear.

"Report over there," the administrator pointed.

"Sure thing." Tom nodded and turned towards the starting point. He looked at the water in the bay and realized that Alcatraz was a long swim away. "Thank God this is only halfway." His stomach fluttered, and his nerves caused him to emit stomach sounds loud enough to draw attention. "Sorry," he said to swimmers next to him. "I'm a little nervous."

"Yeah, me too, and it's not my first mini-triathlon," the contender said next to him.

"It's never easy, but get through the swim and it's a piece of cake."

"I hope so." Tom shook his arms and kicked his legs, ensuring he was loose and ready to go.

Bang! The gunshot started the race, and off Tom went, into the water. He shook from the shock of the cold brisk splash, which he'd expected. He couldn't get going fast enough to warm up. He stroked, kicked, and stroked repeatedly until he settled into a rhythm. Stroke, stroke, breathe, stroke, stroke, breathe - he kept kicking and pulling with his arms. Stroke, stroke, breathe - he pressed on with his rhythm. Tom didn't mind not passing anyone, but he was surprised he'd kept within distance of the guy he'd spoken to before the start.

Fifteen minutes into the swim, Tom was nearing the turnaround point. His rhythm kept him at a good pace, and the swimming he'd done, training in the pool, was paying off. He kicked with ease and continued to pull with the middle of the pack. He didn't care where he landed, but he wanted to finish. Stroke, stroke, breathe, kick - he repeated these without cramping, something he'd heard many people did on the return.

On shore, he was able to get to his station, jump into a tee shirt, and get his shoes on. He grabbed his bike and took off running before jumping on. Tom managed to get on and not fall over, pedaling with power in a gear he'd planned on using after the swim. At first, he felt the muscle transition from swim to bike, but like he'd trained to do, it didn't harm his body nor his spirit. Pedal, pedal - he pressed forward, his breathing increased, and he noticed how his legs started to burn just enough to get his attention. He slowed, listening to his quads and not allowing the burn to have an impact. He pedaled, maintaining a consistent speed. "Middle of the pack," Tom said to himself. "Stay in the middle of the pack."

Tom pedaled like a champion, pressing to maintain speed until they approached a large hill. He stood on the bike and pedaled without hesitation. He smiled because he'd trained on that very hill but not with the burning sensation in his legs. Still, Tom pushed himself, making the hilltop before turning right with the course. He pedaled. "Middle of the pack," he shouted, as if giving himself a support cry. He'd loved the fact that San Francisco had hills, especially when he coasted down them, saving his legs for the run. He managed to get through half of the bike ride, and on his way back, he passed recognizable stretches where he'd trained for the race. He was pleased that he'd practiced on this very race's route. His energy returned when he went near his house and passed Mike and Brianna on the side, cheering him on. Tom waved and noticed some woman standing next to them. He stayed focused on the ride ahead, pedaling his way to the front of the pack. Tom didn't stop; he kept going, driven to be a well-managed machine biking his way to the change point.

It was ninety minutes into the ride when he arrived at the change point. He let the bike coast to a stop and dismounted. He kicked the stand and moved into the tent, picked up a hat, and took off on the run. "Am I a beast today, or what?" Tom asked.

"You're doing great for a first-timer," said the contender who'd started with him.

"Thanks." Tom got into a runner's rhythm. "13.1 miles ahead."

It was eight miles later when his legs started feeling the pain. He'd forgotten to take in additional salt. Tom stopped at a water table and grabbed two bottles, then pushed himself back into the race. One leg in front of the other, he was slower than when he started but still pacing at eight-minute miles. He expected to maintain his pace until he finished the coming hill. It was the largest hill on the course.

"I'm going to make it. After this, it's an easy four miles," he huffed. "One, two, three, fourrrr," he sung, flashing on his Army days of chanting in formation. He repeated, huffing in stride and in cadence.

At the top of the hill he found his second wind, building speed with one-step faster than before and coming abreast to an experienced runner. He knew that passing him would be a remarkable feat. Tom lifted his knees and stretched his legs. Another mile went like the wind. Then he was two miles ahead. "My first mini-triathlon. I can do this," Tom breathed, coasting like the bike ride he'd done hours before. "One, two, three, four," he sang. "Run and run and run some more." His mind wandered to the finish line, and he wished his wife and son were there waiting for him. He blinked and pressed forward.

The last two hundred yards bought a smile to his face, even though the clock time was at five hours and thirty-seven minutes. He pushed himself to get there, running like there was a wind behind his sail. He leaned into the finish line, and his sensor beeped. Tom didn't look at the clock, but he figured it had to be at least the maximum allowed time and added two minutes to it when he saw it was much earlier.

He bent over, catching his breath for a few minutes, then stood tall and walked to the table for water. He grabbed two bottles and shook the administrator's hand as she asked for the sensor from his shoe. "Good race today."

"Thank you," Tom huffed, his legs feeling the impact of the day. "Can I sit next to you for a minute?"

"Oh, sure." She blushed. "I don't mind."

"Thanks." Tom walked to the chair and sat down, holding his head in his hands, closing his eyes and reflecting on his immediate accomplishment. He smiled. "I did it!"

"Yes, you did." The clerk looked at him. "I realize this is your first time at this race. Have you run any others?"

"This is my first," he laughed. "And probably my last."

"Watch out, you get the bug, and you'll be back."

"I don't think so." Tom sat back. "Do you always work these races?"

"No, I volunteered for this one. Usually I'm a supporter on the sidelines."

"You never ran one?"

"Nope, but I watched my ex-husband do it."

"Oh, I am sorry to hear that," Tom paused. "I mean, a failed marriage can be horrible."

"In my case, it's a blessing," she giggled. "I'm Carla, by the way."

"Tom Stetson." He reached for her hand.

"I know." Carla looked at his eyes. "Married or single?"

"You don't beat around the bush." Tom smirked. "I'm widowed."

"I'm so sorry, Tom, I had no idea."

"It's like being divorced, isn't it?"

"I don't think so." Carla shook her head. "I'd think it was worse."

"Maybe, but I think we all mourn when losing a relationship."

"I can see your point."

Carla took another sensor from a contender. "Thank you."

Tom stood and looked at Carla. "Nice meeting you, and maybe we will cross paths in the future."

"I'd like that."

"Make sure you take my number from the form. Call me when you feel up to dinner."

"I can do that." Carla smiled and watched Tom walk away into the crowd.

Chapter 34

It was hot and steaming when the plane door opened to the gangway. Tom had read it was going to be a scorcher, and the environment did not disappoint. The heat met him like a slap in the face during winter.

He followed the flight attendant's instructions, completing the proper documents and was happy to finish the paperwork correctly before debarkation. He got to the checkpoint with his form in hand and passed it to the reception team. They checked it and directed him to the right, straight to immigrations. Tom stood in line, watching the big screen playing different events for the area. He was surprised that most of the advertisements were exactly as he'd seen on YouTube and read about on Travelocity. He couldn't wait to see what the fuss was about. Tom shuffled forward, following the people in front of him. The line was huge, as multiple aircrafts had landed at the same time and it seemed that everyone was a tourist. The lines were amazing because he observed people from all over the continent. He hadn't realized how many different countrymen visited this popular vacation destination.

He made it to the booth, handed the security officer his passport, and stood in front of him. "Are you here on business or pleasure?"

"Pleasure."

"First time here?"

"Yes, exactly, and I hear it's someplace I should enjoy."

"You'll have a blast." The officer swiped his passport into his machine and held it up to compare the picture to his physical appearance. "Here you go."

"Thanks." Tom took his passport and walked through to the luggage area. He grabbed his suitcase and rolled it to the next security checkpoint. "Any fruit?"

"No, I don't have any."

"Okay." The guard waved him forward.

Tom walked past the exit and looked for his name on a placard. Instead, he was met by sharp sales guys who asked him about his transportation. "I'm good, thanks," Tom answered, just like he'd been instructed on multiple websites. He managed to get past the salespeople and walked to the transportation drivers. He saw his name on a placard and walked to the person holding it. "I'm Tom Stetson."

"Welcome, Señor Stetson." The driver dropped his sign and grabbed Tom's suitcase. "I'm Jerome; pleased to meet you. Follow me."

"Hi, Jerome...Okay."

Jerome led Tom to a white van with other passengers sitting in it. He took a seat and put on his seatbelt.

"Mr. Stetson, you're going to the Hotel Krystal. Right?"

"Yes, I am."

"Got it. We're on our way, and we'll stop to drop off other passengers on the route."

"Okay."

Tom looked out of the window and observed the unique trees making up the Caribbean jungle. The brush was not as thick as he'd seen during his Army days when he was deployed in Southeast Asia, nor as green as being in Germany. But it still showed more than Mexico's desert. It was enough to keep him distracted from the way the driver was cruising along the road.

The first stop was a huge hotel, The Mayan Palace: a resort for kings. He knew it had to have been the most expensive resort he'd ever seen. The buildings were impressive: the color of marbled brown, glistening in the sunlight as if the sun were part of their majesty. He looked at the entryway and was amazed at the décor. He shook his head. The chandelier was huge, crystal, and perfectly set, and the floor was marbled, glossy like the outside, but brighter because of the indoor light. The people were dressed well in uniforms and acted cheerful to the guest who got out of the transportation van. Tom nodded in approval. *Wow!* he thought.

On the ride down the main strip, he observed more hotels, public buses passing them, and shopping malls with upscale stores with posters marketing the brands of Paris. He smiled, knowing that had Mary been with him, that would have been one of their tours. He covered his mouth to refrain from embarrassing himself with the other passengers.

Tom was the last to be dropped off from the van. He remembered seeing the center of the Cancun Hotel Zone near the department store, the Market de Negro, and Cong Bongo - a Cirque de Solei type of dance club, all places he'd read about. His hotel was just as impressive. The Krystal Cancun had glass doors and white marble floors, a water fountain in the reception area, and a chandelier you could only imagine at a Ritz Carlton in the South of France. The place was very inviting, with everyone being helpful and courteous. He remembered the Southern charm of South Carolinians when he'd attended boot camp, and Cancun was similar. The bellhop spoke to Tom: "Mr. Stetson, we're expecting you. Please come this way."

"Thank you." Tom followed and landed at the VIP reception desk.

"Sir, I'll keep your bag and bring it to your room."

Tom nodded and stood at the counter. The desk clerk greeted him with a smile. "Mr. Stetson, your room is ready, and here's your band for your wrist."

"Okay." Tom looked at the gentleman. "Does this band signify anything?"

"Oh, yes, let me explain." The clerk pointed at a map of the property and shared what the band meant. Tom read of having an all-inclusive trip but had decided he'd rather explore the multiple restaurants around Cancun. The band gave him access to the property as well as identified him as a guest if he got off the beaten path.

Tom responded, "Thank you for the explanation."

"Yes, sir...Fernando is my name, so if you need anything, please don't hesitate to call."

"I sure will, Fernando." He smiled.

"Your room is 2308, and here's your key." Fernando handed the key to Tom. "If you need any assistance, please give us a call. The bellhop is waiting with your luggage. He will show you to your room."

"Okay, thank you." Tom turned and followed the bellhop to the elevator. His eyes scoured the environment, and he saw the multiple bars, the restaurant, the jewelry and gift shops, and peeked at the pools outside the glass wall windows. Beyond the pools was the blue Caribbean Sea. Tom entered the elevator behind the bellhop. It was an amazing ride because the glass elevator was remarkable with its view of the beach and the ocean. The higher the elevator rose, the greater Tom's view became. He was amazed at how white the sand looked, and the clear water from the beach reached out as far as his eyes could see. "I see why Mike and Brianna like this place so much."

"Yes, I think," the bellhop responded.

"Oh, I'm sorry. I was saying that my friends like Cancun a lot and come back quite often."

"Many people do. It's a great place."

"I can see that."

The elevator doors opened, and the bellhop stepped out first. "Please follow me."

"Yes, no problem."

A turn down the hall and twenty feet midway from the elevators at the end of the hall, the bellhop turned right, tapped the door, and opened it. "Sir, this is your room."

"Thank you." Tom walked in and was amazed at the décor, the earth tone colors, the marble, the massive king-size bed, the huge curtains covering the sliding doors, the marbled bath with bowled sinks, the chrome faucet, and the huge shower. When he opened the toilet room, there was a phone on the wall. Tom listened to the bellhop explain the amenities and followed him to the balcony. When the bellhop pulled back the curtains to the sliding doors, the view impressed Tom. He stood at the glass doors and took in the view, and decided his hotel selection was as impressive as the Mayan Palace.

Tom tipped the bellhop and closed the door after he'd walked out. He turned back to the room and first noticed the large flat screen television, the stereo in-room sound system, and the bar, where the bellhop had reminded him that the first bottle of tequila was complimentary. Tom took out his suitcase, opened it, changed clothes, grabbed his shades and a hat, sandals, and a beach towel, and then spread his sunscreen lotion over his exposed skin. He picked up his room key and went to the elevator. Other people who seemed just as excited to get to the beach or pool joined him. "Hi," Tom greeted them.

"Hi," one lady responded, and her guy looked at Tom with

an interested eye. "You just arrived, I'd say."

"Yes, I got here not even an hour ago."

"Welcome to Cancun. Is this your first visit?"

"Yes, it is."

"It won't be your last." The gentleman smiled.

"He may not like it," the woman said.

"I bet he will." The guy winked.

"I'm already impressed," Tom responded.

"Good, that's the spirit." The guy entered the elevator holding his lady's hand, and Tom followed them. They fell silent on the ride down to the ground floor. The couple walked out and said, "Have fun."

Tom waved. "I will." He followed the signs to the pool and walked directly to the sound of splashing water. He stopped in his tracks, realizing how large the pool was. The videos he'd watched did not give justice to the way the pool was designed. There was a bridge for walking across it. The sun hit Tom, reminding him of his need for shade or some type of cover. He searched for a vacant lounge chair under a canopy.

His eyes found one on the far side of the pool area. He walked over to it, dropped his towel and sunscreen onto it, pulled his shirt off, and sat down. He listened to music while he relaxed, stretching in the cool breeze. In minutes he found himself, eyes closed, listening to multiple languages chatter around him with Latin music playing over the speaker system. Tom breathed as he hadn't since Mary's death. He relaxed his body and mind, breathing deeply, slowly, and easily. His trance shut down everything around him, his chest heaved, and his spirit released the pain of guilt.

The sun shifted, since Tom had been there for two hours. The heat from the direct sunlight made an impact on Tom, waking him from deep sleep. He sat up, looked around, and saw the crowd he'd joined had thinned. He looked at his watch and was surprised that he'd been sleeping for two hours. Tom rose from the chair, walked to the edge of the pool, slipped off his sandals, and jumped in. The cool water hit his body, making him feel satisfied and refreshed. He dipped as low as he could go and surfaced without losing his shades. The water didn't stay cool to him very long; it was perfect. It felt warm, but better than the heat from the sun. He floated on his back for a few minutes and looked at the ocean. When he returned to his sandals, he got out of the pool, put them on, and walked toward the chair. He looked down at the path he was taking and felt eyes on him. Tom raised his head and saw a couple of women gazing at him. Not being the shy type, Tom waved, and to his surprise, they waved back. He smiled, looked at his watch, and got to his towel. He toweled off, sat down, and calculated his next planned activity.

Tom cleaned up and dressed for the evening in short pants, a button-up cotton shirt, and classy sandals. He went to the elevator and ran into the same couple he'd met earlier. "Hi, again."

"Hi," Tom responded.

"Are you headed down for dinner or going out?"

"I thought I'd try eating out first."

"Oh, if you want something close and Mexican, you should try the Hacienda."

"Hacienda?"

"Yes, it's within walking distance and has good food. I mean, *really* good food," the gentleman explained.

"Oh, I can do that right now. I wouldn't mind a good meal and nice environment."

"Yes, it's good, and the environment is nice. I mean, you sit under the stars kind of."

"Oh, good. I like it so far."

"Good." The elevator doors opened. "Have fun, and remember, it's right out of the front door and walk straight across the street to the strip mall. You can't miss it."

"Thanks."

It was only a few minutes after his margarita was served when his dinner arrived. He ordered a local favorite with a Mayan twist of seasoning, something he'd never had before. He looked at the dish and lit into the meal with his utensils. His first bite made him rush for another. The margarita accompanied his second bite, as the heat of the dish was mouthwatering. Tom waved at the waiter and ordered bottled water. About halfway through his meal, the mariachi band serenaded folks around the restaurant. He listened to the band and relished the authenticity of their sound. Tom realized he was really in Mexico.

The two women who had waved at him at the pool sat in front of him. He hadn't noticed until the waiter stood in front of his table and said, "Señor, you have admirers." He smiled and pointed at the table. "They'd like to know if you'll join them for a drink."

"Thanks," Tom replied and went to the table. "Hello, and I'd love drinking with you." He smiled. "I have to warn you. I'm on a tour early tomorrow, so I can't drink with you long."

"Which tour?" asked the woman in red shorts and a white top. She resembled a hometown girl he once knew. Blonde hair, green eyes, and streamlined features. Her lips were full and painted for added excitement. Tom smiled. "The Mayan Ruins at Chichen Itza."

"You'll have fun; it's interesting," the second woman chimed in. She was just as gorgeous, to Tom: more of a full body, brown skin, and piercing brown eyes. Her features were more interesting, as she had full lips and high cheeks with a narrow nose. Her accent struck Tom, identifying she was from Germany.

"Yes, I hear it's going to be interesting. It's why I'm heading there first."

"It's all day - and I mean all day," the brunette said.

"I read about it - and again, it's my first full day."

"How nice," the blonde spoke. "What a smart way to start your vacation."

"Thank you."

"I guess you're not going out at all tonight. I mean, we'd love to dance with you."

"Oh, ladies, I'm flattered, but doesn't the bus come at 7:00 a.m.?"

"There about, but surely you don't have to sleep tonight?" The blonde said.

"Can I take a rain check?" Tom asked.

"We have one more night, so tomorrow night we're definitely going to conclude up our vacation," the brunette shared.

Tom sipped his margarita and scanned the ladies once again. He asked, "How would you rate visiting Cancun?"

"I'd say," the brunette spoke, "it's very interesting. If you like shopping, it's all here, and I mean from local to high-end brands. If you like dancing, it's here, from traditional Latin to Hip Hop. If you like water sports, you're in heaven."

"And if you like people from all over, you're going to meet a lot of them. Some are freer than others, and you may get lucky with a wild experience." The blonde ginned.

"Don't be naughty," the brunette giggled.

"You two must have had a wonderful time." Tom nodded. "I appreciate the review; it's consistent with most I've read." Tom rose. "Ladies, it's been a great conversation. Have fun tonight, and I'll see you around the pool tomorrow?"

"You'll see us." The blonde nodded.

"Oh, have fun tomorrow, and take lots of pictures. Chichen Itza is an amazing place."

"Thanks, I sure will. See you tomorrow."

Chapter 35

The ride to Chichen Itza was as interesting as the ride from the airport to the Krystal Hotel. They stopped at the Riu, another palace-type hotel more impressive than the Royal Mayan. The bus picked up folks at the Americana and at another condominium resort where the condos were decorated like haciendas and unique in their color schemes. Every seat in the luxury bus was filled, and the guide got on the loudspeaker and narrated the itinerary.

During the ride through Cancun proper, Tom noticed the city, filled with people who worked in different industries. He noticed an international port operation, brick manufacturing, and cars: both top end and American-made car salesrooms. He saw common restaurants, some chain types and some local mom and pop shops. He noticed multiple businesses that seemed different from the images he'd been led to believe of Mexico.

The road to the ruins was filled with countryside, and the terrain was full of green trees, but their bottom foliage was scarce, and you could see the ground and quickly spot any animal. It was nothing like the thick brush of Africa or South America, nor like the brush in Germany. He pondered the comparison. He observed old buildings and was surprised to see they were wood huts, sticks made into sheds and lined with electricity. He looked at the rocks and clay structures and heard how poor the original Mayan people were, struggling in the Mexican economy.

Tom heard the tour guide discuss the history of an extremely industrial people long before the United States evolved into a world power. His story was more than intriguing; it was something of great interest. He couldn't believe how the

Mayans had had roadways, mile markers, road lights, and guide maps. He couldn't believe there was a monetary system in place. Tom was totally surprised, so much so that he opened a notebook from his backpack and wrote down facts to research back in San Francisco.

The bus arrived at the rest area, and all of the passengers piled out. One after the other, they walked into the shopping plaza that held unique Mayan arts and crafts. They displayed unique items of the culture based on the history of the Mayan Calendar, such as jewelry, skulls, and native-looking dolls. They made these items by hand, and they were interesting enough for a collector to grab a few items and proudly display them.

Tom bumped into a woman because his attention was on the unique Mayan jewelry. "Excuse me, I'm sorry."

"Oh, it's no problem." She smiled.

"Interesting stuff," Tom pointed out.

"Yes, and beautifully done."

"I think these people are amazing. I can't believe the history behind them."

"It's like my home in Germany. We have unique items in different regions."

"Is that so?" Tom smiled. "I was in Germany years ago, only for a short time. I was in Wiesbaden."

"American Army."

"Yes, but like I said, it was only for a few months. I didn't get to stay there for years."

"I see. You missed a lot."

Tom gazed at the Frauline. "Yes, I would say so."

She smiled and moved to another shelf display.

"I'll see you later. I need to get to the restroom before the bus leaves."

"Okay." She walked further into the store and picked up some silver pieces.

Tom walked to the restroom, competed his business, and returned to the store, walking through the display areas on the way to the bus. He went directly to his seat and took the bottled water the tour guide handed him. He observed others looking at the many trinkets they purchased.

The bus finally arrived at the ruins park. He was excited to finally see the ruins he'd researched. He walked with the group, following the guide's instructions, and like a few others, he protected himself from the sun with the portable umbrella he'd bought in his backpack. He walked with the crowd, intently listening to the guide. There was one story after the other, and he looked at the unique painting, designs, and structures of these ancient buildings. He looked inside, touched the rock, and was amazed at the engineering. "How did they make these buildings without heavy equipment?" he asked.

"It is amazing," the guide responded. "It took them years to build one block at a time, and they created the scaffold from wood."

Tom couldn't believe his ears. "Wood, huh? Wow!"

The guide led them to another structure and shared the remarkable alignment of the top doors with the moon and the sun. He gave instructions to look at how off-centered the doors were, and said: "Look at the sunlight, and now look at the moon. See the alignment?"

Tom was amazed again, and took notes for future reference and study. He was the only tourist writing. "You're really into this, aren't you?" The German lady he met at the store spoke to him.

"I love history." Tom smiled.

"I see."

"Have you visited any other sites yet?"

"No, it's my first day here."

He smiled. "Mine, too."

She turned her attention to the guide and walked with the crowd. Tom followed after putting his pad in his side pocket. He looked ahead and observed the unique features of his new acquaintance. His mind wandered. *Is she with someone?* he pondered.

The group stopped at the middle of two walls with an open field between them. The guide explained what the field was used for and how they played a game. He also explained how the teams played at night, in the moonlight or by the firelight. He pointed out the structure of the walls and how they were curved to reflect sound. Tom took to the story like indulging in hot chocolate and popcorn. He wrote the information down and again took notes to follow up. Amazed, he dropped the pad and pulled out his camera, snapping pictures of the walls. He moved back to the first building and snapped pictures. He looked at his new acquaintance and asked, "Can you snap a picture for me, please?"

"Oh, sure," she responded and walked to him. Her hand was extended to grab his camera, and she took to the tool like a professional. Tom posed in front of the pyramid, and the camera clicked a few times. His eyes widened because he didn't now his camera would perform in such a manner. "You do this a lot?"

"It's one of my hobbies."

"Oh, I am surprised you didn't bring your own camera."

"I did." She pulled the small hand-held camera from her pocket. "This works wonders, believe it or not."

"I heard they do. I guess I'm old-fashioned."

"But I like the old ones, too, because it takes a good eye and not just software."

"You're right." Tom smiled.

The guide instructed the group that there were thirty minutes left before it was time to return to the bus. Tom and his new acquaintance went from ruin to ruin with the camera, snapping shots for each other. He finally noticed that she was alone, like him. His focus was on how unique her features were and how classy her attitude was about simple things. "Hey, it's about time," she said while looking at her watch.

"Yeah, the exit is over here." Tom pointed and waited for her to join him. They walked beside each other on the way over. "I guess you enjoyed this as much as I did."

"Of course; like you, I love history."

"You do? That's wonderful. I look forward to the next site."

"I am not going out tomorrow, but maybe later in the week."

"Shopping, I guess?" Tom asked.

"Yes, the local market. I think Market 28."

"I read about it. But I don't shop much these days."

"Oh, really?"

"No, I think I have enough stuff these days. I should really downsize since I'm all alone now."

"Well, you know better what to do than anyone else."

"For sure."

They arrived at the bus, and she entered first. Tom followed with a drink in his hand from the guide team. "Oh, I didn't see you grab a drink. Would you like one?"

She looked at Tom right after she sat down. "I hate drinking alone."

"No problem." Tom gave her his beer and returned to the front for another. "I'll sit with you, if you don't mind."

"Maybe until my seat partner returns."

"Sure, I can move when they come. Cheers." Tom tapped her beer with his.

It was ten minutes before everyone finally arrived at the bus. Tom rose from sitting next to his new companion and walked to his seat further in the rear. He put his backpack on the shelf and placed the empty bottle in the carton being passed from the front. He looked at others and mingled in on the conversations of what was impressive in the area. The bus took off, moving down the road and leaving the ruin park.

Twenty minutes later, the bus stopped at the same shopping area rest stop they had been to before. The restaurant was open, and the tour included authentic Mayan dishes and some local Mexican dishes for dinner. He was famished, and like everyone else, he stepped off of the bus and right into line. He was surprised to see that three buses were there for the same reason. Yet, he could see there was plenty of food to go around.

Tom found a table, put his hat on a chair, and went to the buffet line. He grabbed a little of everything interesting, including some dishes he knew. He returned to the table and noticed that his new comrade was sitting across from him. "Hey, welcome." Tom smiled.

"Yeah, it was a no-brainer," she said.

"I'm Tom." He offered his hand to her.

"Samantha." She took his hand with a firm grip.

"I like a firm handshake." Tom raised one eye brow. "Do you have plans for the rest of the week? I mean, after shopping."

"I'm playing it by ear, but I will see more sites. I heard Xcaret is a great site."

"Are you swimming at the next spot? I hear it's a great place to take a dip."

"I don't know for sure. It depends on how I feel when we get there." She gazed into Tom's eyes. "How about you?"

"I brought my stuff and probably will, but I hear cliff divers are more fun to watch."

Samantha gave her finished plate to the bus boy passing by the table. Tom followed suit. "Would you like a refill?" Tom asked.

"No, I'm ready for the bus."

"Okay." Tom rose and went behind her chair, pulling it out as she rose.

"Chivalry is alive." Samantha covered her mouth, hiding her elation.

Tom changed in the dressing room for the dip into the cave

water below. It was a unique experience, and the water was cool and inviting. The shade from the natural cavern made it astonishing, and he was amazed that it was fresh water. *How could anyone dive from the top of this opening?* It had to be nearly seventy-five feet, by his estimation. He swam from one side to the other, dodging multiple people who treaded water in the middle. He looked ahead at his destination and couldn't believe his eyes. The body of an angel stood at his destination.

"Wow," he said.

"Yeah, I agree." The swimmer next to him nodded his head.

From her back, he saw perfect curves, the figure most men dream their women could have. He saw the sculptured legs of a woman who definitely runs. He saw her hips and back, which were in perfect proportions. He watched her shake her glistening hair as she stood in the beam of the sunlight. He was surprised at himself for staring. He snapped out of his embarrassing, google-eyed stare to get out of the water and change into his regular clothes for the ride home. When he stepped out of the water, Samantha grabbed his hand. "She could be your daughter," she laughed.

"Oh, I...ah..."

"It's okay. I get that stare sometimes, too."

Tom looked at Samantha in her bathing suit. "Oh, I can see you do." He smiled. "I'll see you at the bus."

Chapter 36

Tom rose at dawn with the birds and walked the beach before having breakfast. He watched the sunrise during his stroll and was impressed at the calm morning. His walk led him to the sea wall near the hotel, and he went to the end of it. Tom stood at the end, watching the pink fusion against the horizon with the blue water changing colors to darkening sky, where both blues touched. His breath was easy and calm as he took in fresh air and felt the soft ocean breeze, listening to the crash of the waves. *Maybe I should cancel my tour and enjoy this? Naw, the tour is first. Stick to the plan.*

After breakfast, Tom stood in front of the hotel waiting for his shuttle to arrive. Like yesterday, a huge bus pulled up, and the guide stepped out, calling his name: "Mr. Stetson."

"Yes, I'm here," Tom responded and moved to the bus entrance.

"Come aboard and enjoy the ride." The guide smiled. "You're our last passenger."

"Thank you." Tom followed instructions and walked to the rear of the bus where the last open row was available.

The bus closed its door and took off onto the roadway, heading in the opposite direction of yesterday's tour. Tom noticed the multiple people on the bus, and he sat with his backpack in a free seat.

"This is the tour for Tulum, the center of Mayan government."

The guide began his spiel on Mayan history as it pertained to Tulum. Tom's ears perked, and he grabbed his notebook and pen. He scribbled comments to remember for future reference.

Tom listened and wrote down quotes to review later. Like his trip to the Mayan Pyramid, he soaked information like a sponge getting wet for the first time.

The bus stopped and Tom followed the group to the canopy path to the ruins. "Hey, this could be exciting," he said to the elderly couple who sat in front of him.

"Yes, it seems the Mayan people were remarkable. Who knew?" responded the woman.

"I sure didn't." Tom walked at a much faster pace than the people in front of him. He found himself abreast of the tour guide and gave his attention to everything the guide said. When he walked around the corner, the canopy shade disappeared, and the cloudless blue sky opened. The sun beamed its powerful rays onto the cliff before them. The ruins were impressive, with square block foundations and partial walls, some freestanding without roofs, and others with roofs. There was a smaller building at the corner cliff, positioned like a beacon at the edge of the cliff. The overlook was perfect for seeing Cozumel in the distance, and with binoculars borrowed from the tour guide, one could see another, similar building down the coast. These were lit at night for the canoes and rafts of the area. Per history, some Mayans traveled on the ocean all the way to Belize from Tulumn. They used the beacons as landmark guides.

Tom returned the binoculars to the tour guide, pulled out his notepad, and scribbled, then drew the building. He sketched the general assembly building, too, which was in view. He took out his camera and snapped picture after picture. He took a picture of the view from the cliff, overlooking the beach below. He zoomed in and recognized people he'd passed at Hotel Krystal.

He turned upon hearing a voice. "Would you like me to take your picture?" a travel companion asked.

"Sure, thanks so much." Tom handed him the camera and stood with the ocean view to his back. His stance was confident as he focused his head and eyes to the adjacent structure at his left. His hand caught his hat right at the snap of the camera.

"Here you go." The travel companion handed him the camera. "If you don't mind, I'd like one of my wife and I."

"Sure, no problem." Tom snapped the photo with their camera and handed it back. "You should check just in case you'd like better shots."

"Thanks, we'll do that."

Tom waited for a response but turned to look at the beach below. He saw the two younger women he'd met the first night he arrived. He lifted his camera and zoomed in.

"These are perfect, you have a great eye."

"Thanks, and enjoy." Tom returned to his camera, eyeballing the beach below. He couldn't believe it: those weren't the women he'd met, after all. Tom snapped pictures of the people on the beach for later review. He turned and walked the ruin's grounds again, snapping the foundations and building structures once more.

An hour later, the tour guide gathered everyone for the walk to the bus. "We're stopping for refreshments." Tom followed the crowd, got on the bus, and looked at his surroundings as the bus traveled the main roads.

After the second margarita, Tom returned to the bus, sat in his seat, and closed his eyes. Between the sun, the tequila, and the excitement, his snooze was automatic. One hour into the ride, he felt a touch on his shoulder.

"Excuse me." The same guy who took his picture was standing next to him. "I think this is your stop."

Tom looked out of the window and nodded in agreement. "Yes, thanks."

"No problem."

Tom gathered his backpack and camera and stepped off the bus and into the lobby of the Krystal Cancun. Tom walked up the stairs into the bar and saw its early evening activity. What he observed amazed him. An all-girl band played music, and they were entertaining. When three couples danced, his eyes went to how each was so different as they danced to salsa music. The swing moves put him in a chair, and his camera became a tool capturing the moment Tom snapped pictures of those couples, the laughter of observers, and the unique rhythmic clapping some people were doing.

Tom stood closer to the musicians and snapped pictures as they played. He snapped pictures of the dancing couples. One couple posed for the camera while others ignored his snaps. At the end of the session, the couple introduced themselves to Tom. "I'm Jorge, and this is my wife Maria." Jorge extended his hand.

Tom shook Jorge's and responded, "Tom."

"Nice to meet you." Jorge glanced at the floor and then at Tom. "I was wondering if we could have a copy of those pictures you took of us."

"Oh, sure, I hope you didn't mind. You two looked as if you were having the time of your life. You're really great dancers."

"Thank you. It's our honeymoon, so we're collecting every picture we can."

"I get it." Tom pulled his camera up and played the pictures on the review screen. "Which would you like?" He stood close to Jorge and Maria, and she pointed. "Let's start from the first one."

"No problem." Tom started from the beginning. After the fifth photo, Jorge said, "Just send us all of them, if you can."

"I can do that. Let me get your email address." Tom went to his backpack and retrieved a pen and notepad. He wrote down their email address and snapped a photo of the couple as a reference. They shared a table and had drinks. Tom talked about his honeymoon, and Maria asked, "Where is your wife?"

Tom energetically said, "She's watching over me, and I'm sure she wants me to have a great time."

Maria touched his arm. "I'm so sorry, I thought she was here."

"I like to think she is." Tom smiled. "But don't let me spoil the evening for you." Tom rose from the table. "I will send you the pictures tonight."

"Oh, thank you." Jorge smiled at Tom and gazed at his wife, and he raised one eyebrow. They waved farewell to Tom and watched him disappear from the bar area. "That was awkward."

"Yeah, I didn't know." Maria shrugged her shoulders.

Chapter 37

Tom woke to the sound of people yelling 'BALL, BALL' outside of his window. The echo made its way through the cracked sliding door of the balcony. He put his feet on the floor and walked to the balcony, sliding the door open. He stepped out to the heat of the day, which surprised him. It was nearly noon, and nothing had awakened him except the sound of shouting. His eyes felt the heat, and his forehead started to bead with sweat.

Tom returned to the coolness of the room, made a cup of coffee, and managed to slip on swim trunks and a tee shirt. He cleaned up, remembering what had transpired last night. His eyes reflected a night of hard drinking. It was something he hadn't done in years, but he remembered being at Carlos & Charley's not far from the hotel. His eyes were bloodshot red, and they barely widened enough to see his full reflection in the mirror. Once he held his head closer to the mirror, he ran to the bed, remembering the last conversation he'd had at the bar. He looked in the bed, and then glanced through the clear chiffon curtains of the balcony. He sighed with relief. "No, nothing happened."

The knock on the door made his head ring. The sound troubled him, and he touched his chest before answering, "Yes."

"Housekeeping."

"Oh," He went to the door, "Can you give me five minutes?"

"Si, Señor."

"Gracias." Tom closed the door and went into the bathroom. He finished the morning routine, went to the coffeemaker, grabbed his coffee, and got his towel, camera, and sunscreen for his backpack. He pulled them together and put the room key in the secure zip compartment, where he added his money clip. Tom grabbed his shades, baseball hat, and flip-flops and walked to the elevators.

He walked through the concierge area near the pool and onto the stone walkway to the beach. The heat of day reminded him of his location. Cancun's sun beamed on him, making him perspire as the cool ocean breeze met him. He stepped onto the sand, flipping his feet free of footwear. Though the sun was beaming with midday heat, the sand was cool, which made Tom shake his head, surprising him as it was unusual to any beach he'd visited. Grateful for the cool experience, Tom picked up his flip-flops and walked to an open lounge chair near a cover. "Is anyone taking this?" he asked the person in the next chair.

"No, it's open," he responded.

Tom dropped his backpack on the table under the canopy and placed the coffee right next to it. He neatly placed his shoes next to the lounge chair and sat down. His eyes were heavy, but the breeze under the canopy helped him settle in. The coffee was perfect, and the afternoon had just embraced his eagerness to relax.

After twenty minutes of staring at the ocean and people passing by, he slipped off his shirt and walked to the water. He waded to a level above his waist and plunged in. The cool water made him shiver. With a couple of strokes, his body adjusted and warmed, and the cool shock quickly faded. He swam with the waves, riding whichever supported him to the shore. He returned to a greater depth to ride another. Tom rode waves for ten minutes, looked at the beach patrons, and watched multiple activities at the resort. He returned to his chair and observed the sounds and people around him.

"Mr. Carlos & Charley's, how are you?"

Tom looked up and Samantha stood there with a smile, looking like a goddess of illusions. "I'm doing okay, I think." He dropped his hat. "Was it you I talked to most of the night?"

"I can't say 'most of the night', but for a while, yes."

"Oh, thank goodness."

"You can't remember?"

"I remember talking," he paused. "But to whom, I can only imagine." Tom laughed.

"Well, I left you with two drinks on the table."

"Why did you leave me?"

"You really don't remember..." Samantha pointed. "My friend and I were heading back."

"Oh, yeah, I know her."

"Yes, you do."

"My apologies for not going with you."

"Why would you?"

"It's a gentlemanly thing to do." Tom rubbed his head after removing his cap.

"She was happily entertained for the night. You kept us laughing after we left," Samantha giggled. "We really had a great time with you, and when we left, there was another table of youngsters waiting to interact with you."

Tom looked at Samantha. "Maybe you can tell me if there were other women at that table."

"Why, you really don't remember, do you?"

"For the life of me, I can't recall everything. I remember a voice that was very unique, and it kept me trying to figure out how she developed that weird accent."

"You had to be some sheets in the wind, as they say. That was the helium."

"What?" Tom laughed. "You have got to be kidding me."

"No, Tom. You were making the entire area laugh about your concern for her voice."

"I should never drink tequila again."

"No, you shouldn't," Samantha laughed and sat at the end of Tom's lounge chair. "What are you doing tonight?"

"Well, I'm not going to Carlos and Charley's." Tom wiped his face and laughed. "I don't think they'd let me in."

"Quite the opposite. How do you think you drank so much?"

"Didn't I buy a lot of rounds?"

"My friend, you bought a few, I purchased a few, and the other table purchased bottles and shots, especially when you danced in the middle of the floor with the staff. You were hilarious. I've never seen a grown man - a mature man - let go as if he was on spring break."

Tom removed his hat and rubbed his head, trying to remember the details of the night. "Tell me how you think I got to the hotel."

"I don't know, but your wrist band helps. I'm sure someone walked you to the concierge of the hotel."

"Honest." Tom looked at his wristband. "Thank God for their system. I swore that some woman got into my room."

"If she did, then she must have been pretty bad herself. I

doubt she took advantage of you."

"There are heroines, after all."

"Or other drunks," Samantha laughed. "Hey, my girl-friend is calling me over." She waved and looked at Tom. "Listen, I have an idea. How about we share our schedule for the rest of the week?"

"I have four days to enjoy." Tom looked at Samantha. "I'd like that." He smiled.

Samantha rose and raised one finger to her waiting friend. "Well, there's no time like the present to talk about the week. Come walk with us."

Tom rose from the chair, grabbed his camera and shades, and put on his shirt. "You don't have to ask twice."

Your Review Counts

Comments about this novel are welcomed. Please take a moment and share your review. Visit www.Amazon.com , www.GoodReads.com, www.barnesandnoble.com, and/or www.LonzCook.net. Or you can write in your blog, or on facebook and share on my page www.facebook.com/warriortoromance or even www.bookblurb.com.

Read other works, (Sisters & Romance Series in order) Good Guys Finish Last, When Love Evolves, and Crossed Expectations. Or enjoy these standalone novels, A Cyber Affair and A Choice to Yield (a feature film of the same title available).

Thank you again for reading a Lonz Cook novel.